HE PRESSED

"You've grown

Oh, I'd show him s

allowed and swept out my leg slamming my skull into his sternum to send him backward. But he didn't go down. He merely stumbled, grasped my waist, and yanked me back into him again.

This time his arms felt like cement blocks as he held me captive, but it put my hands right where I wanted them against his hips. I pickpocketed a knife while he bent to kiss my neck.

"Disappointing," he murmured. "It seems you haven't kept up with your sparring."

"Really?" I pressed the blade against his inner thigh, hard enough for him to feel it through his thin dress pants. One upward swipe would have him pissing blood for at least an hour.

He grinned against my sensitive skin. "Careful, love. You wouldn't want to damage my best feature."

"Try me."

"Are you two done flirting yet?" a deep voice drawled. A scrawny blond demon stood in the doorway wearing a disgruntled expression.

Xai licked a path up to my ear and nibbled the lobe. "Evangeline, this is Tax. He'll be helping us."

I let him feel the sharpness of the knife, metal to skin, as I sliced a hole through his designer trousers. Too bad silver didn't hurt him the way it did a demon. "You don't seem to be understanding the part about my doing this alone."

"You're never alone, love," he whispered.

His words startled me so much that my head spun. It took me a second to realize it had *literally* spun because he'd twirled me around to press my back up against the bar and captured my hands in his. A squeeze to my wrist released the grip on the knife.

Fuck!

Pissed, I kicked out, only to have my legs blocked and pinned by his strong thighs. I glowered up at him. "I hate you."

"I know." He brushed his mouth over mine and pulled back when I tried to bite him.

Dark Provenance Series

A DARK PROVENANCE NOVEL

DAUGHTER
of
DEATH

USA TODAY BESTSELLING AUTHOR

LEXI C. FOSS

Daughter of Death

Editing by: Bethany Pennypacker

Proofreading by: Allison Irwin, Jenny Dillion & Pam Gonzales

Cover Design: Covers by Juan

Cover Photography: R+M Photography

Cover Models: Josie Fox & Michael Scanlon

Published by: Ninja Newt Publishing, LLC

Print Edition

ISBN: 978-0-9993709-4-0

To Allison, Louise, Melissa & Tracey: For keeping me sane when I wanted to kill a certain character. He thanks you too (because without you all, he'd probably be dead).

DAUGHTER of DEATH

SOME ADVICE FROM EVE

The concept of time is relative.
Cryptic, I know, but hear me out.
Time moves differently
            between the planes.

    Heaven, Earth, and Hell.
Yes, they're all real.
    No, I'm not elaborating on them.
        Just time.
A year on Earth equates to roughly
a day in Heaven. Similarly, A year
in Hell equates to a single Earth
day. Mind-boggling, right?
    I think we're ready to begin.

                        — E

EVE'S GLOSSARY

THESE WORDS MAY OR MAY NOT BE USEFUL...

Angel: Pompous immortal beings who are too good for Earth

Archangel: Powerful angels who lounge about at the top of the angelic hierarchy

Dark Angel: Not worthy of a definition

Demon: Immoral immortal beings who want to take over the Earth

Fallen Angel: Me

Genesis: A faction of Nephilim who think they are equipped to protect humanity; clearly inherited their arrogance from their Heavenly genes

Nephilim: Created when angels fornicate on Earth with mortals, or so the theory goes, anyway.

EVE'S DEMON DICTIONARY

FOR THOSE WHO CARE...

Archdemon: Commonly referred to as Princes of Hell; demons who sit at the top of the demonic hierarchy and are the equivalent of an Archangel or higher

Cyclops: Giant, one-eyed monsters banned from Earth because of their penchant for destroying shit

Dargarian: Rare shape-shifters who breathe fire and actually use their brains; not to be fucked with lightly

Demonic Lord: An arrogant class of demons who supposedly lead their kinds and maintain their own regions on Earth and in Hell; notoriously hate each other

Ghoul: Demons with a taste for dead human flesh; also helpful for disposing of corpses

Guardian: Demon bodyguards with persuasive abilities, but not the sharpest blades in the armory

Incubus: Male demon sex gods who can be deadly to humans, but at least the mortals die happily

Ōrdinātum: Part of the whole demon hierarchy, but really just a fancy title assigned to demons who oversee specific regions within a Demonic Lord's territory

Orsini Devil: Devious little demons who enjoy turning invisible and sneaking up on others, but they are the perfect spies when properly motivated

Pestilence: Scary humanoid-looking demons with the ability to create plagues, hence the reason they are banned from Earth

Portal Dweller: Beings with the ability to shift between planes and are the reason demons live on Earth

Royal Guard: An elite class of demons who protect the Princes of Hell and should be avoided at all costs

Scrubber: Demons who can erase or alter human memories but are otherwise generally useless and wimpy.

Slither: Slimy snakelike demons who like to ejaculate paralyzing toxins and are fond of licking their victims. Kill. On. Sight.

Succubus: Female demon sex gods who resemble every male's wet dream, minus the potential death part

Tracker: Little helpers who can track demonic auras and are therefore excellent assets

CHAPTER ONE

TWO DEMONS WALK INTO A BAR,
AH HELL

"EVE, I NEED YOUR HELP WITH A BODY AGAIN."

I glanced at my watch and frowned. "It's only nine o'clock."

"Yeah, my date ended earlier than I expected."

Clearly.

Damn it.

I couldn't close the bar for at least another hour. Sheriff Montgomery was only on his second of the usual four drinks, Billy hadn't passed out yet, and Betsy had just arrived with her worthless excuse of a husband.

It was shaping up to be a typical Thursday night at Violet's Bar, including the call I had just received from my best friend.

I slid a glass of water over to Rosie, who looked ready

1

to fall off her barstool, while balancing the phone between my ear and shoulder.

"I'll be home around eleven."

"Ugh, really? But he's starting to smell," Gwen whined. "And he's oozing all over your rug."

"Rug? What rug?" And why the hell would she wrap a body in it when there were plastic gardening sheets in the garage for this purpose? It wasn't like this was her first bad date.

"It's just a rug," she muttered.

"Wait…" I turned to face the back wall and dropped my voice to a whisper. "Are you talking about my oriental rug?"

"What other rug could I possibly be referring to?"

"Gwen!" I snapped. "That's an antique!"

"Well, what did you expect me to do? You know how I feel about leaving stains on the furniture."

"Then you shouldn't have had sex in the living room," I gritted out. "Neutral territory, Gwen. Remember?" She probably didn't. The woman was a damn Succubus. She had only one activity on her mind when she brought a man home.

"We got carried away," she said, her voice catching at the end.

"Obviously," I muttered. *Since he's dead.*

I pinched the bridge of my nose and closed my eyes.
She's your best friend.
She's a relatively new Succubus.
Yelling at her won't fix anything.

But she buried her latest conquest in my silk oriental rug. "We're going to have a long chat when I get home."

She blew a raspberry at me through the phone. "Fine, but what should I do in the meantime?"

"Call Kevin." He was most useful in these situations.

"The Ghoul? Gross. No."

Leave it to my prissy roommate to be put off by a little bone crunching. "Fine, then I'll call him after work. See you in a bit." I hung up before she could argue or complain about inviting a Ghoul over to the house for a

2

late-night snack.

Rolling up a body in my fucking rug. Of all the things for her to do. Christ.

I swiped the sheriff's now-empty glass and refilled it before tending to the couple at the other end of the bar. It was the usual crowd, all stopping by for a nightcap after work. Well, except Ray, the resident drunk. He didn't work but somehow always managed to afford his tab. I swapped out his beer bottle for a fresh one and smiled. *Mortals and their low alcohol tolerance.*

"How ya doin', Violet?" Betsy asked as I approached. The blonde bombshell was far too good-looking for her old, overweight husband and his wandering eye. Right now that rusty gaze was settled on my cleavage. One of these days, I would shove a blade down his throat and force him to swallow, but not tonight. Betsy still adored the old bastard. I'd wait until she left him.

"Livin' the dream," I replied as I started preparing her usual rum and Coke. "You?"

"Same old, same old," she drawled. "Are y'all goin' to the country fest this weekend up in Nashville?"

Ha. That'll happen the day a Demonic Lord concedes his territory to an Orsini Devil.

But I couldn't say that without offending everyone at the bar.

I opened my mouth to voice an excuse, but it died in my throat as electricity danced over my skin. Oh no. Not tonight.

Demons.

At least three.

My nostrils flared. A human wouldn't be able to scent them or notice the subtle change in the air they created, but I would.

I set Betsy's drink down on the bar top with more force than necessary and focused on the door. The inhuman impostors had chosen the wrong bar to play in tonight, and they were about to be taught a lethal lesson.

Three.

Two.

Ding.

Sheriff Montgomery glanced over his shoulder with a smile ready, as did several of the others, but the man who sauntered in didn't return the Southern gesture. He didn't even acknowledge them. His eyes were for me, and me alone.

Fuck.

Not a demon, but something far worse.

Sin dressed in all black.

And damn, did he look good. He *always* looked good.

"Gin on the rocks." His deep baritone brought up a flood of unwelcome memories and sensations. All of them centered between my thighs. I knew that body well, every lean, muscular inch, and I remembered what it could do. *Pleasure and pain.*

The small room had gone quiet, as it always did when a stranger arrived. This was the local bar—they weren't used to out-of-towners, and Xai definitely resembled a foreigner in his hand-tailored suit. His tousled midnight hair, matching eyes, and sun-kissed skin marked him as clearly *other*. But it was his accent and gestures that really set him apart. He always stood out wherever he went.

My gaze drifted over his shoulder as two of his companions entered, both in suits far too expensive for this cheap establishment. They strolled up to flank Xai.

Guardians. I smiled. *Glorified demon bodyguards.* The angel thought he might need protection for this visit. At least I couldn't fault his intelligence.

"They'll have the same," he added in that low, sexy murmur as he straddled the stool beside the sheriff.

"Sure," I replied, mostly because I sensed my bar patrons were starting to grow uneasy by the newcomers. They might not be able to sense their demonic auras, but the three men oozed danger. Especially Xai.

I selected a bottom-shelf gin, knowing he would hate it, and poured three drinks as requested.

"Intriguing," Xai said as I slid the glasses across the bar. He wasn't referring to the cheap drink but to my willingness to serve him and his cronies. The latter eyed the liquor with distaste, clearly finding the alcohol beneath them. They probably wanted to get this party started but wouldn't make a move without their keeper's permission, and Xai loved a drawn-out game.

I leaned against the counter behind me and waited for his first move. Those wicked eyes danced appreciatively over my red halter top and jeans as he openly searched me for knives. He wouldn't be able to see or sense them and he knew it, but he did it just the same.

"You look different," he mused. "Did you lighten your hair?"

I snorted. Neither of our appearances had changed since our Fall to Earth all those millennia ago. I would forever remain the light to his dark with my pale complexion, blue eyes, and ash-colored hair, and he knew it.

"You must be seeing the gold halo hovering over my head," I replied dryly.

"Ya know this guy, Violet?" Sheriff Montgomery interjected.

"Violet," Xai repeated, his lips twitching at the corners. "Hmm…" His gaze slid over me in a way that said he was picturing me in purple lingerie. "How beautifully appropriate."

I didn't shift my focus away from the dark angel as I replied, "Yes, we're acquainted."

"That's putting it a bit lightly, isn't it?" Xai turned to the sheriff, and I could tell by the curve of his mouth that he was about to say something devastating. Something that would require cleanup in the form of mortal corpses. He always did enjoy a good slaughter. That was the problem with immortals our age. No humanity.

But some of us still cared.

At least a little.

I sighed, annoyed. If I didn't intervene, all Hell would break loose, and I already had one body to clean up tonight. Adding a bloody bar to the mix would make for a very long night.

Damn it.

Xai would call me soft, but it was the practical option. Their mortal lives were short enough already.

"All right, y'all, time to call it a night," I said before Xai could create a scene. Since everyone was still gawking at the out-of-town guests, I didn't have to raise my voice to be heard. But a few of them did look at me as if I'd grown two heads. "Seriously, the bar is now closed, but all your drinks are on the house." *Because I'll be sending the bill to the man in the expensive suit.*

Xai smirked. "How quaint."

"Yes, having a heart is a weakness." My retort knocked the amusement right off his handsome face. Those starless eyes glistened with memories better forgotten and a hurt neither of us would ever soothe.

Xai snapped his fingers. "Now."

"Leave," his Guardians said at once. The single word command reverberated around the room and forced the mortals into action. Damn compelling demons. They were useful in certain situations, but this wasn't one of them.

"That wasn't necessary," I muttered.

Xai set his untouched drink off to the side—as if he couldn't stand the sight of it anymore—while saying, "There's a Scrubber waiting outside. They won't remember anything except that they had a good night."

It took conscious energy not to gape at him.

He brought a Scrubber demon? That explained the additional demonic presence I felt outside. *But why?*

Bringing a demon along who specialized in altering human memory implied he wasn't here to harm. But the Xai I knew would never care about that. He considered our kind superior and never hesitated to play God.

"Don't look so surprised, love," he murmured, seeing right through me in that same way he always did. "I'm not always in the mood for blood."

"Debatable," I replied flatly.

He shrugged one shoulder as if to say, *True.*

I watched as the last of my patrons disappeared. Already I could see their brains working to formulate a logical reason for their sudden desire to leave. Mortals were always quick to ignore their instincts and fabricate stories to explain supernatural occurrences. It was the reason Hell had found sanctuary on this plane.

"Now that we're alone…" Xai steepled his long, elegant fingers against the bar. "Care to dispose of your knives?"

That was an easy question. "Nope."

He clucked his tongue, his expression one of amusement. "Are you going to make me come get them?"

I smiled sweetly. "Are you going to make me kill you?"

His grin grew with anticipation. "The last time we fought, you ended up naked beneath me," he sighed. "A moment I cherish and would love to repeat. However, there's the matter of Lord Zebulon's message that we must discuss first. He wishes to see you."

I should have known that was the reason for his visit. Everything Xai did was for Zeb.

"When?" I asked.

"Sunday." Xai reached into his suit jacket and pulled out an envelope. "I believe all the information you require is in here."

I didn't take the envelope. "What does he want?"

"To talk."

"About?"

"That is for him to explain, not me."

Typical Xai answer. Oh, he knew exactly what Zeb wanted, but he wouldn't tell me. It had nothing to do with morals or loyalty to his Demonic Lord. He just wanted to annoy me, something he excelled at better than others.

Rolling my eyes, I took the envelope and opened it. It was filled with travel documents. "Miami," I said, reading the destination. I looked at Xai, my expression cynical. "There's this great invention called the telephone. Perhaps you've heard of it?"

"Perhaps I wanted to see you," he countered, a slow,

sensual smile forming on his lips.

"I was referring to Zeb flying me to Miami with less than three days' notice, not your surprise appearance." Though, come to think of it, he could have used the phone, too, and just sent me the plane ticket electronically.

"It's an urgent matter."

"Regarding?"

"Nice try," Xai replied as he stood up. The Guardians took that as a sign of permission to leave and did so promptly. "I'll be picking you up from the airport. And it is a business meeting, so please remember to dress appropriately." The look he gave me said my current attire wouldn't cut it. He started toward the door, his mission seemingly accomplished.

"You're forgetting something," I told him when his back was to me.

He glanced over his shoulder, his look dangerously seductive. "Oh, I haven't forgotten our little fight, Evangeline. I have every intention of picking up that particular argument when you arrive in Miami."

"I wasn't talking about my knives," I replied, my voice dry again. "I'm talking about a little thing called 'agreement.' I might have plans this weekend." I didn't, but that wasn't the point. I didn't succumb to anyone's demands, including the Demonic Lord of North America. If he wanted to arrange a meeting, he could call for my availability and schedule some time in Nashville.

Xai smiled. "I have no doubt you'll arrive on time."

"And why is that?"

"Because, Evangeline," he said as he started toward the door again, "you're curious."

Damn straight I was curious. Zeb never summoned me. Even when I worked for him, he would send me a note via courier with his request, and I either accepted the job or refused it. But to send Xai here, and demand my presence in Miami, was suspicious, to say the least. Zeb notoriously hated the southern states. They were too close to the borders with Valentino, the Demonic Lord of South America.

This couldn't be about a job.

First, I was retired.

Second, he would never risk discussing an assassination so close to another Demonic Lord's territory.

So this is personal, then.

Damn.

This really was going to be a long fucking night because now I needed to get my affairs in order. Nothing good ever came from having a personal discussion with a demon lord.

"Oh, by the way," Xai added as an afterthought. "My apologies about your oriental rug. I imagine that will be difficult to replace, yes?"

For the second time tonight, I fought my urge to gape at him. He'd obviously shown up prior to his demon counterparts and deliberately listened in on my phone call with Gwen. I couldn't sense him the way I did demons. Angelic auras were different from the underworld.

But that wasn't what bothered me. Spying I could handle, but his falsely casual statement revealed a lot more about our current situation. And the potential for blackmail.

He knows about Gwen's control issue...

I folded my arms to distract my hands from fondling my knives. Knowing Xai, that was the purpose of his statement. He loved a good fight, and we both knew I was the best fighting partner alive.

"Eavesdropping isn't an attractive trait, Xai."

"Yes, and neither is this soft side you've been showing lately." His sardonic tone grated on my already-tried nerves. Then he grinned, and I stopped breathing.

Wicked.

Cruel.

And downright mean.

This was going to hurt.

"It would be a shame if Lord Zebulon found out about Guinevere's control issues, yes? I suspect he would

9

send her back to Hell for more training, and we both know what that would require."

His sable irises gleamed as the threat settled in the pit of my stomach. I read the hidden meaning behind his words. *Show up on Sunday, or I'll tell Zeb about Gwen.*

"Do it, and I'll kill you," I promised.

He knew my one weakness was my best friend, and he used it against me.

This was why I hated him.

And also why I once loved him. He knew how to play me better than anyone did, and time only strengthened that bond.

"Don't worry, Evangeline. Your secret is safe with me." He fucking winked, the bastard. "Have a lovely evening, darling. I look forward to strip-searching you on Sunday."

CHAPTER TWO

TO-DO LIST:
CREMATORIUM AND THE SILVER MAKER

"YOU DIDN'T NEED TO BURN IT," Gwen muttered, her slender arms folded around her torso. "I mean, the mortals have dry cleaning."

"And how would I explain the stains?" Not to mention the stench. She'd created a corpse burrito by rolling up her date in my oriental rug and then left him in the living room. Even Kevin had gagged a little, and he literally lived for that shit.

"I don't know. Maybe say an animal died?" she suggested as her cute little button nose scrunched.

"Too late now." Not that it would have worked anyway. Handwoven silk was not meant to be deep cleaned, nor was it meant to hold dead bodies. "Next time, remember the plastic sheets, Gwen. I don't want to do this again."

"It hasn't been enjoyable for me either," she murmured, broken. Her cerulean eyes were a shade darker than normal and underlined with unshed tears, and her full lips trembled. Most Succubi didn't kill during sex unless they wanted to, but Gwen couldn't seem to help herself. She always got caught up in the moment, feeding a little too hard, and by the time she realized what she'd done, it was too late.

I wrapped my arm around her small shoulders and hugged her to me. "You'll get there."

"You say that every time, Eve. And every time, you're wrong."

"Then maybe you should take Zane up on his offer." The Incubus had offered to supervise her feedings in the form of threesomes, but so far she'd refused. Mostly because she was secretly in love with the gorgeous man, something he seemed completely oblivious to, and also because a relationship would never work out. They both needed to feed sexually, and it could never be from each other.

"I know it's not what you want to hear," I continued. "But you really need to consider it before someone else finds out." Demons were under strict rules in this region regarding mortal kills, and Gwen had more than exceeded her allotted quota. If Zeb found out, he would send her home, and I'd never see her again.

Hence Xai's parting comments. I had no doubt he would follow through on his unveiled threat if I didn't board that plane Sunday morning. And then my roommate would be in serious danger.

Ultimatums and cryptic games.

Oh, I'd show up all right. If anything, so I could reacquaint the bastard with my knives. The man always did look good in red.

Gwen sniffled. "I'm not sure what would be worse at this point. Sean was so sweet, Eve. He didn't deserve to die like that."

His frozen expression of ecstasy said he hadn't minded all that much, but I kept that thought to myself.

12

She fiddled with a strand of her long, almost-black hair and bit her lip to keep it from trembling. "My heart can't take much more," she admitted. "He's the fourth one this month."

I nodded but remained quiet. There wasn't much to say other than, *I know*.

Gwen sighed and looked upward at the Heavens, as if my ancestors held all the answers, then shook her head. "Ugh, you're right. I need to stop being selfish and talk to Zane. He couldn't possibly hurt me more than I'm hurting right now."

A partial truth. I had a feeling Zane could do a lot of damage if she let him, but her heart was in the right place.

"You're a good person, Gwen." A demon with a conscience was an oddity in this world and probably why she had become my best friend over the years. I hoped she never changed, but I knew there was a strong probability that she would eventually. Most immortals did.

"I'm really not," she replied. "But I'm trying to be."

"And that's what counts." I hugged her again and started toward the crematorium exit. My rug was incinerated, as were the body parts Kevin hadn't wanted, and I'd already fiddled with the building's security tapes. Time for the next stop on our early morning tour around Nashville.

Gwen figured out my intentions about ten minutes into our drive, her lips curling down. "Why are we going to your armory?"

"Errand," I replied vaguely. Gwen was one of two people who knew about this place, and because I had trust issues, it was the only one she knew about. But this weaponry superseded the others because it contained my favorite asset: Danny Gleason, also known as the other person I trusted with this location.

The parking lot was vacant except for an inexpensive gray sedan. With the amount of money I paid Gleason, he could afford better transportation. I hopped out of my considerably nicer SUV, and Gwen followed with a grumble. The bar didn't help me afford this lifestyle, but rather my former career did. A few millennia as the top assassin on Earth had set me up for, well, eternity. It quite literally paid to be the Daughter of Death.

I tapped twice on the side-entrance door, paused, and then added a third knock. A sleepy and slightly irritated Gleason greeted me with his trademark scowl in place.

"Hello, handsome," I said with a kiss to his cheek. His deep-red stubble tickled my lips. So sexy. His thick auburn hair and muscular build weren't bad either. Gwen knew better than to touch him, so she just gave a finger wave. This was the one mortal on Earth I forbade her from fondling, no matter how much she might want to. I needed him alive and would go to great lengths to keep him that way.

"This better be good," he grumbled.

"I'm always good," I teased.

His green eyes shifted upward in his version of an eye-roll before settling on me. "Stop flirting and tell me why I'm here."

"Such a sweet talker, Gleason."

"It's three o'clock in the morning, Eve. If you want sweet talk, then fuck me first."

I patted his sturdy chest. "All in good time, my love."

He snorted. "Right."

We both knew I couldn't sleep with him, not because I found him lacking in any way, but because I considered him invaluable.

Silver didn't exist on Earth thanks to demons eradicating it over a millennium ago. They replaced element 47 with a new version that was considerably less harmful to underworld beings, and then they unleashed an army of Scrubbers to alter mortal perception. Humans no longer knew the substance existed and were hardwired to not even consider the potential chemical properties. All because pure silver could kill demons.

Which was why Gleason meant so much to me— because despite the mental blocks in place, he had figured out how to reproduce the precious metal. It helped that I provided him with the source material in the form of an old blade.

"Do you have my toys?" After Xai left, I had sent Gleason a list with what I needed from the vault.

"Yes." He led the way to his lab. "You realize you have a key, right? That you don't need me to pull this shit out for you?"

"But then whom would I flirt with?" Not a lie, but not the truth either. I would tell him why I wanted him here after I reviewed the merchandise. Then the fireworks would start.

He just shook his head and kept moving.

Gwen admired his ass with a seductive smile, and I flashed her a look. She just shrugged—her way of saying, *He wears those jeans well.* Which, yes, he did, but my heart only seemed interested in a certain tall, dark, and handsome angel in a black suit. Two-thousand-plus years, and I still found him attractive. Unbelievable.

Gleason stopped at a table and folded his arms. It stretched his gray shirt across that strong chest, which elicited a sharp intake of breath from the Succubus beside me. Or maybe her reaction was to all the silver tools on the wood surface. I picked up the one closest to me.

Pure silver was too soft to form solid weapons, but even a tiny amount fused with a harder metal could kill a demon. The hair sticks in my hand were exactly what I needed. I twisted up my blonde strands with one hand and slid them into place to test their weights. The sharp, pointy ends rested against the back of my neck at the perfect location.

"Nice," I said, grabbing the shoes next. They were the right size and fit, with a sharp silver-infused heel. A necklace and matching earrings were up next, all holding sharp edges in the right places, and last was a set of handcrafted blades with an *E* carved into the handle. I caressed them in reverence as I met Gleason's impatient gaze. "I just fell even more in love with you."

He wasn't amused. "Are we finished here?"

"Not quite." I secured the blades from the table and

prepared for a verbal battle. One that would put me on one side and Gwen and Gleason on the other. "Xai came to see me tonight."

"*What?*" And there was the shouting I expected from Gwen. "We've been together for the last *four hours*, and you're just mentioning this to me?"

"We had other problems to deal with."

She scoffed at that. "Oh, please. We deal with dead bodies every week, and Xai is so not the norm." Her eyes narrowed as speculation tainted her features. "Did you fuck him?"

Of course she would ask that. "No, it was a business visit. Zeb wants to see me."

Her jaw dropped while Gleason paled. He knew of the Demonic Lord because I'd warned him years ago that his work for me could get him killed. But the insanely smart chemistry professor had been too intrigued by the "new metal" to ignore the opportunity, not to mention his fascination with the underworld. I told him everything because I considered it a fair trade for more silver products. Most of mine were centuries old and tarnished. The effect didn't dull, but the look and feel did.

"Why?" he asked, all his earlier grumpiness replaced by concern.

"He wouldn't tell me." Hence the reason I called this impromptu meeting. "But I'm flying to Miami on Sunday."

"Like hell you are," Gwen snapped. "The last time you went to see Xai, he…" She trailed off after remembering the mortal in the room. "Yeah, well, you know what he did."

I did. Only too well. "I can handle Xai."

Her eyes told me just how much she didn't believe that. Fair enough.

"Anyway, there's a small chance Zeb knows about our arrangement," I said, bringing us back to the point. "It's unlikely, but he isn't following our established protocol, and something feels wrong." I couldn't put my finger on it, but my instincts flared with warning. Nothing good was waiting for me in Miami.

"Yet you're going," Gwen muttered.

"Yes." Here was the part I dreaded having to say, but I had to tell her. She deserved to know. "Xai overheard our call tonight about the rug." Her rosy cheeks whitened as my words translated. "It wasn't enough to cause an immediate issue, but it could pique Zeb's interest if he tells him." Which he would if I didn't show up on Sunday, and then we'd be dealing with not only an irritated Zeb but also a curious one. And the last thing Nashville needed was a pissed-off Demonic Lord to arrive with his entourage.

"If?" Gwen sounded both incredulous and nervous. "You mean 'when.'"

I pursed my lips. "Maybe, but Xai's more likely to stay quiet if I show up on Sunday." He loved to piss me off, but he never crossed the line into unforgivable territory, and he had to know this would do it. "Besides, he doesn't have ample proof of anything. We've disposed of the body, and it's only the one occurrence. But I'd rather Xai not give Zeb a reason to watch you."

"What do you think he wants?" Gleason asked, his expression more curious than afraid. "Because I have a feeling if he knew anything about me, I wouldn't be standing here right now."

I shook my head. "Zeb's a master manipulator who loves a good game of chess. Your being alive may only be temporary, which is why I need you to take a vacation."

His scowl returned. "It's the middle of summer semester, Eve."

"Then it's a good thing you have teaching assistants, Professor Gleason."

He didn't appear impressed by that response. "And where do you want me to go?"

"Europe." The Demonic Lord in that region loathed Zeb. It would take months for them to work out any kind of mutual agreement, and by then, Gleason would be somewhere else. "It's just a precaution," I added. I doubted this meeting had anything to do with my silver maker, mostly because I'd done a fantastic job hiding him. If Zeb had discovered my secret, I would be more impressed than anything else.

"He probably just wants you for a job," Gwen murmured, her earlier concern replaced by thoughtfulness. "And Xai used it as an excuse to see you." She added that last part with an eye-roll. "Fucker."

"Most likely, but they both know I'm retired." Not that either of them cared.

"Right, and they want to change your mind. Especially Xai."

"If anyone wants to force me out of retirement, it's Zeb." He always did enjoy a good negotiation, and he loved confusing his opponent, which could explain his sending Xai to the bar.

"Or maybe," Gwen continued, her tone speculative. "Maybe it's not a job at all." Her brow furrowed. "You haven't done anything to piss him off, have you?"

"Not recently." I could think of over a dozen things I'd done in the last decade alone, but something drastic enough to warrant punishment? Doubtful. Zeb liked me too much.

"Not a convincing answer," she replied knowingly. "What about Lord Valentino? Miami is near his territory. Maybe he's requested a meeting through Lord Zebulon?"

"I haven't seen that arrogant bastard in over fifty years, so I doubt it. Besides, Zeb would never hand me over to him." He hated Valentino more than I did and would never agree to a trade.

Gwen sighed. "Well, I have no idea, then."

"Me neither." But as Xai predicted, I was curious. Why Miami, and why Sunday? "The way I see it, Zeb's provided me with a fully financed trip to Miami. Might as well enjoy the mini-vacay on his dime." The lightness in my voice was more for their benefit than mine. This would in no way turn out to be a fun trip, but they didn't need to know that. The last thing I wanted was for them to worry. I could handle myself.

My attempt at humor seemed to work, because

Gwen's lips lifted at the corners. "Right. Because you need free vacations."

"It's the beach. I'd be a fool to turn it down."

And a fool to go, her eyes seemed to say.

I couldn't argue with that.

It seemed to be a common theme with Xai, ever since the day I Fell. Love made you do crazy things, and this trip would be no exception.

CHAPTER THREE

DEMONS DON'T WALK ON WATER; THEY FLOAT

"AIRPORT SECURITY STILL SUCKS," I told Gwen as I walked through Miami's baggage claim toward the airport exit. "They can't seem to see beyond stereotyping."

When I went through the metal detector in Nashville, it had beeped loudly. The agent took one look at my violet bikini, nearly translucent blouse, and short jean skirt and smirked. "Have a safe flight," was all she said before giving me a not-so-thorough pat down. She erroneously assumed a woman of my fashion sense couldn't be a threat to society. A misconception of epic proportions. I couldn't be deadlier if I tried.

"Maybe you should consider a job with the STA," Gwen suggested around a mouthful of food. I'd obviously caught her eating a late lunch when I called. "If anything, fabricating the credentials to get in could be fun."

"It's called the TSA, as in the Transportation Security Administration, and it would bore me to tears." Going through luggage all day and patting people down for weapons? Yawn. Unless they let me keep the weapons. I would totally agree to those terms.

"True," she agreed. "So, any sign of tall, dark, and dead yet?"

I started unfastening the buttons of my blouse as I continued my journey. "Not yet." A few males trained their eyes my way as my shirt gaped open to reveal my string bikini top.

"Send the asshole my love when you do." Gwen's voice was saccharine sweet.

"Would that be a kick to the groin or a slap across the face?"

"Both, clearly. And give his balls a good grab and twist for me as well." She sipped loudly through a straw and let it go with a pop. "What is all that rustling?"

"I'm juggling the phone while stuffing my shirt into my bag." Xai had said to dress professionally, so I'd opted for Miami Beach attire. I zipped up the backpack and swung it over my shoulder.

"You're stripping at the airport?"

"Yep." Much to the amusement of the security personnel standing near the doors. "It's July, it's hot, and I need to work on my tan."

She snorted. "I hate to break this to you, Eve, but you don't tan."

"Even angels can dream, Gwen."

"Uh-huh." She sounded amused.

I spotted Xai just outside the exit, leaning against a sleek black automobile with his long legs stretched out in front of him and crossed at the ankles. His hands were tucked casually into the pockets of his black dress pants, and his thick hair was lightly ruffled thanks to the warm Miami breeze. He was the picture of nonchalance with the sleeves of his white dress shirt rolled up to the elbows and the top button undone. A sliver of tanned skin peeked out, alluding to the hot, solid male that existed beneath.

My blood heated with memories of his touch, of his body hovering over mine, him claiming me as his… Him throwing me away like trash…

One day I wouldn't react to him. Today was not that day.

I cleared my throat. "I found tall, dark, and dead."

Xai raised his gaze from my purple bikini top upon hearing my description of him. Then both of his eyebrows shot up when he overheard Gwen reply. "Good. Don't forget to deliver my message to his balls."

"I won't," I replied. "Try to stay out of trouble while I'm gone."

"I'm the one who should be telling you that," she grumbled. "Call me after your meeting."

"Yep." I hung up and dropped my phone into my purse.

Xai studied me as he tried to figure out which point to address first. He chose the one most men would choose. "And what, pray tell, would the Succubus like to say to my balls?"

"Hasn't anyone ever told you that eavesdropping is rude?" I knew he couldn't help it. Our hearing wasn't exactly human.

He smiled. "Just because you choose to ignore your natural talents, Evangeline, does not mean I choose to ignore mine."

"Keep talking like that and I'll stop ignoring said natural talents," I replied, returning his smile.

"Tease." He took my bag and placed it in the trunk. "Tall, dark, and dead?"

"Gwen's new nickname for you," I replied as I settled into the leather bucket seat beside him. "And to answer your earlier question, she requested that I give you a kick to the groin, followed by a pull and twist."

Xai's amusement was palpable as we left the arrivals area. "Well," he murmured after a moment of contemplation, "I do enjoy her enthusiasm."

"I'll be sure to let her know."

"Please do," he replied. "And also let her know that although I truly appreciate her giving you fashion advice, your attire does not quite meet the required business-professional standards I stressed during our last meeting."

"Oh? Are you going to make me change?" I asked, silently daring him to try.

"Mmm, unfortunately, we don't have time for such pleasures."

"You sound disappointed."

"Hardly, love. I'm sure I'll find a reason to strip you later. But for now, we need to discuss your meeting with Lord Zebulon."

"Are you going to tell me why I'm here?"

Xai's expression took on a brooding air, causing my stomach to churn. I didn't like that look. He rarely used it, but when he did, our conversations never ended well.

"You're going to need to leave your silver in the car." Apparently, that was his way of saying no to my previous question. Fine. He didn't have to tell me why Zeb wanted to meet, but he had to be crazy if he thought I'd meet with a demon lord unarmed.

"Not going to happen."

His hands tightened on the steering wheel, making his exposed forearms flex. "I'm not playing, Evangeline. You cannot enter with weapons, or there will be severe consequences."

I studied his immaculate profile. "I've always carried weapons around Zeb."

"Lord Zebulon," he corrected. "And not this time."

"What the fuck is going on, Xai?"

He rubbed his eyes and shook his head. "I can't, Eve. Just show Lord Zebulon some respect today. It'll go a long way."

A sarcastic reply tickled my tongue, but my instincts held it back. Xai excelled at lying. He could talk a woman out of her clothes in seconds or bring an enemy to his knees with a few well-argued words, but his tone and body language made me believe him now.

Something was wrong.

Very, very wrong.

I fidgeted with my skirt as we continued the journey in silence, considering his request. No way would I meet with Zeb empty-handed, but I could try for respect. And maybe I would grab a shirt from my bag as well.

The Demonic Lord rarely pissed me off, and most of the time, I actually liked the guy. He had a sardonic sense of humor I could respect, not to mention his chess skills. I enjoyed a challenge, and he was certainly that.

After twenty or so minutes, Xai exited the highway and headed in the direction of the beach. I counted the palm trees as we passed them and admired the crystal waters beyond. When he turned in to a marina, my assassin brain clicked into gear. Boats were a great way to isolate prey and then dispose of the remains. Even a mile away from the coast could do the trick.

Definitely not leaving all my weapons in the car.

Xai killed the engine and stepped out without a word, his expression stoic and body language unreadable. That alone told me what to expect from this meeting. If this were a simple job, he would have told me and continued our playful banter.

He opened my door and placed his elbow on the roof of the car to block me from exiting. "Please," was all he said.

Both my eyebrows popped up at that single word. Xai begging? Hell no. That did not happen. Ever. And I knew exactly what he wanted too. My knives, items he usually had no problem physically taking from me in a sexy little fight. But not this time.

I pressed my palm against his hard abdomen to nudge him back while I stepped out of the car. My flip-flops clacked on the concrete, reminding me that I'd left my new heels in the backpack. No worries. I still had my hair sticks.

He stared down at me, that elbow still on the car and

his body heat radiating into mine. Despite the humid air, I shivered at his nearness. That special spicy scent that was all Xai wafted over me, melting my insides and speeding up my heart. He always did this to me, even when I hated him.

"I don't know what's going on," I admitted. "But we both know I won't go down without a fight."

I unsheathed the knives at the top of my thighs and handed them over. Three blades total. I kept the sharp silver cross at my neck and the items holding up my hair. His eyes danced over them with recognition, but he didn't request I remove them; he simply pocketed my weapons and pressed his forehead to mine.

No words.

No warning.

Just a gentle touch that left me wondering what the hell had gotten into him. Xai did not do sweet gestures. It wasn't in his blood.

"Let's go," he murmured. His hand slid to my lower back to urge me forward. I kicked his passenger door shut behind me and tried to ignore the way his skin burned against mine. It felt right, too right.

This was the part where a sane person would probably try to run. No, not quite. Most people wouldn't have even gotten to this point. But I never shied away from a challenge, nor was I the type to flee. I tackled my problems head-on because that's the only way I knew how.

I kept my footsteps light, my stride confident, and my head held high, even as an eerie sensation crawled over my skin. There were at least a dozen demons surrounding us, some of their auras more ominous than others. My nostrils flared at the acrid scent underlying their presence. A human would catch the faint hint of sulfur, while it hit my sensitive nose with the force of a freight train. *So many demons.*

Xai's palm flexed as he shifted me toward a dock leading up to a pristine yacht. I eyed the beauty with interest. Elegant furnishings, fresh paint, new flooring, and untarnished wood all suggested this was a recent purchase.

"Underworld 6," I said, reading the name on the side. "That's original."

No comment from the dark angel, but his mouth curled slightly at the edges. Clearly, I wasn't the only one who found humor in it.

He led us onto the deck and then down a set of stairs into a plush meeting area with a fully stocked bar. The hallway at the back likely led to a bedroom or two, or maybe those were in the area above. I doubted a tour was on the agenda for the afternoon, not that I needed one. There were at least three escape avenues in this room alone should I need one.

Xai slid behind the bar and grabbed a bottle of whiskey from the top shelf. Then he set two glasses on the granite countertop and poured a healthy portion into each before pushing one my way. I accepted it and shot the liquid back into my throat, enjoying the burn on the way down. He followed suit, then poured himself another as two Guardians strolled into the room.

"I confiscated them," Xai said by way of greeting. I assumed he meant the knives because the demons relaxed at his words. Interesting that he didn't mention my other accessories. The demons would be able to sense them, but perhaps they assumed the slight irritant to be a result of residue or from the close proximity of the weapons in the car.

The two bulky demons positioned themselves beside each doorway, folded their thick arms, and trained their beady eyes on me. Their defensive postures practically dared me to try to escape. I suppressed a smirk. I could immobilize two brainless goons in my sleep. It was the Dargarians outside that concerned me. The fire-breathing shape-shifters were not only fast but also intelligent and a very rare demon breed. I didn't sense them, but I knew they were there. Zeb didn't go anywhere without his favorite pets.

"Hello, Evangeline." Zeb's smooth voice floated

through the room as he appeared out of thin air, almost as if my thoughts had conjured him.

I maintained a bored expression during his exercise of power. Corporal shifting might be rare, but he wasn't the only demon who possessed the ability. "Lord Zebulon," I greeted, mostly to see what he would do and to get a rise out of Xai. It worked. Both men raised their brows at my formality, making me smile. "See, I know how to mind my manners. Now, how about you return the favor and tell me why the fuck I'm here."

Xai visibly cringed at my bluntness, while Zeb's lips twitched in amusement. His crisp white shirt glowed against his dark skin, giving him an angelic appearance I knew to be a lie. He clasped his hands behind his back before sauntering toward me.

"As direct as ever," he murmured as he invaded my personal space. "I've always liked that about you."

I didn't react to his nearness, because I knew that was precisely what he wanted. This display of power was nothing new, and neither was the dangerous gleam in his brown eyes. He cocked his bald head, that knowing gaze sliding over me. My hands hung open at my sides, legs spread, shoulders relaxed. Despite his intimidation, I didn't feel threatened. If he wanted to dance, I'd change my stance, but for now, I remained at ease with the bar and Xai behind me, and Zeb to my front.

"You were right, Xai," he murmured.

"I usually am," was his casual reply.

Zeb revealed his hand then, holding it palm up, and my eyes zeroed in on the familiar item he held. "I believe this belongs to you."

I gaped at it, not only because he held it without flinching but also because it was covered in blood. Demon blood.

"What's going on?" I asked as confusion and shock ran through me. Zeb was holding one of my original blades. It was an antique with my initials etched into the corner, and the metal hadn't tarnished. Red welts littered his palm as his skin reacted to the silver-laced handle, but he held it the way one would a utensil.

"Where did you find that?" I asked, curious.

Xai moved to take his place beside Zeb. He had served as the Demonic Lord's right-hand man since the day I Fell, which made both of them very old. They stared at me with the same inscrutable expression, which showered goose bumps down my arms. I took it as a positive sign that the yacht remained docked, but their show of solidarity left me uneasy. It always did.

"It was found near a pile of ashes," Xai explained, his voice low and even. Meaning they'd found my blade near a demon's corpse, because that's what silver did. It incinerated demonic beings from the inside out when shoved into their hearts, similar to a cremator for humans, only without all the hassle. Underworld crime scenes were always easier to clean up.

"Okay." They found my knife at a questionable scene. "So, who did I supposedly kill?" Because that had to be the point of all this. Once I had a name, I could refute it and be on my merry way.

Both men continued studying me in that eerie way, but it was Xai who broke the silence. "The blood on the knife belongs to Kalida."

My heart stopped.

Or maybe I wouldn't be on my way.

Because that was no ordinary name. It belonged to Zeb's only child. His daughter.

Oh, shit.

CHAPTER FOUR

WARNING: ASSASSINS DO NOT PLAY WELL WITH OTHERS

BETRAYAL PUNCHED ME IN THE STOMACH. Xai led me here, all the while knowing I would be accused of murdering a Demonic Lord's daughter, and never thought to warn me. Or rather, didn't *care* enough to warn me.

Bastard.

It shouldn't have surprised me, but it did. It fucking hurt. He knew what would happen if Zeb found me guilty. Punishment—and it wouldn't be my death. It would be something much worse because I couldn't die. But I could feel pain. Excruciating, unending pain. And Xai had subjected me to that fate without blinking an eye.

My heart ached as hatred thickened my blood. He always hurt me. Always. And this time was no different. When would I learn not to trust him? Not to love him?

I caught his gaze and let him see, just for a moment, what he had done. Not that he would care. He never did. And the stoic glance he gave me back said just that.

Another piece of my soul broke in that moment. A tiny, infinitesimal fragment that I would never see again. Gone to join the others that he'd previously destroyed. It was at moments like this that I wondered if I would ever be whole again. If I even had enough energy left to try.

I closed my eyes, and when they reopened, I made sure they were as unfeeling as Xai's and refocused on the too-calm Demonic Lord. The fact that he hadn't tried to punish me yet suggested he knew what I was about to say, but it needed to come out just the same.

"I may not have liked Kalida"—an understatement— "but I didn't kill her. And even if I did, I wouldn't be careless enough to leave a weapon with my initials on it at the crime scene. Not to mention, all my blades are in far better shape than that one. Check Xai's pockets for exhibit A. Furthermore—"

"Enough." Power underlined that single word as Zeb asserted himself as the ruler in the room. His aura surrounded me, suffocated me, and demanded my submission, but I held my position. No way would I bow to him. Not even for this. But I would stop talking. And I inclined my head in a measure of respect before meeting his gaze.

We stared at each other for too long, and I knew my fate was being decided. If he found me guilty, I would fight. It didn't matter that he had me outnumbered. I wouldn't be punished for something I didn't do, no matter how compelling the evidence.

Xai tucked his hands into his pockets. "For what it's worth, I don't believe Eve did this." I didn't bother to look at him or acknowledge his vote of confidence. If he truly considered me innocent, he should have warned me. But he didn't.

"Yes, you've mentioned that already," Zeb replied, eyes smoldering. A touch of that fury underlined his voice as he added, "I allowed this meeting because of your conviction and also because I don't recall Eve ever making a mistake on this scale before. Although, maybe she's grown soft in her retirement."

"*She* is standing right here, and you're more than welcome to test your retirement theory," I said. I'd love a reason to fight Xai right now. To drive a knife through his gut, twist, and yank it out, all the while staring deep into his eyes to see the flash of pain. Maybe that would give him a brief glimpse into how he made me feel every day.

"Yes, testing your skills is exactly what I want to do." Zeb looked to Xai, and I felt a grin coming until he continued. "You suggested I give her a week to discover the one responsible. I'm in agreement, but should she come back empty-handed, I'll have no choice but to seek retribution."

Xai tilted his head in acquiescence. "Certainly."

"You will work with her," Zeb added. "And should she disappear while under your watch, her impending punishment shall fall to you, plus whatever else I have in mind."

I expected some form of argument to that, but my arrogant ex merely shrugged. "I see no problem." Of course he wouldn't. He assumed I couldn't outrun him. An assumption that would be his downfall someday. But not this week, because I had no intention of running anywhere.

Someone had set me up, and that someone was going to die. Painfully.

"Then I shall leave the two of you to get started." Zeb finally addressed me again, his hypnotic gaze dancing over my attire, or lack thereof. "It's lovely to see you again, dear. Good luck." His tone held a touch of warmth that suggested he meant it, then he disappeared in a whoosh of energy. It tickled my skin and left a blast of heat in its wake. The move surprised me enough to widen my gaze. Zeb hadn't just teleported; he'd left this plane. For Hell. A move that usually required a Portal Dweller.

"He's gotten stronger," I whispered to no one in

particular. *How?*

"A lot has changed since you left, love." Xai reached out to touch me, and I stepped backward away from him.

"Don't."

His lips curled in challenge. "You know that only turns me on more."

I did, because anger had the same impact on me. No one fought me the way Xai did, meeting me move for move until he found a weakness to exploit. And whenever he pinned me, I always caved. Every fucking time.

My hands curled into fists. "You could have warned me."

He didn't seem particularly worried about it. "Zeb needed to see your reaction in order to believe it, Eve. Especially on this."

I almost laughed. "Is that your justification for waltzing me into a death sentence? That Zeb wouldn't have believed my reaction otherwise?" I shook my head. "You're an asshole."

His eyebrows shot up. "I am. That's never changed, nor is it anything new, but I kept you in the dark to protect you. Your reaction just now saved your life today, and the only reason you reacted that way was because I didn't tell you about Kalida ahead of time."

I snorted. "Bullshit. If you'd told me, I could have walked in and told Zeb point-blank that I didn't do it. The scene was clearly staged, and we both know I'm not suicidal enough to kill his daughter."

"Do you have any idea what I've had to do to keep him from killing you outright?" Xai countered, his tone harsher and less controlled than before as he stepped into my personal space. "His only child was just murdered, and all evidence points to you."

"Which is pretty fucking convenient, don't you think?"

"Of course it is, but Lord Zebulon isn't in a rational frame of mind. There's a reason he's in Hell right now torturing inferior demons for sport. He's hurting, he needs an outlet for his rage, and up until four days ago, *you* were his primary target. *I* changed that." He wrapped his hand around the back of my neck and forced me to hold his smoldering gaze.

"I didn't warn you, because he needed to see your shock and indignation. If you came in here spouting denials, he would have snapped. You forget how well I know him, Evangeline. I did what I did to protect you, just as I've always done."

"As you've always done," I repeated. "Right."

"You're infuriating," he growled.

"And you're insufferable," I threw back, eyes narrowed. "There's no way in hell I'm working with you on this case. Just give me the information you have, and I'll handle the rest."

I could see in his eyes how badly he wanted to dominate me with his mouth, but he held back. Probably because he knew I'd stab him. His explanation held merit, but centuries of hurt kept me from forgiving him outright or acknowledging that he probably did save me from a painful punishment today. Whatever he did, it wasn't for me, but for him. He was the most selfish being I'd ever met, and no way had that changed over our latest decade apart.

His breath feathered over my lips as he chuckled dryly. "Oh, darling, you forget that it's not only your life on the line, but also mine. If you disappear, I'll be the one Lord Zebulon punishes."

"Is that supposed to encourage me to work with you? Because I've gotta be honest, that kind of makes me want to run just for the hell of it."

Xai tightened his hold around my neck and bit my lower lip in response. The metallic taste of blood seeped into my mouth, propelling me into action. I shoved him away, only to be spun around and yanked backward into his chest. He pressed his mouth to my ear. "You've grown soft, Eve."

Oh, I'd show him soft. I dropped as low as his arms allowed and swept out my leg to knock him off balance before slamming my skull into his sternum to send him backward. But he didn't go down. He merely stumbled, grasped my waist, and yanked me back into him again.

This time his arms felt like cement blocks as he held me captive, but it put my hands right where I wanted them against his hips. I pickpocketed a knife while he bent to kiss my neck.

"Disappointing," he murmured. "It seems you haven't kept up with your sparring."

"Really?" I pressed the blade against his inner thigh, hard enough for him to feel it through his thin dress pants. One upward swipe would have him pissing blood for at least an hour.

He grinned against my sensitive skin. "Careful, love. You wouldn't want to damage my best feature."

"Try me."

"Are you two done flirting yet?" a deep voice drawled. A scrawny blond demon stood in the doorway wearing a disgruntled expression.

Xai licked a path up to my ear and nibbled the lobe. "Evangeline, this is Tax. He'll be helping us."

I let him feel the sharpness of the knife, metal to skin, as I sliced a hole through his designer trousers. Too bad silver didn't hurt him the way it did a demon. "You don't seem to be understanding the part about my doing this alone."

"You're never alone, love," he whispered.

His words startled me so much that my head spun. It took me a second to realize it had *literally* spun because he'd twirled me around to press my back up against the bar and captured my hands in his. A squeeze to my wrist released the grip on the knife.

Fuck!

Pissed, I kicked out, only to have my legs blocked and pinned by his strong thighs. I glowered up at him. "I hate you."

"I know." He brushed his mouth over mine and pulled back when I tried to bite him. The spec of blood on his lips had my thighs clenching. Fighting with him like this set my blood on fire, and the erection against my belly wasn't helping matters. "You're not doing this alone, and if you fight me each step of the way, we'll never exonerate you. So either you work with me or we both end up in the fiery pits of Hell. Your choice."

Both? Pretty sure only I would end up there.

"We work well together," he reminded, his voice softening to the one he used in the bedroom. Coaxing, seductive, and deceptively sweet. God, I loved and hated that tone. I started to squirm, but he held me steady, his gaze burning into mine. "I'm not going anywhere, Evangeline, so either deal with it or start stripping. Again, your choice."

His tongue traced my bottom lip, soothing the already-healing wound he created minutes ago, before dipping inside to gently explore my mouth. Whiskey, mint, and a taste that was all Xai teased my senses and forced my body into submission. I craved him more than air, and no matter how hard I fought it, I could never deny my attraction to him.

The clearing of a throat reminded me we weren't alone. Not only was Tax watching us, but two Guardians were as well. The former looked irritated, while the latter were a little too interested in the show, which effectively killed the mood.

Xai dropped my hands and bent to retrieve the item I used to slice his trousers. Then he held it out to me, extending his version of an olive branch. *Work with me.*

Damn it. What choice did I have? Seven days resembled an instant for an immortal. I would need all the assistance I could get, especially since I hadn't kept up on demon politics during my retirement. And although I could name all my enemies, I didn't have complete lists for Zeb or Kalida. And who better to acquaint me with those than Xai?

"I assume you have a place to start?" I asked as I accepted the item from his hand.

His swoon-worthy grin melted the last of my resolve. There were harsher chores than staring at that handsome face for a week. "Oh, I have more than that. I already have a lead."

My breath halted. What? That implied he'd started investigating on his own. Why? To prove my innocence? No. That wouldn't fit his style. He only did things for himself. But he didn't care about Kalida, unless their relationship had changed over the last few years. Had they become lovers in my absence? My stomach revolted at the idea.

Him taking her to bed... That was an image I did not need in my head.

"Come on," he murmured, wrapping an arm around my stiff shoulders to pull me away from the bar. "I'll brief you in the car. Tax will follow us."

"Yes, because that's what we Trackers do," the other man muttered. His snarky tone and timely interruptions had me liking him already. I gathered from his comment that he was a Tracker demon, which meant he would be useful, just as Xai had implied.

I sighed. *Fine.* We could collaborate on this mission, but that didn't mean we were partners. Assassins worked alone for a reason; we didn't play well with others. But we did know how to play along to obtain information, and that's exactly what I would do, for now.

I reclaimed my other knives from Xai's pockets and sheathed them as we walked. He pretended not to notice, but his smirk said he'd felt my wandering hands.

His allowing me to recover my silver seemed to be another olive branch. I extended one back by not knocking his arm off my shoulders. Or at least that's what I told myself.

Logic would be the only way to survive the week, because the second I let any emotion in, I'd be done for and Xai would no doubt ruin me all over again.

Just like the night I first Fell.

CHAPTER FIVE

WHISKEY ON THE ROCKS WITH A SIDE OF CONFUSION, PLEASE

SCOTT STREATOR.

A thirty-seven-year-old male with a smile meant to turn heads and a charming personality to go with it. He was built for the beach, with his blond hair, hazel eyes, and toned physique. I flipped through the file again before setting it on the table.

"Your best lead is a human?" Incredulity colored my tone. Kalida was never very capable or strong, but she could have easily handled a mortal.

Xai finished his whiskey and signaled for the hotel bartender with a nod. "I'm not suggesting he actually killed her, but I suspect he knows something that could be useful." His expression turned bored as the busty female flounced over to do his bidding. "I'd like a refill."

"Whiskey or something else?" she asked in a sultry

tone that beckoned sex.

His gaze fell to her ample cleavage before slowly rising to her lips. "More whiskey, darling."

"Coming right up." She put an extra sway in her hips that Xai admired as she walked away.

I rolled my eyes. "That girl wouldn't survive ten minutes in bed with you." He might feign interest, but I knew his tastes, and that redhead was all curves and no flair. Xai preferred a woman who could fight him in the bedroom, and sometimes win.

"Mmm, I would break her in less than five," he murmured. "Not that I would ever invite her to bed to begin with."

"Then you'd better let her down gently, because I think she's expecting a huge tip tonight."

He didn't look impressed in the slightest, despite having checked out her ample assets. "I can admire a confident woman, but not a blind one. She has to know that no sane man would choose her when he has you as a date."

"A line?" I teased, trying to lighten the suddenly somber mood. We so did not need to go there. "You can do better than that."

"It's not a line, Evangeline, but the truth." No hint of humor or jest, just Xai. He always did this—uttered what he considered to be facts without having any idea how they affected me.

Our mutual attraction wasn't the problem. We always wanted each other and likely always would, but while Xai craved my body, he didn't desire my heart, and that was our downfall. I wanted more, and his selfish nature wouldn't allow it. He'd proven that time and time again, yet my body sang for him even now, despite a lifetime of duplicity. One touch, and I caved. Every. Single. Time.

"Always living in the past," he whispered.

"And always damning my future," I replied softly.

His pupils dilated with an intense emotion that singed the air between us. "One day you'll understand."

"You've been saying that for centuries."

"Yes, and still you're blinded by what you choose to believe, and fail to *see*." He wrapped his hand around the back of my neck to hold me in place, effectively silencing my pending retort. The small table between us suddenly felt infinitesimal as he leaned over it, entering my personal space.

"Xai…"

"Shh." His lips brushed mine just as the waitress returned. He didn't acknowledge her but merely kissed me in that deceptively soft way of his. I fought not to return the gesture, but my mouth moved on autopilot, and when my lips parted in anticipation of his tongue, he pulled back.

"Was that gentle enough, love?" he asked against my mouth, his dark eyes holding mine. "Or should I be less subtle?"

"Please don't," Tax said as he dragged a chair over. He'd arrived shortly after us but disappeared without an explanation. None of our rooms were ready yet, according to Xai, hence our impromptu meeting at the bar.

Xai released me and picked up his glass to take a sip. "Is he here?" he asked, his tone bored. The missing redhead suggested his message had been received loud and clear. Poor girl. At least she wasn't left shivering in the aftermath of his warmth. *Teasing bastard.*

"Room 2517," Tax replied. The thin demon eyed the expensive furnishings of the bar with interest. "At least he has good taste in hotels."

"I assume the 'he' we're discussing is your human lead?" I picked up the file again to reread the notes regarding his employment. A smooth-talking criminal with ties to the Miami drug trafficking industry and a propensity for hurting women. No permanent address because he preferred to move from hotel to hotel as the industry required.

My kind of former assignment, but not what I expected for this case.

I dropped the papers and allowed the uncertainty to

color my tone. "I'm not seeing how he has anything to do with Kalida."

"They were lovers, darling. Though, what she saw in him is beyond me."

"You sound a little salty about that, Xai."

"Hardly," he scoffed. "I would just expect a woman of her background to have higher standards."

Yes, because a Demonic Lord no doubt raised his daughter with specific relationship values in mind. Right.

"So how do you know they were lovers?" All the surveillance photos were of Streator and his business associates. Nothing on Kalida.

"Tax," he replied simply.

"I tracked her essence to him," the Tracker elaborated.

"Was he one of her human feeders?" I asked, referring to Kalida's need to feed sexually, like Gwen. Despite Zeb being her father, she'd inherited her mother's Succubi genetics. Demon breeding was unpredictable at best.

Xai swirled the contents of his drink. "I can't imagine another reason for their involvement."

"Maybe, maybe not." Tax frowned. "He reeks of demon, and not just Kalida."

"Interesting," Xai said, thoughtful. "He's scheduled to stay here a few days and has a meeting lined up with business associates tomorrow by the pool. Fancy some sunshine, darling?"

"You're the eavesdropper, Xai. Maybe you should work on that golden tan of yours while I go through Streator's room."

"I'll go check out his room," Tax interjected. "I want to familiarize myself with the various demon auras surrounding him and his men. From what I sensed, Kalida isn't the only one who has fallen into his bed."

My eyebrows rose. "A man capable of seducing multiple demons? Does he have Incubus ancestors?" A glance at his photo had my nose scrunching. "No, definitely not good-looking enough for that."

"So you agree with my assessment that he's an intriguing lead?"

I met Xai's amused gaze. "I'm more impressed than ten minutes ago, but I'm not confident in his involvement with her death. It seems much more likely that one of Zeb's enemies is responsible, one who either desired my punishment or thought to set me up."

The culprit clearly had a death wish, because I did not take lightly to being framed for murder in such a sloppy manner. As an assassin, retired or otherwise, I applauded my cleanup efforts. To leave my degraded, bloody blade at the scene only added insult to injury. As if I could ever be so careless.

"We also need a list of Kalida's competitors," I continued. "Specifically, those who didn't approve of Zeb appointing his daughter as Ōrdinātum of this region." That designation was typically reserved for high-ranking demons with a propensity for power, but Zeb had the authority to assign leadership roles in his territory to whomever he wanted. And his daughter had desired the southern states, hence his assignment of the sought-after role to her.

Xai conceded my point with a single nod. "We'll compile a list of likely candidates tonight and start researching where appropriate. In the meantime, I'd like to learn more about the mortal with underworld connections. Something tells me Lord Zebulon would be fascinated by him as well."

His subtext was not lost on me. *A bargaining chip should we fail.* If we presented Zeb with an alternate case, he might be willing to grant us more time. A risky game, but if anyone knew how to play it, it was the dark angel across from me.

"I'm going to need sunscreen." Not to prevent a sunburn, but for something else entirely. "I have the swimsuit covered."

Xai's gaze fell to my breasts, which were covered by my translucent blouse thanks to the bar's clothing policy. "I can't wait to see the bottom."

I grinned. He knew me too well. "I'm sure you'll approve."

"Indeed," he murmured as his phone started to ring. "Our room must be ready."

My grin slipped a little. I didn't like the lack of a particular plural in that sentence. "You mean 'rooms.'"

He merely smiled.

"Xai, I'm not sharing a room with you."

"You'd prefer to sleep with Tax?"

"Hell no," the Tracker inserted flatly. "My skin is on fire just being this close to her silver. Fuck if I'm sleeping next to that."

Well, at least it wasn't so much an aversion to me as to my proclivity for metal toys. "I want my own room."

Sometimes I swore Xai resembled Lucifer more than his actual father, and this was one of those moments. His eyes glistened menacingly as he curled that delicious mouth into a devastatingly handsome smile.

"Perhaps you missed Lord Zebulon's warning regarding what will happen to me should you disappear. So let me be clear, Evangeline. The threat of my accepting a punishment on your behalf is far too great for me to ignore, because we both know how much you would enjoy watching me burn. Therefore, we will be sharing a room, if nothing more than to ensure you don't try to run."

My hands itched for a sharp object to throw at him.

"I hate you." Mostly because he was right.

The temptation to do just as he said—disappear and leave him to fry—appealed to me more than I cared to admit. It also grated because a part of me broke at the idea of him hurting for me. Yet we both knew he more than deserved to feel pain on my behalf. I was stuck on this godforsaken plane because of him and his manipulative games—something he'd never been punished for or shown an inch of regret about.

"Yes, darling, that look is exactly why I'll be keeping a very close eye on you, not that I mind." He cast an admiring glance over my breasts, increasing my urge to cut him.

"Touch me, and you'll regret it." An empty threat since we both knew fighting only turned us on more. Fucking hormones.

"I always do, Evangeline." With that pronouncement, he stood and sauntered over to the reception area.

I had half a mind to leave, but the damn Tracker beside me would ensure my eventual return. *Here to help, my ass.* Oh, he might be useful in the Streator case, but now his presence took on a whole new meaning.

"He hired you to track Gwen down if I run." Not a question. Because he wouldn't be able to follow my angelic aura, but he could easily trace and capture my demonic best friend. And Xai knew I wouldn't allow her to face punishment for my sins.

Clever bastard.

"It's nothing personal," Tax replied with a shrug. He beckoned the redhead from the bar to request a drink. She was considerably less flirty this time around and didn't even look at me. Probably a good thing because my expression would have scared her.

Fury mingled with hurt. I understood Xai's desire to babysit me after Zeb's threat, but his general involvement in this case perplexed me. He obviously had nothing to do with Kalida's disappearance, yet his boss seemed adamant that we work together. Why? A punishment for standing up to the demon lord for me? Or something else?

Zeb mentioned something about already knowing Xai's feelings on the subject, which suggested they'd discussed it prior to my arrival. Had he argued on my behalf and encouraged this seven-day deal? It seemed so unlike him, yet here we were, in an expensive Miami Beach hotel. Why the hell would he even bother? There was nothing in this situation for him to gain except potential pain.

Two thousand years, and I still didn't understand the angel I Fell for. His convoluted reasoning made my head spin, and his incorrigible behavior left a lot to be desired.

But then he went and did something like this, causing me to reevaluate everything I knew about him. As if I didn't have enough to figure out with this case, Xai had to go and give me one more question to ponder.

Why is he helping me?

CHAPTER SIX

MEN ALWAYS TRUST
A BLONDE IN A THONG

XAI, being his usual pompous self, booked us a suite on a high floor of the hotel. It boasted three bedrooms with en suite bathrooms, a kitchen, a living area, and a dining room big enough to host ten people. Another olive branch, or perhaps a habit of luxury— most likely a bit of both.

After a long night of compiling a list of suspects, I crashed in the master bedroom, while Xai slept elsewhere. When I woke, I found breakfast, a stack of documents, and a note waiting for me on the oversized dining table.

Meet me at the pool around noon. —X

From the notes we reviewed on Streator, that would be in the middle of his first meeting and a prime time to saunter into the pool area wearing my skimpy violet bikini. I nibbled on the toast and eggs he had left for me—no doubt courtesy of room service—and reviewed the file he had left under the note.

"Holy hellfire…" I had assumed he went to sleep when I did, but the report he'd compiled on all our suspects suggested otherwise. He'd already ruled out a third of the suspect list based on conflicting timelines and known locations. No way he found all this information online, which meant he had called in a favor, likely to another Tracker or someone with technical skills. If I needed proof that he would take this case seriously, he'd left it on the counter for my perusal. But it still didn't tell me *why*.

I polished off the last of the food on my plate before gulping down the freshly squeezed orange juice. Pure heaven, and undoubtedly my favorite Floridian treat. The beach and palm trees were a close second.

A glance at the clock suggested I had just enough time to call Gwen before heading down to the pool.

"So, he hired you for a case, then?" she asked after I vaguely reviewed yesterday's events. I left out a few key elements because I didn't want her to worry.

"Yeah, he needs me to help figure something out. Should be done in a week or so." And if not, then I'd see her in a few years or decades, maybe centuries.

Demons weren't allowed to cross borders without permission, but I didn't live by their rules. Most Demonic Lords in the other territories respected me enough to grant me entry without question, and since they didn't play nice with others of their stature, I wouldn't have to worry about being extradited back to Zeb. I considered that to be a last resort, as I refused to accept punishment for a crime I didn't commit.

"Uh-huh. A vague assignment in Miami for a week where you're working with Xai—I assume, anyway—and you don't sound angry about it." I grimaced at Gwen's summary. "You realize I know you better than that, right? What's really going on, Eve?"

I picked up the cute swim bag I bought from the

hotel gift shop and slid it over my shoulder. It contained a hot-pink towel and sunscreen. No knives needed today. If I needed a weapon, I'd create one. Even the simplest item could be turned into a lethal tool if used right.

"Gwen, you know I love you," I said as I headed toward the front of the suite. It was almost noon. "But I need you to trust me right now, okay? I've got this."

Her silence painted a clear picture in my mind of her current expression. Eyes narrowed, lips pursed, body rigid. She didn't like being kept in the dark, and I hated putting her there, but involving her would only complicate matters. If Zeb thought he could use her against me, he would, and I refused to put her in that position.

"Please," I added, my hand on the doorknob in the marble foyer of the hotel room. This place reeked of elegance and charm and no doubt cost Xai a pretty penny. Not that he would care. His assets rivaled mine.

She blew a raspberry over the line. "Oh, fine," she drawled. "But if I find out this was all a ruse to force you into spending a week alone with Xai at some fancy hotel, there will be hell to pay."

I rolled my eyes. "No chance in that."

"Uh-huh."

Two could play the incredulous game. "How's training going with Zane?" I asked as I walked down the hall toward the elevator, wearing nothing but a pair of silver stilettos and a translucent black top that revealed my lush purple bikini beneath.

"Cute," she muttered. "Fucking cute."

"You give me a hard time about Xai; I'll give you a hard time about Zane."

"Yeah, well, only one of those two is a threat to our sanity, hmm?"

Fair point. "I'm staying sane. Promise."

"Good, because I can't lose you again."

The memory of the last time Xai betrayed me shivered down my spine. He left me in Hell. Literally. If I hadn't found a Portal Dweller when I did, I would have suffered excruciating pain. Angels, Fallen or otherwise, were not meant to visit the underworld for extended periods of time.

"You won't lose me, Gwen." Because I would never trust him that way again. I hit the elevator button a little harder than necessary. "I've gotta go."

"Be safe and check in soon," she said, her earlier teasing replaced by sincerity. "Miss you."

"Miss you too." We exchanged a goodbye before I hung up and descended to the main level of the hotel. Heads swiveled my way as I journeyed toward the pool with an innocent expression on my face. I'd mastered this alias long ago, the one with a sheepish look and a faint blush that drew male admirers.

I pressed the phone to my ear and pretended to be in the middle of a conversation as I entered the pool area. My mark stood on the opposite side at a high table with two other fully dressed men in polo shirts and khakis. All three were enjoying afternoon drinks, but their serious expressions indicated their topic to be anything but lighthearted.

There were four bodyguards stationed around the deck, all of whom failed to blend in with the vacation crowd, but I suspected Streator liked it that way. Xai, on the other hand, was relaxing in the hot tub, his muscular arms draped over the edges as if he owned the place. He resembled a confident man hoping to get laid, and the three women in the water with him appeared happy to oblige.

I ignored him as I sauntered by, and I felt his eyes caress my ass along the way. He said he wanted to see the suit bottom, and he could see straight through my sheer top to the purple thong beneath. His favorite.

"Are y'all kidding me?" I asked my imaginary friend over the phone. "What am I supposed to do?" I paused for effect as I stopped right by Streator's table. "Well, I don't care what Billy said. No. I can't believe y'all are bailing on me!" I tapped my heel-clad foot and popped a hand on my hip. "And what am I supposed to do now?

Hang out by myself?" I gasped in mock disbelief. "Y'all know how unsafe that is!"

Streator and all his men were looking at me now with interest. Perfect.

"Fine. You'd better." I hung up with a flourish and huffed, "Crud muffin," under my breath. Then I feigned a shudder before throwing my bag onto the chair beside the businessmen. "Then I'll just make do," I muttered to myself as I pretended not to notice them. "Hangin' out at the beach by myself all week. Unbelievable."

I pulled my swimsuit cover over my head and folded it neatly off to the side, all the while allowing the men to admire my scantily clad figure. The strings of my bikini tickled my back and upper thighs as a light breeze hit the pool area. My blonde ponytail fluttered a little with it, painting a seductive picture that seemed to have silenced my audience.

"Well, sugar honey iced tea," I said as I picked up the sunscreen. "Hmm…" I dabbed a little on my arms and legs, purposely bending at the right angles to attract attention, and rubbed slowly. Xai's amusement was tangible across the pool. I always sensed him, even when I didn't want to. He wouldn't like this next part, but it had to be done.

Once I finished rubbing lotion all over my flat abdomen and the crease of my breasts, I attempted to reach my back.

"And this is why a girl doesn't travel to Miami alone," I grumbled to myself as I gave up with a sigh. My eyes danced around shyly as I tried to find someone to help. When I found the three men behind me, I forced a flush into my cheeks and gave a little squeak. "I'm so sorry! I've gone all up in your business without meanin' to. Do y'all need me to move?"

Streator's hazel eyes danced appreciatively over me as he murmured an approval to his buddies. My lips curled into a bashful smile while I fantasized about driving a blade into his black heart.

"You're welcome to stay, sweetheart." His file labeled

him as a charmer, and I could see it in the way he grinned at me now. Suave, confident, and powerful. Too bad I ate men like him for breakfast.

I pressed a hand to my breast and sighed in relief. "Oh, thank you. I can't tell ya how much that means to me. This trip is not turnin' out at all like I planned." I allowed my eyes to mist a bit to emphasize my frustration. Damn friends not showing up when I expect them to. "I promise not to bother y'all."

I started to turn, then bit my lip and looked back at them. I gave my head a little shake, as if I decided against something, and went to leave them alone when Streator took the bait.

"Do you need some help with that?" he asked, eyes gesturing to the sunscreen.

"Oh, I couldn't..." I swallowed and glanced at the ground before gazing up at him through my lashes. "Um." I bit my lip again for show. "Would ya mind applyin' this to my back? I tried, and um..." My voice trailed off as he stepped forward and held out a hand.

"Sure, babe." He flashed a practiced grin my way as I gave him the sunscreen.

"You're a lifesaver, sugar. Thank you." I pulled my ponytail over my shoulder and presented him with my back. His hot palm slid over my skin in a caress far gentler than I expected, and I feigned a shiver in response. It helped that he wasn't horrible looking, but knowing the truth beneath the surface certainly dampened any feelings I could have toward him. I pretended it was Xai applying the sunscreen, which helped heat up the moment as Streator's fingers traced my thong.

"What's your name?" he asked as he slipped just south of the string to fondle the top of my ass.

Since he'd finished massaging all the lotion in, I turned to face him, which sent his hand to my hip. "Violet O'Hara," I breathed. My lashes fluttered as if his touch had lulled me into a sense of deep comfort. "And you?"

"Scott Streator." Arousal had darkened his hazel eyes to a deep green.

"It's great to meet you, Scott." I licked my lips. "Thank you for helpin' me out with, uh, my back."

"Anytime." He handed over the lotion and took a step back. Then he signaled for a waiter in a manner similar to Xai's last night. "Put her drinks on my tab," he said when a young guy in board shorts and a polo shirt approached.

"Yes, sir." Gray eyes met mine. "What would you like?"

"Oh." I pressed my palm against my chest in mock surprise. "How generous. It's truly not necessary…"

"I insist," Streator replied, his charm fully in place. "Consider it my way of improving your vacation."

I forced my cheeks to heat as I smiled at him. "I'll accept, but only if you join me for a drink at some point too." I tugged on my lip after I said it, as if second-guessing my boldness. It had the desired effect.

"I'll certainly take you up on that, Miss O'Hara." He rejoined his amused colleagues and gave the one to his left a look that said, *I'm going to have a fun night.* Too bad our definitions of a good time varied significantly.

I caught the waiter staring at my cleavage and pretended not to notice. "Can ya do a Manhattan? I tried one the other night, and they are to die for." I tilted my head back as if praying to Heaven above for creating such an amazing drink. Really, I should be glancing at the ground since Hell invented alcohol.

My excitement caused his eyes to snap up to mine, and a real blush colored his cheeks. If he couldn't handle me in a bikini, then he needed a new job because there were similarly dressed women all over the pool deck. My angelic ancestry gave me a slight edge over them, but I noticed a few bombshells as I analyzed the scene earlier.

"Uh." The kid cleared his throat. "Yeah, we can do that."

"Thanks, sugar." I gave him a smile and relaxed into the lounge chair. Streator and his men had eyed the exchange with amusement. I read their expressions with an internal smile. They saw me as adorable and harmless. Just as I wanted.

Game on, boys.

CHAPTER SEVEN

FALLEN ANGEL OR NOT,
ALL MEN ARE POSSESSIVE BEINGS

FIVE STRONG MANHATTANS lulled me into a pretend sleep. My arms were stretched out over my head while I rested on my stomach, ass fully exposed. I parted my lips to give the false appearance of a drunken slumber and listened as Streator met with his colleagues.

They had taken over the lounge chairs behind me, which I gathered was not part of the original meeting plan. Streator had suggested it, saying they could admire the scenery while discussing business. Too bad said scenery kept distracting him from the important stuff.

"She's fucking perfect," he murmured, going off topic again. Apparently, my bikini worked a little too well.

"Do you think she's a virgin?" George asked. Not his real name, but a nickname I'd given him. With his bald head, deep voice, and stocky build, George seemed appropriate. I referred to the suaver one to his left with the full mane of dark curls as Calvin. So much shorter than Associate Dumbass Number One and Associate Dumbass Number Two.

"With a body like that? I doubt it, but she's definitely inexperienced. She clearly has no idea how to work her assets."

Oh, if you only knew, Streator. I hoped Xai overheard that. He'd enjoy it too.

"Too bad. She'd be worth a fortune." George's response was unexpected. A fortune? "Hell, with a body like that, a lot of bidders wouldn't care."

"You read my mind, and she's alone too." It seemed playing the abandoned card had worked in my favor, but not in the way I expected. I just wanted an excuse to sit close to the men and listen in on their conversation. Now it seemed Streator had other ideas. His file didn't mention anything about prostitution or human trafficking, but it fit his criminal profile and proclivity for hurting women. He was shaping up to be the kind of human I wouldn't mind killing.

"You want me to run a background on her, just to make sure it wouldn't be an issue should she disappear?" Calvin's tone held a hint of boredom, suggesting this kind of conversation occurred frequently between them. Which confirmed my trafficking suspicions.

None of this had anything to do with Kalida's murder, or framing me, but Streator had officially piqued my interest. Once I figured out who had framed me, I'd have to take on his case pro bono. Ridding this plane of his appalling ass would be my gift to humanity.

"Yes, I'm very curious to know more, and I'll solve the virgin question tomorrow night." So confident. Streator no doubt planned to use alcohol as a tool to learn more about my virtue. Should be fun. "I'd do it tonight, but the incoming shipment takes precedence. I'll consider her my reward for a job well done."

Ah, and now we're getting back to the point of this meeting. They'd referenced the shipping container a few times, as well as an arrival time, but nothing more. Despite having labeled me as harmless, they weren't as forthcoming with information as I wanted. Hence my drunken slumber.

"My contact stated he's on schedule for pickup, so it should be a smooth transition," Streator continued. "We'll have guards in place to avoid a repeat of last month's issues, but the additional metal should keep them in line."

"How many more shipments are we expecting?" The hint of hesitation in George's voice intrigued me. What were they trafficking that had him so nervous? Definitely not women, if his earlier tone was anything to go by, and it couldn't be drugs. Weapons, perhaps?

There was a pause as Streator sipped his beverage, and then he replied, "Geier says at least three more."

The familiar name sent a chill down my spine. I'd been alive too long to believe in coincidences. The Germanic surname wasn't necessarily unpopular, as several humans used it, but so did a certain former Demonic Lord. The same one who Zeb dethroned when he took over this territory, sending Geier crawling back to the underworld.

I stood corrected. This man could very likely be tied to Kalida, or perhaps be the one who led Zeb's oldest enemy to his daughter.

The trio continued their discussion, mostly about the logistics of the transfer, timing, and jobs for the evening. I gathered the general location of the shipment, but not the container number. After an hour of feigning rest, I yawned with a little mewl I knew men enjoyed and rolled onto my back to stretch. I needed to touch base with Xai. His inhuman hearing likely allowed him to catch most of the conversation, but I'd listened to every word.

Streator's aroused gaze met mine as I peeked at him. I blinked, as if trying to remember how I ended up by the pool, and sat up quickly in mock surprise.

"Oh my word." I covered my mouth with a hand as I giggled. "What time is it, y'all? I think I fell asleep."

Xai's gorgeous form grabbed my attention as he stood

off to the side of the pool. He'd been lounging in a chair similar to mine and working on that delicious tan. His black swim trunks sat low on his hips, exposing the deep V of his abdomen. And Gwen wondered why I couldn't resist him. He had the body of a Viking and the complexion of a Spartan. *Mouthwatering.*

Catching my appraisal, he glanced over with a wink. *You're not the only one who looks good in swimwear, darling,* he seemed to say.

I suppressed a grin and refocused on my target. Xai had only distracted me for a few seconds, and he stood just out of sight of the trio beside me, so no one noticed my gawking. It worked to my advantage as natural heat suffused my cheeks. They'd assume embarrassment brought on my blush, when it was really my body reacting to the perfect male specimen across the pool.

Streator glanced at his watch to answer my question. "Just after four thirty."

My eyes widened. "Shut the front door. I've been sleepin' this whole time?" I shook my head. "You must think me an awful bore."

"Hardly, sweetheart. You're adorable."

Do you say that to all the girls you want to sell? I bit my lip, mostly to keep from asking that out loud. "You're a peach," I murmured as I stretched again. His gaze fell to my breasts and then to my hips as I rolled off the chair onto unsteady feet. Alcohol didn't actually affect me, but they didn't know that. I pretended to stumble just a little and giggled again. "I definitely need some food, y'all. Any recommendations?"

"The pool bar makes a good burger," George replied, speaking to me for the first time.

I scrunched my nose. "Oh, that sounds greasy." And absolutely delicious, but not appropriate for my alias. "Hmm, I wonder if I can get a nice salad inside, or a sandwich." I pulled my swimsuit cover over my head, much to their disappointment. "Will I see y'all around this week?"

"Definitely," Streator replied. "Tomorrow night."

My eyebrows popped up. "Tomorrow night?" I repeated.

"For dancing and drinks." He exuded a confidence I usually found sexy. I liked a man who knew what he wanted and went for it without faltering. Too bad this one possessed a proclivity for harm. "I'll meet you in the lobby at eight. Wear a dress."

I pretended to consider. "I do like to dance…"

"And I promised you a drink," he added, referring to my earlier request to share a beverage at some point as payment for adding my Manhattans to his tab.

"Eight o'clock." My lips curled as I picked up my bag and slipped on my heels. "I'd be delighted."

"Good." He flashed me the kind of grin most women would swoon over. "See you tomorrow, Miss O'Hara."

"Until then," I replied and tripped over myself as I stepped away. His resulting chuckle was music to my ears. A true gentleman would ensure the drunk solo woman arrived safely to her suite, but Streator only expressed amusement. Something told me he'd be plying me with ample Manhattans tomorrow night, assuming I showed up for our *date*.

Once out of his sight, I straightened my shoulders and walked normally. He could potentially check the security feeds, but I doubted he'd go that far. I'd given him the name of my current alias. When Calvin checked into it, he'd find that Violet O'Hara was a Vanderbilt dropout who went into the family business of maintaining the local bar for her recently deceased uncle who happened to name the property after her. She had no other family alive today and a bank account that left a lot to be desired. In other words, the perfect prey.

I used my key card to enter the suite and tossed my bag onto the kitchen counter.

"Did you hear his comments about Geier?" I asked as Xai rounded the corner in nothing but a towel. The water glistening in his dark strands suggested he'd just taken a shower. My heartbeat kicked up a notch at the sight, while my brain remained focused on work.

"No way is that a coincidence," I added.

He said nothing as he approached me, those black eyes intense and fixated. I stepped back into the counter as he crowded my personal space.

"Xai…"

His fingers knotted in my ponytail as he yanked my head back to the angle he preferred.

Oh, fuck… I knew that look. Nothing good ever came from that look.

I flattened my palms against his bare chest, but he pushed right through my physical barrier and took my mouth with a ferocity that screamed possession. His tongue demanded entrance, and when I tried to fight him, he bit my lip hard enough to bleed. On my gasp, he entered and unleashed his desire in a kiss that deprived me of oxygen.

My knees threatened to buckle under his assault. He fucked my mouth the way he did my body, reminding me who we were to each other with a few bold strokes. I melted for him, as I always did, as arousal raced through my system.

God, I missed this.

I missed *him*.

I hated it. Loved it. Craved it.

My arms wound around his neck to pull him closer, and he reciprocated in kind by grabbing my hip and yanking me into his hard body. The hand in my hair tightened to the point of pain as he devoured my mouth, and I scratched him in response.

Sadistic bastard and his dark yearnings.

He grinned against my lips. "Mmm, do it again."

I tried to knee him instead, and he spun me around to face the counter, his chest to my back. He dragged his teeth over my neck as he wrapped his arm around my waist to hold me in place.

"Not what I requested," he murmured as he ground his erection into my ass. The whimper that escaped me was both a result of need and him tugging sharply on my hair, forcing my head backward and to the side. His mouth found mine again, and this time his kiss was meant to punish.

I tried to squirm out of his grasp, but he held me with the ease of a stronger man who knew his opponent too well.

There were few who could do this to me, and I hated how much I loved his show of dominance. I'd only topped him a handful of times, which I suspected he'd allowed more out of amusement than anything. My leg swept out behind me to unbalance him, but he outmaneuvered me and bent me over the counter.

The marble felt cool against my stomach and chest. I shifted my hands to push myself off the surface, but Xai caught my wrists and twisted my arms up behind my back. A shiver traversed my spine as he secured them with one big palm.

He wedged himself between my thighs, effectively trapping me in the weakest of positions. "Your sparring needs work, love."

"Give me a blade and let's try again."

His fingers skated up my thigh, beneath the sheer fabric of my cover-up, to the crease of my bare ass. "The sunscreen was a clever ruse that nearly ruined our only lead."

I glared at him over my shoulder. "Excuse me?"

He grinned. "Oh, you were perfect, love. Too perfect."

His hand drifted to the top of my thong before lovingly stroking the exposed skin below. "When he touched you here, I almost killed him just for thinking that he had the right."

The possession in his tone solicited a quiver from deep within. Only Xai had the ability to do this to me.

I'd never allow another man to claim me, because my heart only belonged to one man, even if he didn't truly want it. But in moments like this, I wondered if that was really true. I understood the line between lust and love, but what we had far surpassed an emotional label.

We belonged to each other in a way few people did.

Our bond was quite literally not of this plane.

His thumb traced the strings over my hip as he murmured in approval.

"You slay me, Evangeline." The passion in his voice caressed my senses and scattered goose bumps down my arms. He leaned over me, pressing his blazing chest to my back, and nibbled my ear. "Every damn time."

I trembled beneath him. *This* was the Xai I couldn't resist. My first lover, the angel I Fell for, the man I wanted more than a holy purpose.

I'd given up everything for him, including my reason for existing, only to be tricked time and again.

Just when he convinced me things could be different, that he'd finally found his humanity, everything crumbled. The charade, the feelings, my heart— everything shattered, leaving me alone to pick up the pieces until his next round.

Toxic relationship didn't even begin to cover it.

If only I could find a way to break this damn eternal bond between us. My only saving grace was knowing he felt it too, that despite all his efforts to run away, he always came back for me because he couldn't help it.

Sensing my shifting mood, he sighed. "Over two thousand years, and you still don't understand." He pressed his temple to mine briefly before pushing away.

"Maybe you should explain it," I suggested bitterly. "Oh wait, that would be the easy way out."

A chill swept over me as cool air replaced his body heat. I shoved off the counter and found my footing easily before rounding to face him.

The storm brewing in his ebony gaze belied his patient expression. "You said Streator mentioned Geier, as in the former Demonic Lord. In what context?"

I swallowed my growl.

Now that he'd ravaged me against the counter and staked his claim, he wanted to discuss business. No commentary regarding my supposed misunderstandings, as usual.

Fine.

We'd focus on the job, if nothing more than to solve Kalida's murder and to return me to my life without Xai. And then wait until the next time he decided to waltz in and destroy everything.

"He mentioned him as a business associate. Weren't you listening?"

"Not well," he muttered. "I didn't trust myself to stand any closer."

Right. Because he wanted to murder Streator. Damn possessive, heart-destroying angel.

I ignored my mental tirade and relayed all the pertinent details of the discussion. He folded his arms while I spoke, and listened without interruption.

"So, I want to grab a shower and some food, then we'll head over to the shipping yard because I want to see what product he's moving. Hopefully, that'll tell us if drinking and dancing tomorrow is necessary." I cringed a little on that last part. Spending the evening in Streator's company without killing him would prove to be a challenge.

"I'll let Tax know about our plans," was all he said before turning away. His towel-covered ass taunted me as he moved. Frustration be damned, my body still wanted him. Badly.

Xai was the only man who could truly satisfy me. It didn't matter whom I took to bed; they never measured up to expectations. He never admitted it, but I knew he felt the same about me. Hence our never-ending sexual battle.

Well, at least we had something else tonight to distract us. We both enjoyed sex in kinky places, but there was nothing even remotely appealing about a shipping yard.

Time to go to work.

CHAPTER EIGHT

EVEN THE SON OF CHAOS GETS SERIOUS EVERY NOW AND THEN

I WAS SURROUNDED BY ORSINI DEVILS. Devious motherfuckers with no loyalty except to their bank accounts.

They kept disappearing and reappearing all over the damn place, like excited little minions awaiting their orders. I twirled a silver blade between my fingers and dared them to try pickpocketing me. None of them seemed all that eager to take me up on the lethal offer. No idea why.

Tax kicked his leg out to trip one as he popped up in front of him, and the short, chubby excuse of a being fell. The tracker's ability to sense auras gave him an advantage.

The tiny devil jumped to his feet with a disgruntled snort, his humanoid features set in a scowl that was almost comical.

"Sorry, didn't see you," Tax deadpanned. The Tracker was growing on me.

Xai hopped down from a shipping container and landed deftly on his booted feet. His black jeans and dark shirt accented his lithe form. The man resembled a god when he wore his trademark suits, but the casual look gave him an almost humanlike appeal. Except his face gave him away. No sane person could ever mistake his angelic features as human.

He'd been off scouting the locations I suggested for our mission, because he didn't trust my judgment. Retired or not, I could handle a reconnaissance mission.

I raised an eyebrow and waited for the words I expected.

"It seems you've retained some of your natural talents after all, Evangeline." Okay, not the phrase I anticipated. "Maybe there's hope for you yet."

The knife flew from my hand, and he caught it deftly by the deadly side before it could pierce his cold heart.

"Good thing you're wearing black, Xai." I'd thrown it hard enough to slice on impact, which was evident by his now-bleeding palm. Rather than return the silver to me, he squeezed it tighter, embedding the sharp edges into his skin without flinching.

Blood dripped from his hand as he held my gaze. "At least you've maintained some of your lethal proclivities."

"I'm still Azrael's daughter." Death ran in my blood. Literally.

"Indeed." He returned the dagger in the same manner, but instead of aiming for my heart, he went for my femoral artery. Jackass.

I caught it by the handle and wiped the blood off against my black jeans before sheathing the dagger along my forearm. His gaze smoldered with unveiled arousal in response. This was our version of foreplay, and we both played the game at an expert level.

"The shipping container Streator desires is on the opposite side of the industrial park." Xai returned to business as usual. "Tax, I want you by the entrance to read the auras of our quarry and his entourage. Let us know via the comms if there's anything off."

The Tracker nodded once with a bored expression. Not much seemed to faze him.

"Nick," Xai continued, addressing the taller of the Orsini Devils, which wasn't saying much. My five-foot-seven-inch height still dwarfed the man by at least six inches. "You and your devilish friends can take up positions near the pier. You're to observe only. Any behavior beyond that is out of my protection. Do I make myself clear?"

The little minions bobbed their heads vigorously, which meant nothing. If they wanted to fuck around, they would, at their own risk. Because neither Xai nor I would help them out if they got caught thieving.

The three of them scurried off on their short, stocky legs while chattering amongst themselves like a pack of hyenas. They had the right skills to be spies, but the maturity of five-year-old mortals.

"I hope you're not paying them much." Because I doubted we would get anything useful from them.

He lifted a shoulder in his version of a shrug. Money meant little to him, as it did to most immortals our age. "Come. I want to show you something."

He grabbed the side of the container to start his upward climb with the gracefulness of an Archangel. The blood from his palm painted a path as he went, but he didn't seem to notice. All that sinewy muscle flexed as he moved, distracting me from obeying right away. His tight ass looked fantastic in those jeans. And Gwen wondered why I rarely dated. How could a mortal ever compare?

I shook my head and started after him. The combat boots were new, as were my jeans and long-sleeved shirt. I hadn't anticipated the need for practicality when I packed. It was Miami. I'd brought shorts, swimsuits, cover-ups, sundresses, heels, and flip-flops.

Xai's irritation was palpable when I mentioned my need to stop by the mall. Lucky for him that I hated shopping, or I would have tortured him a little more. Instead, I ran through the store, grabbing what I needed, and changed in the car. That last part he had enjoyed a little too much, despite my telling him to focus on the road.

He leapt from one container to another, his long legs propelling him farther than mine.

When he ascended a taller stack, I sighed. The angel always did have a thing for heights. It was a love we didn't share. My heart gave a small pang as I followed him. The sky always reminded me of home, of a former life that now existed only in my dreams.

I pulled myself up onto yet another container and nearly ran into Xai's back. He'd stopped near the edge, hands on his hips and face tilted upward, eyes closed. We were at least fifteen stories in the air, placing us on the same level as the top decks of the cruise ships docked at the passenger port next door.

"What did you want to show me up here?" The container in question was now far too small for observation, not to mention the fact that we were nowhere near the entrance. "This location holds no tactical advantage, nor is it a suitable sniper point."

Rifles weren't my preference, but I knew how to use them. My genetics preprogrammed me with the ability to handle weapons of all kinds and to also make even the most innocent object deadly. But even I would have difficulty being effective at this vantage point.

"Don't you feel it?" he whispered, his expression more relaxed than normal.

My stomach knotted as a warm breeze ruffled my ponytail. The familiar caress elicited a shiver from deep within my soul. My shoulder blades flexed on instinct, remembering the weight they used to carry so long ago and the feel of the wind beneath my feathers. I palmed my chest to stave off the ache blossoming there, but it was useless. Standing up here, in the darkening sky, and feeling that missing part of my being, hurt.

I had half a mind to shove Xai over the edge and

watch him fall. How was that for symbolism?

"You think I mean to torture you," he whispered, eyes still closed. "But I don't. I miss it just as much as you do."

"Is that why you brought me up here? To commiserate?" I couldn't help the bitter note in my voice, but this was a waste of fucking time. We had more important things to worry about than a past we would never be able to fix.

"No, Evangeline." He looked at me then, his fiery gaze intense. "I brought you up here because the warm air reminded me of home, and for just a few seconds, it afforded me a moment of peace. I thought you might want to share it with me."

"Peace is not what I feel up here." My low tone held a broken quality that couldn't be helped. He had to know what he was doing to me.

"That's because you refuse to accept fate." He wrapped his unwounded hand around the back of my neck and pulled me to him. I grabbed his hips to push him away, but his opposite arm snaked around my waist to hold me in place. "Until you let go of the past, you'll never embrace the future."

"Cryptic as always, Xai."

"Stubborn as always, Evangeline." His lips feathered over mine with the words. "If I could return your wings, I would. But I can't." He captured my mouth before I could formulate a reply.

Holy hell, was that some backward form of an apology? No. Xai never apologized. He was too selfish to understand the concept. But regret underlined his tone, just as it did his kiss. The dominant side of him took a back seat to a gentler version I didn't know how to handle. There was a reverence to this embrace that I didn't understand. It left me feeling cherished, an emotion I'd never experienced in his company.

Who is this enigma, and what did he do to the cruel version? It all started with his allowing my patrons to live the other night, such an uncharacteristic act. Then his essentially volunteering to help me with this mission, and now this. His possession earlier was all Xai, but this tender side of him left me unbalanced. He didn't use his tongue to deepen the kiss, just allowed his lips to softly move against mine as if memorizing the feel of my mouth.

It was arousing as hell and so unlike anything he'd ever done to me. Was this a new tactic? Had he identified another avenue to harm me? Or... had something changed? I quivered at the dangerous line of thought. The second I believed that, he'd destroy me. Just as he had done every time before.

He squeezed my neck with just enough force to say he'd sensed my conflicting emotions. Neither of us possessed the ability to read minds, but our unworldly bond granted us a unique understanding of each other. Sometimes, though, like now, I swore his intuition surpassed mine.

"It's time." He nuzzled my nose before letting me go. Another new gesture, and it left me baffled.

"What the fuck has gotten into you? Why are you acting like this?"

A sharp nibble or a slap to my ass was more his style.

This nuzzling shit? No.

I preferred jackass Xai over this tender side of him. I could handle the former by hating him, which worked for me. This new strange behavior, however, threw me off my game. I could actually like this form of him, and that terrified me.

"Perspective," he replied vaguely.

"Perspective of what?"

"Of what life would be like without you, Evangeline." A note of despair trickled through his tone, but it was gone when he added, "Now try to keep up."

With that, he stepped backward off the edge of the platform.

CHAPTER NINE

THERE ARE WORSE SMELLS
THAN DEAD FISH

THE COOL METAL seeped through my thin shirt as I rolled into my scouting position. If I'd overheard Streator's conversation right, then his future meeting spot lay about fifty feet away. If I was wrong, then Tax would tell us through the earpiece and I'd find a new spot, but for now, this one was perfect. It lacked overhead lighting, a weakness the yard designers obviously hadn't taken into consideration when placing their posts.

"Mmm," Xai murmured as he dropped onto his stomach beside me. "Seeing you like this brings back all sorts of memories." From his warm tone, I knew which moments from our past he meant. "Admit it, love. Part of you misses it."

I shifted onto my elbow and looked at him.

Sleek, solid male encased in black.

My kryptonite.

Did I miss this? Oh, yes.

Did I regret leaving? No. Okay, maybe a little.

Living with Gwen and running a bar had its positive moments, but it led to a boring existence. I thought it would help me find purpose, and I desperately craved change. But normal life was boring. I missed the rush and adrenaline that came from being on a mission, and above all, I missed my lover and the way he set my blood on fire.

Xai made me feel more alive than anyone ever had, but with that came the inevitable pain. For every sensation he evoked, an equally uncomfortable one awoke, leaving me a dysfunctional mess. One would think that two thousand years on this plane would deaden my emotions and humanity, but being with Xai had the opposite impact on me. He brought out a side of me that cared more than it should, and I both loved and hated him for it.

He reached over to drag his thumb along my lower lip and tracked the move with his hypnotic gaze. "I missed you too, Eve. More than you'll ever know."

"I didn't say I missed you."

"You didn't have to. Your eyes said it all."

"You're seeing what you want to see, Xai." A lie. I could hide my emotions from everyone else, but never from him. He always saw through me no matter how hard I tried.

"I am," he agreed. "But that doesn't make it any less true."

This new softer side of him was going to get me killed. Not that I could actually die—the weapon for that didn't exist on this plane—but there were worse fates than death. Like living an eternity with a broken soul. I suspected that was Xai's endgame. To see me completely destroyed, just to say, *I did that*. He loved a good challenge, and that's what I presented. I was the prey that always got away.

"Uh, guys?" Tax's voice came through the earpiece.

"Streator just arrived, and I sense three Guardians in his caravan."

Xai glanced sharply at me before looking toward the entrance. I rolled back to my stomach, my arm touching his as I followed his gaze.

"You're sure?" I asked.

"There might be four. Something isn't right about this, like, at all." Apparently, Tax was vying for the role of Captain Obvious tonight. "But they're heading your way."

Guardians couldn't sense demonic auras the way a Tracker could, but they were innately attuned to their surroundings. Even the subtlest change in atmosphere would alarm them, and if they sensed a disturbance from Tax or the Orsini Devils, they would be particularly alert. I wasn't worried so much about the former as the latter.

Xai relaxed his chin on his hands, and I followed suit. Maintaining an air of calm would keep our location hidden. And even if they found us, we could handle a few Guardians.

"Your file on him didn't mention the demon entourage, only his ties to Kalida," I said. Although, Tax had mentioned sensing other auras on Streator. Perhaps these were the ones he felt.

"Because I didn't know. My findings on him were enough to pique interest, hence my suggestion we look into him."

"It was a good suggestion."

His lips twitched at my admission, but he remained focused on the mission. "Showtime."

A caravan of black SUVs approached the container. "That's a lot of cars."

"Thirteen," Tax confirmed over the earpiece.

"There's no way he's picking up weapons." He wouldn't need that much room for a few guns, or even drugs. "I bet there are girls in that container." I couldn't help the disgusted note in my voice. There was a special place in Hell for monsters like Streator. I intended to send him there after I finished dicing him up. His death would be slow and purposeful.

"Easy, love," Xai murmured. "We need him alive for now."

He'd no doubt read the lethal desire in my eyes. My blue irises deepened to a sapphire shade when I wanted to kill. A trait I inherited from my father.

"Dibs," was all I said as I stroked the silver blade near my wrist. An action that calmed my instinct to seek justice. A man with Streator's record sang to me in a way few mortals did. Most of my marks were demons, and even then, I only assassinated those who deserved my version of punishment.

"He's all yours," Xai replied softly as one of the cars parked beside our container. All the others stopped in line behind the first SUV, creating a long black snake.

Their conspicuousness confirmed they'd paid off port authority or had contacts on the payroll. Either way, they were clearly unconcerned about being caught here tonight. Our team had parked down the street, scaled the fence, and hidden along the perimeter. Xai hired someone to interfere with the video surveillance, just in case. It'd clearly been an unnecessary precaution on our part.

Streator stepped out of the vehicle closest to us and was immediately flanked by two men in tailored suits. Both human, and way overdressed for a Miami summer night. My jeans and shirt were sticking to me from all the running and climbing. It didn't irritate me as it would a mortal, mostly because I'd been far more uncomfortable at certain points in my long life.

Xai nodded over to the second car as a Guardian exited, his stumpy arms folding. Two more joined him, all bulky muscle and no brains. They reacted to danger, and that was about it.

"Open it," Streator demanded.

To my shock, the Guardians moved to do his bidding. It took genuine effort not to say anything and to continue to observe.

Then the doors opened to reveal the contents of the

crate, and the energy required to remain silent quadrupled. I grabbed Xai's arm to keep him beside me, or perhaps I did it to steady myself. I wasn't sure. But his muscles were locked—as though he wanted to pounce—and my limbs agreed wholeheartedly.

Because the contents weren't girls.

They were demons.

Of all kinds.

I watched in horror as a snakelike creature with two heads slithered out first. He reeked of the underworld, more so than the average demon. My nose twitched, confused. How had I missed that stench? Xai seemed to be wondering the same thing as his frown deepened. We both should have sensed it.

A giant stalked out next. *Cyclops*—brutal demons who wreaked havoc on the world a few millennia ago. They were on the "banned list," something I knew Zeb took very seriously. Only demons with humanoid forms were allowed on this plane, and clearly, neither of these guys fit the bill.

The atmosphere thickened as the underworld spewed several more of its more infamous monsters onto the concrete below. My eyes watered from the overwhelming stench, but the mortals below seemed unfazed. I suspected it was my Heavenly genetics reacting to the dangerous beings and functioning as a warning system. Xai appeared to be suffering the same ill effects, which he fought by breathing through his mouth.

When a particularly gruesome-looking fellow stepped out, my stomach revolted. His fingers oozed with some sort of green liquid that sizzled against the pavement. My lips parted on a gasp as recognition hit me square in the gut. Xai's gaze flew to mine, his horror evident.

Pestilence demon.

What the fuck was Streator doing with a being who could bring about a mortal plague? He at least resembled a humanoid, but his kind was strictly prohibited from this plane. All it would take was a sneeze, and he'd wipe out millions.

The rules were not about humanity but about a way to prevent war. Angels granted the underworld permission to take up residence on Earth so long as they kept their populations low, behaved themselves, and remained a secret. That's where the Demonic Lords came into play. They governed their specific territories, nominated Ōrdinātums to oversee specific regions within the territory, and kept the demonic population in line.

What was happening below broke all the laws.

My head spun as the line of hellish beings continued to stroll out of the container. Each one of them was escorted to an SUV by a Guardian, where they squished inside without protest. Streator observed with his hands in his khaki trousers, expression bored.

Clearly, this had happened before. So where were all these ghastly creatures hiding? What was their purpose for being here? Surely they weren't wandering the streets of Miami.

"That's the last one," a voice from inside the container said after a handful of what seemed to be Earth-sanctioned demon types exited. I suspected they weren't actually on the welcome list, however, since they arrived with this unsavory lot.

"Same time in two weeks?" Streator asked.

"Yes," the unseen male confirmed. And the door shut from the inside. My brow furrowed. The voice belonged to either a Portal Dweller or someone who had arrived with the help of one. Which explained the sudden stench. At least my senses were still intact, but I kind of wished they weren't.

This is bad, I told Xai with my eyes.

He gave a slight nod in response. *I know.*

"Wrap it up." Streator clapped his hands as if that would encourage everyone to move faster. The Guardians were trying to fit the Cyclops into a vehicle. His fifteen-foot frame appeared quite unwilling to oblige. He blinked that big eye in irritation and grunted like a toddler. I would have laughed if it weren't so dire.

A sharp crack caused me to snap my neck to the left

to where the mortals stood. It sounded like a whip hitting concrete, yet Streator's hands remained in his pockets. Was he holding some sort of mechanism that omitted a high-pitched signal meant solely for immortal ears?

When it happened again, I flinched. Xai appeared discomforted by it as well, but not nearly as irritated as the demons below. A whimper through the earpiece said the Orsini Devils weren't pleased either. Tension rolled through the air as two of the Guardians glanced around, sensing the disturbance.

I held my breath, waiting. If they found the little guys, our cover could be blown, and as much as I wanted to kill Streator, we needed him alive now more than before. Because I had a lot of questions, and he would be answering them.

The Cyclops finally maneuvered his way into the car, dispelling some of the anxiety radiating below, but not all of it. My nails dug into Xai's arm—I hadn't let go of it this entire time—as Streator and his men reentered their vehicles. The revving of engines never sounded so sweet, and then they were leaving in the same order they arrived.

I expelled the breath I'd been holding as the last of the cars disappeared.

Fuck.

What the fuck just happened?

I'd expected a crate full of human bodies, not Hell spawning its worst creations onto Earth. Angels, even Fallen ones, were predisposed to good, and to be faced with such malevolence all at once created an imbalance. It was why our kind didn't fare well in the underworld.

Even that small dose left me unsettled.

Hell is close. Too close.

I could handle most demons in my sleep, but those beings below were the purest of evil and had no business on this plane. Unless someone intended to start a war. *Again.*

I rolled into Xai on impulse and inhaled his spicy scent, needing to replace the acrid one clouding my senses. He said nothing and simply wrapped me in his arms while I regained my bearings.

The familiarity of his touch soothed my soul on the deepest level, lulling me into a state of peace I so desperately craved after the horror show we'd just witnessed. He needed it almost as badly as I did. I could feel the unease in his taut limbs and could hear it in the shaky breath that ruffled my hair as he kissed the top of my head. He tightened his grasp as if needing to remind himself that I was still here.

"They're gone," Tax said through the earpiece. "Everyone else okay?"

Jabbering started over the comms as the Orsini Devils all spoke at once. I ripped the speaker from my ear and curled deeper into Xai's chest. I wasn't ready yet. He gently rubbed my back as he loaned me his strength and comfort.

"We're here." The flatness of his tone was a stark contrast to the way he held me. His lips brushed my forehead, an apology for spoiling the moment, but he needed to respond to our team. And I silently thanked him for being the one to do it.

Xai tilted my chin back and pressed a kiss to my mouth. Gentle, tender, and for once, I welcomed it. It was what I needed in that moment, and as always, he knew. He nuzzled my cheek before kissing me again, firmer this time. I sighed against him and let his tongue in to slide against mine.

Whiskey, peppermint, and a taste that was just Xai overwhelmed the last of the underworld's hold over my psyche, placing me firmly back in the present. I grasped his shirt, clinging to him as I deepened our embrace and returned the favor, granting him all the access he needed to ground himself. And by the time we pulled away from each other, we were both panting with a mixture of lust and confusion.

I blinked up at the half moon and let out a laugh that was part hysterical, part relief. What a messed-up way to respond to such a bizarre situation. But it encompassed us completely.

Terror, I realized, was the culprit. Seeing those horrific creatures enter this plane—a plane I considered my duty to protect—invoked a fear inside of me that only Xai could calm. And I'd returned the favor in kind, whether he wanted to admit it or not.

His eyes glistened as they met mine, and compassion floated between us. He stood first, then held out a hand to help me to my feet. Normally, I would have scoffed at it, but nothing about tonight was normal. Not anymore.

"We need to meet with Lord Zebulon. Now." I couldn't tell if he was talking to me or Tax, but I assumed he meant that command for the Tracker. He confirmed when he added, "Good." Then he drew his thumb over my cheekbone, down my neck, and all the way to my hand. He gave it a squeeze. "Ready?" That soft question was for me.

I cleared my throat and swallowed all the emotions bubbling inside me. I'd had my moment to react, and now it was time to pull it together. Because what had started as a horrible assignment had just gotten so much worse, and I would need a level head to get through it. And maybe a touch of sarcasm.

"Am I ready to tell a Demonic Lord that Hell has literally broken loose in his territory?" I pretended to consider. "Sure. Why not?"

CHAPTER TEN

WHY ARE KNIVES SO SEXY?

"ILLEGAL DEMONS PASSING through an unauthorized portal," Zeb murmured as he paced the hotel suite with his hands behind his back. His light-colored trousers and baby-blue polo shirt were destined for the golf course. An appropriate outfit for blending in with the Miami humans. "And you believe this to be related to my daughter's murder?"

"Yes," Xai replied. He stood beside my chair, leaning against the wall with his legs crossed at the ankles. His relaxed position belied the tension in the room, and his next words didn't help matters. "It's the perfect distraction. While you're mourning and seeking vengeance, the real enemy is creating an army. Furthermore, framing Evangeline for the death of your daughter removes one of the strongest players on the board."

Warmth tickled my chest at the unveiled compliment. I knew my worth in this territory, but it was nice to hear Xai acknowledge it. The two Dargarian bodyguards lurking in the kitchen snorted at the comment, or maybe they'd choked on a fireball. Their green eyes glowed with suppressed embers as they surveyed the living area, searching for the silver they no doubt sensed on me. If they decided to heat it up in here, we'd have a problem, mostly in the form of my daggers implanted in their chests.

Zeb scratched his chin, thoughtful. "There is logic to this assessment," he admitted. "My immediate reaction was to punish, and then you came back without Eve last week, which diverted my focus."

Xai shrugged. "No harm, no foul."

Doubt colored the Demonic Lord's features. "You mean to insult my creativity."

"I wasn't all that impressed, no."

"Is that an invitation to try again?"

Another shrug from the dark angel. "If you deem it necessary."

Amusement filtered through Zeb's expression. "I might."

I glanced back and forth between them. Clearly, I'd missed something, but I knew better than to ask. They both adored puzzles, and I was not in the mood to solve one right now.

"Can we get back on task, boys? There's a Pestilence demon roaming about, and I'm dying to put a blade through his heart."

The Dargarians in the kitchen narrowed their fiery gazes at the threat in my tone. I blew them each a kiss. *Come play with me. I dare you.* My blood craved vengeance more than oxygen. A side effect of the horrors we'd witnessed three hours ago. I needed to kill something, and preferably a demon.

"Easy, love," Xai murmured. "They can be useful."

That remained to be seen. I preferred not to rely on

dangerous creatures, hence my volatile relationship with Xai. He was the most threatening being in the room, which, considering present company, said quite a bit.

"You believe Geier to be behind this?" Zeb asked, ignoring the sidebar conversation about his bodyguards.

"Streator mentioned the name earlier. I don't have proof yet that it's the same Geier we all despise, but you know how I feel about coincidences." I'd lived too long to believe in happenstance. "Seems someone wants his old job back."

"Or something far worse." Xai's speculative tone held a quiet quality that felt ominous. "Introducing a Pestilence demon to the territory you want to own feels counterintuitive to a Demonic Lord's goal. Lords are here to protect the balance, which requires proper management, and there are some creatures that cannot be governed."

I shivered at his mention of the beings unleashed from Hell tonight. They were all *creatures* that would never listen to reason. Their entrance to Earth created a disturbance that would be felt on all planes. If this tipped the scales of power too much, Heaven would be forced to intervene, and then mortals would learn the true meaning of the word *apocalypse*.

Xai laid his hand on my shoulder. A small touch that warmed my chilly skin and went straight to my heart. I hated how well he read me, and yet I loved how he soothed me with the simple gesture. The conflicting emotions left me itching to stab something. Like the smoldering demons in the kitchen.

"What is your plan?" Zeb asked. "As I assume that's why you called this meeting at two o'clock in the morning."

"Evangeline has a date with the human tomorrow. I propose that she go and learn more."

"The same one Kalida used for sustenance?" Of course that was the way Zeb would word it. Humans were inferior to the demons, similar to how a mortal might view a chicken.

"Yes, he propositioned her at the pool earlier." Xai's grip tightened subtly with the comment, as if to remind himself that I sat beside him and not Streator. He never did enjoy missions that involved me seducing other men.

"He didn't so much proposition as demand," I corrected.

"Do you think the mortal possesses a gift for compulsion?" Zeb asked curiously. "That would explain his ability to command his superiors."

"If he does, I didn't feel it when we met earlier." Streator possessed a certain charm, but I chalked that up to confidence. It came naturally to some men, and he struck me as one of those.

"A demon succumbing to human demands. What is this world coming to?" Zeb mused. "In any case, Xai, your suggestion seems lacking. Why not take him now and demand answers? Surely Eve can extract information from him."

I grinned at the prospect. Sometimes the Demonic Lord did provide sound ideas, but Xai had to throw a wrench in the glorious plan by shaking his head.

"No. If we take him now, we risk only obtaining the answers he can provide and losing our lead to his boss, which may or may not be Geier."

"How is going on a date with him going to lead us to his boss?" I asked. It would be far more prudent to use a knife strategically on him to carve out some answers and move on. No sense in letting that asshole touch me again.

Xai shook his damn head again. "From what you said, he's interested in procuring you, perhaps, for illegal means, yes? Would that not grant us deeper access to his business and potential partners?"

Oh, hell. I could see where this was going. "You want to use me as bait."

He grinned. "Come now, darling. This will no doubt afford you an opportunity to save some of your precious mortals from a horrible human. And once we have our answers, I'll happily let you kill him in any way you choose."

Ugh. Xai knew too well how to play me. *Fucking sweet talker.* "You want me to play the virgin card." Because that's what intrigued Streator and would guarantee me entry into his version of the underworld.

"So you believe his trafficking business to be related to what you observed tonight," Zeb inferred, still pacing. "And you would like to test that theory. But if you're wrong?"

"Then I lock him in a room with Evangeline for thirty minutes where she'll introduce him to her penchant for knives." He sounded so bored, but affection darkened his gaze as he said that last part.

I wholeheartedly approved of this backup plan. "Yes, please."

Zeb paused, his gaze on the dark angel beside me. "I assume you would like an extended timeline?"

Xai shrugged. "It's unnecessary. We still have six days."

Right. My punishment deadline. I would have liked a few extra months or years, but apparently, my vote was null and void. Not like it wasn't *my life* on the line or anything. Seeing the relief in Zeb's features kept me from remarking sarcastically about it. Demons had a strange relationship with vengeance. It didn't matter whom they took it from as long as it happened, hence the reason I would be the one serving time in Hell even if Zeb knew I was innocent.

Underworld politics baffled my mind. I much preferred angelic justice.

"Excellent," Zeb murmured. "Keep me posted."

Sulfur overwhelmed my senses as the demon disappeared, just as he did on the yacht. Except this time his Dargarian bodyguards went with him.

I jumped to my feet, while Xai remained impassive beside me. Our hotel suite was empty, minus the fresh stench of Hell. Tax and the Orsini Devils hadn't been part of our meeting, mostly because they weren't allowed in a Demonic Lord's presence without a formal invitation. More demon politics, and not what I cared about at the moment.

Zeb had created a portal not only for himself but also for his minions. Xai's expression told me this information didn't shock him as it should. Which meant he was used to it.

"Oh, you had better start talking, and fast." Because that was one hell of a show of power, even for a Demonic Lord. "He shouldn't be able to do that."

"I did mention that times have changed, Evangeline."

"Cut the arcane bullshit, Xai. *How* is Zeb doing that?"

"It would appear he's grown in power."

"No shit?" I rolled my eyes at his vagueness. "Stop being an ass, and tell me what the fuck is going on here."

The look he flashed me said he didn't appreciate the command in my tone and had no interest in complying. He pushed off the wall and headed toward his bedroom without a word. Typical Xai. And I was over it.

Adrenaline thrummed through my veins, setting my blood on fire.

I hated the silent game. Normally, I could ignore it, but not after Zeb's display of unnatural power. This wasn't a joke or information to be withheld. Not after everything we'd seen tonight. An increase in power suggested either an imbalance that needed addressing or a potential promotion within the underworld.

"Xai." The warning in my voice begged him not to ignore me, but he did. His stride didn't even waver as I followed him down the hall.

Fine. I'd grab his attention a different way.

A blade slipped into my hand as I dropped to sweep his legs out from under him, but he anticipated it with a jump. His responding kick missed my face by a millimeter as I leapt backward, and then I charged him.

All the pent-up frustration, fear, and fury from the last few days crashed down at once, and I let it out in the only way I knew how. By fighting.

Xai countered each of my punches and kicks, reminding me just how fast he could move, and when his arms came around me in an unyielding hold, I growled. I hated to be restrained and he knew it, but he also wanted to remind me that he had the power to put me in any place he wanted.

"Are you quite done?" he asked without a hint of exhaustion. *Asshole.*

I slammed my heel into his booted toe in response, which elicited a curse from him. A backward kick to his shin forced him to release me because he knew my next kick would be to his knee. I spun around and sliced my blade across his stomach.

He glanced down at it in minor annoyance. "Now you owe me a shirt in addition to the pants you nicked yesterday."

"Bill me."

"Oh, I intend to." He pulled the shirt over his head to reveal every inch of his golden torso. His muscles rippled as he tossed the fabric to the floor, then his hands went to his belt. "I suppose I did promise you a workout tonight." He loosened the buckle and slid the black leather through the loops of his jeans.

My mouth went dry at the sight. "That's not what I had in mind," I managed.

He shrugged as if to say, *Too fucking bad*, and whipped the end of his belt at me. I grabbed the smooth material and yanked it from his hand before he could try to pelt me with it again.

But that was precisely what he wanted.

While I was distracted with the makeshift weapon, he took a step forward, wrapped those steely arms around me, and threw me onto the bed. I tried to use the momentum to continue the roll, but he was too damn fast. His hand wrapped around my ankle, and the next thing I knew, I was beneath a very hot and heavy man. Both of my wrists were captured in one of his hands above my head, and his thighs pinned mine to the mattress.

"Mmm," he murmured. "Feel better?"

Yes. "Ask me that again after I stick a knife through your heart."

He tsked. "Now, Evangeline…" He trailed his free hand down my side to the hem of my shirt and back up to the dagger sheathed against my ribs. "How do you intend to stab me without your blades?" He casually tossed the item onto the floor before slipping his fingers into the front of my jeans to remove a second blade.

I squirmed beneath him, eliciting an amused chuckle from him that stirred vibrations in all the right places. Retirement had really weakened my skills, and the ease with which he restrained me proved it. Fuck.

He unbuttoned my jeans, then slid the zipper down before lifting just enough to slide that treacherous hand inside. But rather than explore my lacy black panties, he moved to my inner thigh to slowly remove two more weapons and dumped them unceremoniously onto the floor.

Goose bumps scattered down my arms. I hated the silent game, but this one? Oh, this playtime I adored, even if it was his way of dominating me.

"How many more?" he mused quietly.

I responded by trying to throw him off me again, which failed. Despite hovering over my hips, his thighs held my legs in place, as did the powerful fingers wrapped around my wrists.

It didn't help that he was inhumanly strong. All angels were, but Xai was the son of two Archangels, which placed him above me in the angelic hierarchy. I could never best him, even when in top shape. He was one of the select few with the ability, hence the reason why his dominance enthralled me.

I shivered beneath him, both loving and loathing his show of control.

He gripped my hip and squeezed in a sensitive place that caused my pelvis to buck upward into his prominent erection. I tried to fall back to the mattress, but his hand snaked around my back to stop me and captured the final piece of silver resting against my spine. Rather than add it to the pile on the floor, he dragged the sharp point up my ribs to the base of my throat, where he pressed the blade hard enough to tingle but not bleed.

"Oh, I do love having you beneath me like this, Evangeline. I've missed it terribly." He relaxed his lower body and pressed his hard member into the sensitive place between my thighs.

I bit my lip to hold in my moan. He wasn't the only one who missed this. He felt so heavy, so *right*, against me. Desire thickened my blood, sending the world into slow motion. I felt every move, throb, and tremble and luxuriated in the tranquility of it all.

Xai always had this impact on me. A few touches and strokes were all it took to melt me inside and out, until I lay pliant beneath him.

The sharp edge at my neck only added to the effect. Rather than feel threatened or scared, I felt safe and protected. Such a bizarre reaction to a clearly predatory position, but I knew Xai. He was the jackass who always betrayed me, and yet he never physically harmed me. Oh, he might draw blood, but not to evoke pain. Everything he did was meant to draw out pleasure, and my body loved him for it.

He brushed his lips over mine in a chaste kiss before drawing the metal across my collarbone and then down at a purposeful angle that sliced the fabric of my shirt along the way. The skill in that single move left me panting as he exposed me from sternum to belly button. I knew my blades were sharp, but he cut through the cotton as if it was butter, something that took the right amount of pressure and precision to accomplish. And he did it all without scraping my skin.

"I consider us even on the shirt, love," he whispered against my mouth.

"Xai…"

"Shh, I know." The kiss that followed scorched me from the inside out and left me quaking beneath him. It'd been so long, *too long*, since I'd felt him like this. He was my one addiction, and my life never felt complete when we were apart. Hate and love mingled in my heart, brewing a maelstrom of emotions in my blood.

I wanted to fuck him, kill him, and find forever with him.

The feelings were so conflicting and overwhelming, and I unleashed them all with my mouth. Our tongues engaged in a strenuous battle for control. My fingers itched to knot in his hair, to yank him away and hold him to me.

So much confusion.

Heat.

Passion.

Memories.

So many moments in the past where I let myself go, only to burn.

"My darling Evangeline. Why would I ever want forever with you?"

"I never chose you, darling. And I'll never choose you."

"Love is such a naïve notion. When will you stop expecting it from me?"

"Enjoy Hell, darling."

"When will you learn, Evangeline? I don't want you. I've never wanted you."

My heart ached with all the cruel words, but it was my back that hurt the most. Always in these moments, that tender place between my shoulder blades wept with the loss of my most precious assets.

My wings.

I longed to fly again…

To feel the wind ruffle my feathers.

To live.

Xai pulled back with an agonized gasp and shuddered over me. I'd not meant to telegraph my pain, but he must have sensed it. Part of that abnormal bond neither of us understood, the same one that always tied us back together. The same one he fought with every grain of his being and swore didn't exist.

"Evangeline," he whispered hoarsely. He tossed the knife away and palmed my cheek. His thumb beneath my eye battered my already-bruised heart and unsettled my memories. This was the moment he usually belittled my emotions and berated me for becoming more human. But rather than do or say as I anticipated, he held me tighter and kissed my damp eyelids before pressing his forehead to mine.

He freed my wrists and cupped my face between his hands, holding me reverently. I shuddered beneath him as his comfort seeped through my barriers and caressed my very soul.

Why is he doing this to me?

"I can't." He sounded so broken, so unlike the Xai I knew. "I've tried everything, and no matter what I do, you stay. You exhaust me, Evangeline."

I stilled beneath him. "What are you talking about?"

He just shook his head against mine. "It's not our time. Not yet." With a sigh, he went to his elbows on either side of my head and pulled away to stare down at me. "Have you felt uneasy lately? Perhaps a little off balance, or maybe light-headed?"

His abrupt change in subject jarred me into speaking the truth. "I always feel that way around you." I didn't mean it to come off as sarcastic, but it probably sounded that way to him.

"You haven't felt the power shift?" he asked. "From the underworld, I mean. Has it impacted you at all?"

"I…" *Power shift?* "I really don't know what you're going on about."

His lips curled downward. "You truly don't feel it?"

"I obviously felt something earlier tonight."

"But not before that?" The severity in his tone forced me to consider. This clearly meant something to him. After a minute of thought, however, I shook my head.

"Other than tonight and the two times Zeb created his own portal, no. But I don't spend a lot of time with demons, besides Gwen."

That wasn't the answer he wanted. I could see it written clearly in his intense gaze.

"Something is coming," he whispered. "I don't know what it is, but I feel it in every fiber of my being. Like there's an ominous cloud of doom approaching." That was rather colorful for him, which implied the seriousness of his words. "Lord Zebulon's increased strength is a recent development, and he's not the only one showing signs of new gifts."

"The other Demonic Lords?" I guessed.

He nodded. "Some are reveling in it more than others, as you would expect. But something else is coming."

As the Son of Chaos, he would feel the disturbance before others would, I imagined, since he could always detect darker elements.

"I don't feel it," I whispered. Death called to me daily, whether it be a sick mortal or a soul requiring vengeance, but those feelings were a part of my nature. "I don't sense anything."

Another nod, this one slower and measured. "There's something else I need to tell you." This talkative side of Xai was new, but I didn't question it.

"Okay... ," I prompted when he didn't elaborate.

"Lord Zebulon..." He paused as if the words were difficult for him to say. "Evangeline, someone gave him a holy blade."

"A holy... ?" My voice faltered as terror seized hold of my heart.

"Yes, and he's keeping it in the underworld." Which meant someone could steal it. Such a rare artifact would call to a damned soul, not to mention the power it held.

I had no words.

No feelings.

Nothing other than horror.

Because a holy blade could kill... not demons... but beings of angelic descent.

Like us.

CHAPTER ELEVEN

EVEN AN ANGEL LIKE ME NEEDS
A LITTLE RELIEF SOMETIMES

XAI'S ADMISSION FOLLOWED me into my nightmares. One where Zeb administered a punishment that felt too much like death. When I woke on a silent scream, Xai wrapped me in his arms and kissed me back to sleep.

It was the strangest night I'd ever experienced in his bed, and not the least of all because we both wore clothes. I'd swapped my shredded shirt for one of his, shucked off my jeans, and fallen asleep beside a boxers-clad Xai.

We spent the afternoon digging into Streator's illegal businesses. The original file provided a preliminary overview that lacked some pretty significant details, like his involvement with human and demon trafficking.

Xai, using one of his more influential aliases, managed

to locate an exclusive slave auction with ties to our mark. Streator didn't own it, but he partook in the festivities and "donations" frequently. Given the conversation I'd overheard yesterday, the asshat planned to make me one of those donations. I had my doubts about his penchant for selling women being related to what we witnessed last night, but there was only one way to be sure. Hence my date tonight.

I slipped on my silver-heeled stilettos and meandered into the living area, where Xai stood waiting for me.

Appreciation lit up his expression. "You wore the purple one."

I gave him an exaggerated curtsy before playfully fondling the silver cross hovering above my cleavage. "Seemed appropriate for Miss O'Hara."

"Hmm, and matching panties?" His eyes burned as they roamed over my exposed legs. The violet dress flared to midthigh, making it perfect for a night of dancing.

I grinned. "Who says I'm wearing any?" I'd meant it as a tease, but he took it as an invitation. His hands went to my hips as he pushed me into the wall of the foyer. I flattened my palms against his sturdy chest to shove him away, but my nails curled into the soft fabric instead. He resembled the dark angel of my dreams in his sinfully tight jeans and a black dress shirt rolled to his elbows. A look I would never tire of on him.

My dress bunched as he slid a thigh between my legs and pressed upward into my most sensitive area. The rough fabric felt delicious against my silk-covered mound, especially as he shifted subtly to test the barrier. If I were truly bare, he'd sense it.

"Tease," he growled.

I held on to him as he rubbed a little harder with that muscled thigh. After millennia of practice, he knew exactly what angle affected me most, and God, did it feel amazing. Especially after the foreplay from last night. Our afternoon of research did little to dampen the lust thickening between us, though we both chose to ignore it. Until now, anyway.

"Are they black or violet?" He whispered the words against my parted lips.

"Black," I mouthed.

"Not necessarily virginal, love."

"I didn't wear them for Streator." He might try to sneak a peek at the goods, but I'd shove my stiletto through his eyes first.

"Mmm, then I approve." He took my mouth in a punishing kiss meant to remind me of his place in my life.

My soul wept with the familiarity of it as my body broke to his will. I wrapped my legs around his waist as he hoisted me into the air, and cried out as he pressed that perfect part of him against my hot center. He was going to make me late for my date, but I didn't care. Not when he touched me like this.

Xai commanded control of my being, and I gave it up willingly. There was no other way. He owned a part of me no one else would ever touch, just as I owned a part of him that he would never admit.

His tongue explored the deep crevice of my mouth. Memorizing, tasting, remembering… I returned the kiss, luxuriating in the intimacy flowing openly between us. When he pressed hard into my core, I jolted, and a flood of warmth went south.

My body knew what he wanted, had been trained to respond to even the subtlest of motions. I grabbed the back of his neck, then threaded my fingers through his thick, dark strands and held on as he pushed his hips into mine again. His rhythm and finesse sang to me on a deep level, calling my pleasure to the forefront like a siren's song.

"Xai…" I could feel the bundle of nerves tightening, but I needed more.

This teasing put me on the edge, but without the right pressure…

Oh…

His hand slid under my dress to the top of my panties to slip inside.

There…

I moaned as the pad of his thumb parted my folds, and then he was right where I needed him.

"Your panties are soaked, darling," he murmured. "Just as I want them."

He tugged my bottom lip into his mouth and sucked hard while rubbing my clit with expert skill. Each stroke brought me closer, fogging my mind with desire, and forcing me to forget everything except him. I loved these moments.

"Every move you make tonight will remind you of who last gave you pleasure. Of what you have to look forward to later." He kissed me hard, his tongue diving deep as he shoved two fingers inside me. Rough, hot, and so very Xai. My body quivered, waiting and longing for the word it needed to let go. Because I knew him. If I started to climb over the finish line without his expressed approval, he'd stop, and I so needed him to continue.

A whimper of unsuppressed need escaped from my mouth.

"That's what I wanted to hear, love." He grinned against my lips and pressed down hard with his thumb. "Come for me, Eve. Now."

Fuck.

I couldn't deny the command in his voice. A spasm shot up and down my spine, sending shivers of excitement through my limbs. He swallowed my moan with his mouth as he massaged my center.

"Mmm," he murmured in approval. "Don't you dare change these." He snapped the elastic panties to punctuate his point. "I want to pull them off of you later with my teeth."

I trembled both from the promise underlining his words and from the aftershocks of my orgasm.

"Okay." The acceptance tumbled from my lips of its own accord. My pleasure-induced mind couldn't think beyond the moment or the delicious waves of heat rolling through my lower belly. It was always this way with him. Explosive and addictive.

The back of my head hit the wall behind me as I shuddered through the remains of my ecstasy. He still hadn't stopped touching me, his fingers deep inside and that thumb playing wickedly with my oversensitive nub.

"Xai…" It was part plea, part desire. "I'm going to be late." I probably already was.

"I know." He nuzzled my cheek before pressing his lips to my ear. "And the beautiful flush of your cheeks will tell him why."

I swallowed. "Not helping with my virgin charade."

"Even virgins masturbate, darling. He'll think it was for him, but you'll know the truth." He shoved those fingers deep before pulling them out to lick them while holding my gaze. "As will I."

Those three words sent a shiver down my spine. The good kind. "Marking your territory, Xai?" It came out on a husky breath.

"Your body already knows her master," he replied, his gaze darkening with arousal. "It's your mind that required the reminder." His hands went to my hips to help me stand and smooth out my dress.

"You'll have to do better than that to trick my mind."

Challenge dilated his pupils. "Oh, darling, we both know that wasn't even a warm-up."

My thighs clenched with the memory of what I knew he could do.

He was right.

That orgasm paled in comparison to the pleasure his touch provoked.

I wanted more. So much more. And I knew he did too. Yet he smoothed out his shirt, readjusted his pants, and gestured toward the foyer rather than demand me to kneel. He always required reciprocation. Not that I minded. Xai ensured I orgasmed multiple times first, but he partook as well. Except now he seemed to be delaying his own gratification.

A new game.

One I liked.

Grabbing his neck, I pulled him down for a kiss that

expressed gratitude and a harsher element. It served as both a promise and a threat.

Two could play the ownership game. He belonged to me just as much as I belonged to him, and my mouth strived to remind him of that. My tongue branded his as my nails scored his scalp. And when he palmed my lower back to pull me up against the hard ridge of his erection, I smiled. "You share that with anyone else, and you'll never win my mind."

His mouth curled against mine. "Don't worry, love. My body knows his mate too." He nipped my lower lip to keep me from replying to that surprising response. "Now let's go. You have a mortal to seduce and, hopefully, kill."

"Sweet talker," I murmured. He always did know the right words to motivate me. I brushed my mouth over his before I pulled away. "You'd better bring my toys." Blades didn't really pair well with my short dress.

He smirked. "Of course, darling. You know how much I love watching you dance."

Let the show begin.

CHAPTER TWELVE

EH, I'VE HAD WORSE DATES

STREATOR STOOD IN the center of the lobby wearing a button-down shirt and khaki trousers. He drew the eye of several women who passed by, and the curl of his lips said he knew it. But his gaze was all mine as I stepped out of the elevator at ten after eight.

"Oh my goodness," I said as I rushed up to him with my hand pressed against my chest. "I lost track of time and…" I trailed off and bit my lip. Let him make what he wanted of that. "I'm sorry, darlin'. Can you forgive me?"

"Hmm," he murmured, looking me over with an appreciative grin. "I think I can find a way for you to make it up to me."

I peered up at him through my lashes. "What did ya have in mind?"

"It's a surprise." He glanced at my empty hands. "I

assume you're ready?"

"Um." I gave a giggle as I fingered my neckline. "Didn't wanna bother with a purse, so I used my, uh, old-fashioned pocket." My identification card, money, and hotel room key were all in my bra, and I'd purposely not brought a phone. It added to my helpless, naïve virgin vibe.

His grin spread to his eyes. "You're adorable, Violet."

I preened for him. "Thank you, darlin'. You're not too bad yourself."

"Shall we?" He held out his elbow, and I threaded my arm through it.

"Yes, please."

The nod he gave his bodyguards was well practiced and subtle. They both fell in line behind us at a respectable distance, one a normal date probably wouldn't notice.

Streator opened the passenger door to a fancy black two-seater parked just outside the reception entrance.

"Oh my Lord. Is this your car?" I asked, feigning shock and excitement.

He smirked. "It is today."

Cocky. I caressed the leather bucket seat with false reverence. "Wow…"

It wasn't the sexiest brand on the market, and I much preferred the one pulling up behind it. Xai sauntered outside without a glance in our direction and handed a tip to the man stepping out of his sleek black car. I hid my grin as I folded myself into the two-seater and watched in the side mirror as my dark angel indulged the valet in conversation. A stalling tactic to follow us to our destination, one neither bodyguard noticed as they climbed into a SUV parked at the corner of the drive.

"Hang on, sweetheart," Streator murmured as he started the car. "I'm going to give you a ride you'll never forget."

I nearly choked on my tongue. What a line. Idiot. I buckled myself in anyway and gripped the seats to stop myself from stabbing him with a hair pick. He chuckled at what he assumed was my nervousness. If he only knew.

His hand fell to the gearshift as he expertly navigated us away from the hotel. At least he opted for a manual. Nothing annoyed me more than an automatic transmission in a fast car. What the fuck was the point?

"Tell me about yourself. What brings you to Miami?"

Oh, good—small talk. My favorite.

I played along all the way to our destination, answering every question with information he already knew.

Xai had reserved a room under my alias to maintain the facade, giving Streator all the details he needed to run an initial background check. The human had connections, both politically and otherwise, so I had no doubt he knew everything about Violet O'Hara. A businessman with his background didn't go on a date without having obtained all the necessary information in advance.

"Oh my." I let my lips part in awe.

Streator had chosen one of the more affluent clubs in Miami. The exterior boasted a gorgeous patio with steps leading down to the beach, while the interior was upscale, decadent, and filled with elite clientele.

Couples mingled and danced, clinking crystal glasses and basking in the exuberant atmosphere. Several celebrities were in attendance, something that would enthrall my tabloid-loving roommate. Gwen used the gossip magazines as a way to stay informed of human affairs and passed that trivial knowledge on to me.

"Impressed?" His lips brushed my ear as he settled us into the booth of a VIP section near the bar.

Not really. "How'd you get us in here, sugar?"

He placed his arm around my shoulders and trailed his fingers over my upper arm. "Mmm, I might know a few people."

I blinked up at him. "What do you do?"

He shrugged. "I'm an entrepreneur specializing in the trade of exotic goods. Nothing interesting." He lifted his hand to call over a waiter and ordered us a round of martinis. "Ready to share that drink?"

I grinned. "You know I am."

My eyes wandered while he peppered me with more trivial questions. He asked about my family, friends, and general relationship ties. All typical date questions, but I knew his curiosity ran deeper. He wanted to know whether anyone would come looking for me if he chose to procure me for his nefarious means. I welcomed him to try.

When he suggested switching from talking to dancing, I accepted, mostly because I wanted to see more of the club. His bodyguards had hung back just outside the VIP section, while Xai remained missing in action. Though, I *sensed* he was lingering somewhere. But not in the same way I could feel a demon's presence. This went deeper.

Streator grabbed my hips and pulled me into him in the center of the room, moving us in tandem to the beat. He wasted no time acquainting our bodies and exploring my curves.

The desire to eviscerate my date entertained my thoughts.

It was a good thing Xai had my knives.

Speaking of…

I lifted my hands over my head as I swayed to the beat and scanned the club. No sign of my dark angel anywhere.

Where are you hiding?

Streator trailed open-mouthed kisses along my neck and up to my ear, where he nibbled the lobe. I squirmed and giggled in response, and his arms wound around my waist. He pressed his prominent erection into my backside, telling me how much he liked my virginal act. I gasped for effect because that seemed like something an innocent would do, and he spun me around to kiss me.

Escalation.

Good.

The seductive game was starting to bore me. I needed him to move this forward so I could get to work. Obviously, he didn't work in this club, and his bodyguards weren't relevant. I wanted more details about his illicit dealings and business partners. Some of their names were in the files, but none of our research explained the demon parade from last night.

I needed to learn more. Not just about the drug and human trafficking, but the contacts in his elite circle. I'd hoped a few would meet us here, but it seemed Streator had only one activity on his mind tonight.

His tongue felt wrong in my mouth, but I let him explore while tentatively returning the kiss. The temptation to bite down and knee him in the nuts crossed my mind a few times. But something told me he wouldn't enjoy that nearly as much as I would.

When his hands drifted up my legs, beneath my dress, I stopped him.

First, ew.

Second, only Xai went there.

Third, a virgin wouldn't allow such behavior.

I tore my mouth from his and gave him an alarmed look. "I… We… But…"

He smiled at my inability to form a sentence and pulled his hands from mine to palm my ass. "Not into a little exhibitionism, hmm?" He spoke the words against my ear.

Not with you, anyway.

"It's not that," I said loudly back as heat crept up my neck. Picturing him with a knife through one eye excited me greatly. "I… Oh Lord, how do I say this?" I bit my lip and averted my gaze. "I'm… This isn't something I do!" I had to shout to be heard over the club's noise.

I cleared my throat in a false attempt to speak again, then opened and closed my mouth as if I couldn't get out the words. He lifted my chin to force my eyes up to his, and whatever he saw on my face seemed to appease him. His lips found my ear again.

"Talk to me, sweetheart."

Wow, he was good. Just enough charm and concern to put a woman at ease, and looks to go with it. He didn't need to engage in human trafficking to get laid, but something told me he enjoyed the power exchange in sex. And not the consensual kind.

"Um…" I cleared my throat again and elevated my voice to be heard over the obnoxious beat. "I told ya my parents are gone, but they raised me with certain ideals. Like not lyin' with a man until my weddin' night."

His sharp intake of air was music to my ears.

Meanwhile, somewhere, I sensed Xai laughing. I tried to find him as Streator manhandled me off the dance floor, but my dark angel had clearly found a decent shadow to hide in against one of the walls.

"You're waiting until marriage?" Streator asked once we were in a quiet location. His curious tone didn't match the excitement running through his gaze.

Hook, line, and sinker.

Done deal.

I gnawed on my lip. "Well, no. Yes. I don't know. I've never really found anyone who made me want to, uh, test the boundary?"

He nodded thoughtfully. "I see."

"I totally spoiled our night, didn't I?"

"Oh, no, definitely not." He rubbed my arm in a comforting manner. "How about we get out of here so we can talk some more."

Talk. Yes, I'm sure that's what you have in mind.

Game on.

I went for a sheepish smile. "I think I'd like that."

He did another one of those subtle nods to his minions before palming my lower back and escorting me toward the exit. We didn't speak as we waited for his car, and I fidgeted with the hem of my dress.

I half expected Xai to appear, but he didn't.

My stomach churned with apprehension. It wouldn't be the first time he abandoned me midmission.

Where are you?

Had I manufactured his presence in the club? An amusement to taunt my heart?

Streator opened the passenger door, and I slipped inside.

The hairs along my arm danced with uncertainty.

Something felt off.

My earlier confidence dwindled as my *date* joined me in the car. The abrupt shift unsettled my nerves.

Millennia-old instincts flared in warning.

Trusting Xai had burned me so many times before, but he'd been different this time. A ruse to lure me into a sense of comfort? Just to double-cross me in a moment of need?

Had he duped me as smoothly as Streator duped Violet?

My soul cried in refusal as the fractures of my heart ached in protest.

What could he possibly have to gain by leaving me alone on this mission?

Streator was a human. One who consorted with demons, apparently, but a mortal nonetheless. I didn't need a knife to bring him down.

"Violet," he murmured as he expertly navigated us away from the club.

"Hmm?" I glanced at the side mirrors for any sign of Xai.

A dumb fucking move.

One I knew better than to make when in the presence of someone like Streator.

The prick in my neck caught me completely unawares, and by the time I swung around to meet his icy stare, it was too late. He'd already injected me with some kind of drug. My body would metabolize it faster than a human, but it'd still knock me out.

Fuck.

I knew this was the point, but *fuck*.

"Shh…" Streator had the audacity to cup my face with one hand, while the other focused on steering the car. "Enjoy the dream, sweetheart. It'll be the last one you have for a while."

"You basss…" Fuck, I was already slurring.

What the hell did he inject me with?

More petting.

All the way down to my breasts, but my hands were suddenly too numb to shove him away. He fondled me with the ease of a man who did this often while driving.

"Too bad I can't keep you for myself," he murmured almost sadly. "But you'll be worth a fortune."

My growl came out as a gargle as black spots clouded my vision.

Damn it.

When I woke up, someone would die. And that someone would be Streator.

His chuckle followed me into the darkness, where I didn't dream. Not entirely, anyway.

Whatever narcotic he gave me put me in a state of subconsciousness. I'd never experimented with drugs, but I suspected he'd just pumped me full of one, because wow.

Doors.

So many fucking doors.

And the hallway I stood in was stark white.

The Heavenly ideal, I supposed. Except not.

I grabbed the handle to my left and stepped into a nightmare.

My past.

CHAPTER THIRTEEN

NOTE TO SELF:
DON'T DO DRUGS

WINGS THE COLOR of midnight painted a path through the clouds scant inches from me. I loved this game despite the inevitable outcome.

He would win.

He always won.

But still I tried, my purple-tinted feathers beating hard at my back as I chased the Son of Chaos. His laugh prickled my skin, sending shivers of delight to my lower abdomen.

We both knew what would come next.

A long night in each other's arms, loving one another until dawn.

"Tired yet, love?" Xai taunted.

"Never."

He dove headfirst through a cloud, but I recognized this trick and stayed straight instead of following. Warm hands grabbed my hips as he came up beneath me, aligning our bodies in flight and guiding me with his stronger wings.

"You're learning," he praised against my lips. His rewarding kiss left me dizzy, or maybe that was from the spinning of our wings.

Xai let me go just as suddenly as he caught me and swirled downward through another cloud. This time I trailed after him with a laugh.

He chanced a glance back at me, that smile of his radiant. "Want to try something new?"

"What did you have in mind?"

"Follow me," he replied vaguely.

And I did.

Because I always did.

I landed in the dreamy hallway again with a thud and hopped to my feet. Still surrounded by white. My shoes echoed as I paced, and an eerie silence fell when I stopped. This mind game was new. I'd been knocked out before, but never quite like this. I tried another door and instantly regretted it.

Falling.

It burned.

Fuck, it hurt.

My wings sizzled, my feathers crying as they melted into ash.

By the time I landed, I couldn't move, couldn't breathe.

I curled into a ball and screamed, and screamed, and screamed.

Agony.

Confusion.

Nothingness.

I knew it would hurt, but I had no idea it would rip my heart from my chest.

My eyes drifted upward to the canopy of branches and leaves above me. I couldn't even see the sky. Not that it mattered. What was the point if I couldn't fly?

And then I saw him. My dark angel stood not ten feet from me, leaning against a tree with his arms folded. The trademark smile I expected didn't appear. Instead, he remained stoic, almost bored.

"Well, that was impressive." I flinched at his sardonic tone. Had he hit his head when he Fell? "You shouldn't have followed

me here, Evangeline."

I frowned. "You asked me to." After we last made love, he begged me to find a way to follow him, so I did.

His brows shot up. "I never expected you to believe me." He pushed himself away from the tree. "Well, I hope you can find a way back home. You shouldn't be here."

My breathing faltered as he turned away. "Where are you going?"

"Does it matter?" he asked with a dark look over his shoulder. "It's not like I want you."

His words were sharper than my knives. They struck me in the middle of my chest, shredding my heart.

"Xai…" It came out as a broken plea. "You don't mean that. Y-you can't mean that."

His starless eyes narrowed in disgust. "You can't possibly think I want this version of you? Broken, battered, and bruised?" His smirk hurt me more than my broken wings. "Oh, you did." He tsked and shook his head. "My darling Evangeline. Why would I ever want forever with you?"

Tears filled my eyes as the hallway materialized around me. I wrapped my arms around my tender stomach to stop the dry heaves from unnerving me completely.

The memory was too real. It felt like yesterday. The pain, fear, and loneliness. He'd left me in the forest without a backward glance. Almost a century went by before I saw him again, and by then, my love had turned to hatred.

Until he tricked me into his bed again.

I wiped the dampness from my cheeks and gave my head a shake.

Whatever drugs Streator had given me had royally fucked me up.

This place was my own personal hell.

An endless corridor of pain and memories.

"Wake up," I demanded with a smack against my cheek. The impact burned, but I remained very much alone in this vapid state.

The knob beside me twisted by itself, and I jumped

backward. A mistake, because the door behind me had been opened without permission.

Blood.

Sweet, blissful death.

I smiled as the demon shattered to ash at my feet. A girl could get used to this. As the daughter of Azrael, I craved retribution but rarely sought it. However, this child-eating asshole deserved his fate, and my soul sighed in relief at having relieved this plane of his wretched existence.

Applause broke out behind me, sending a chill down my spine. I'd recognize that essence anywhere.

"Xai," *I growled and tossed a blade over my shoulder in greeting.*

He caught it deftly between his fingers before admiring the craftsmanship. "Lovely," *he murmured.* "Make it yourself?"

"What do you want?"

"You," *he replied as he pocketed my weapon.* "Or rather, I have an opportunity for you."

My eyebrows inched upward. He acted as if several centuries hadn't passed since our last encounter. Typical. "No, thank you." *I bent to retrieve my silver from the demon's ashes and turned to leave.*

"Perhaps I didn't phrase that correctly." *His smooth tones held a lethal edge that caused my footing to falter.* "It's more of an ultimatum."

"Excuse me?" *I faced him with an incredulous expression.*

"You heard me." *He ran his gaze over me in a way I knew too well. Distance and time never seemed to matter. The moment we laid eyes on one another, it was as if yesterday never happened. But not this time. I refused to fall prey to his bed once again.*

"What ultimatum?" *I prompted as I crossed my arms to hide my hardening nipples.*

"Lord Tardís requires a favor, and in exchange, he'll grant you sanctuary in his territory. Something I fear you may need after slaughtering Lord Slanderin's Órdinátum."

I rolled my eyes. "Demon politics don't concern me."

"Oh, but they do, darling. Far more than you realize. Hell runs this plane now, and as such, we must play by their rules."

"Or what?" *I asked.* "They'll send me home? Oh wait, I can't* *go back." I'd tried and failed numerous times.*

"No, Evangeline, they'll send you to Hell." His blunt reply sent a chill down my spine. "And don't think to run. They'll only send me after you, and we both know I'll have no issue handing you over."

I gaped at him. "You wouldn't." He might be a coldhearted bastard, but our history had to mean more to him than some ridiculous bargain he'd formed with the Demonic Lords.

"How soon you forget," he mused. "I never chose you, darling. And I'll never choose you. This would go so much better if you simply remembered that."

The door slammed shut on that memory, sending me flying backward into the white wall. I collapsed with a shudder as his cruel words washed over me.

Why was my subconscious doing this to me? As if it wasn't enough to endure the original experience, I had to relive each one of my most hated moments again?

Fate was a cruel bitch.

I exhaled roughly and shot to my feet again before pounding against my cement prison. My hands came away bloody, yet I felt nothing, so I punched over and over again. But the hard surface didn't give, and all the doors surrounding me opened at once.

Blaring heat seared my skin before I fell into the worst memory of them all.

Hell.

The way time moved here was all wrong. I couldn't run as fast as I wanted, and my head pounded from the severity of this place. Xai set the pace, and with each step, he increased the distance between us.

"Slower," I panted. And wasn't that a weird sound. I never breathed heavily from a run. Only a night in my dark angel's bed left me feeling winded, but we'd certainly not been doing that down here.

"Keep up," he called over his shoulder, and I swore he sped up.

I pushed harder, but each stride seemed to weaken me more. Fire slithered through my veins as a sense of dread settled in the pit of my stomach.

This place courted death.

Mine.

Purple flames raced along the walls while my feet skipped over obsidian-crusted rock. I didn't understand Hell's geography, but I knew this maze of corridors was not where we wanted to be.

"*We need to get out of here,*" *I rasped.* "*Xai, please.*"

His chuckle sounded wrong to my ears. How could he laugh in a place like this? I tried to grab his arm, to stop him, but he swiveled away from me.

"*What's going on?*" *He'd led me down here, claiming my most recent mark had ducked into Hell to hide and only Xai knew the demon's hiding spot.*

I'd trusted him to guide me because he'd shown me that soft side of him again, but as Xai turned to look at me now, I saw the harsh version had returned. The one that loved to punish and hurt.

My sadistic angel had come out to play.

"*When will you learn, Evangeline?*" *he mused, his gaze running over me mockingly.* "*I don't want you. I've never wanted you. Perhaps now you'll leave me alone for good and go back to where you came from.*"

I gaped at the cold man smirking down at me. "*Don't do this. Not again. Things can be good between us, and you know it.*"

The bastard laughed and shook his head. "*Love is such a naïve notion. When will you stop expecting it from me?*"

My eyes narrowed. "*Stop.*"

I couldn't utter another word as exhaustion settled over me. Angels were not meant to visit this plane. Our souls were too pure, though Xai seemed perfectly fine. Perhaps his had been tarnished enough that the underworld welcomed him. Or maybe his Archangel bloodline had something to do with it. He always did thrive on chaos and pain.

For a brief second, I swore concern etched his features, but then it was gone and replaced by a mask of indifference.

"*Enjoy Hell, darling.*"

He took off at a pace my legs couldn't match under this level of fatigue, but that didn't stop me from trying to chase him.

"*Xai!*" *My yell came out as a hoarse whisper. Every part of my body seemed to be shutting down under the stress of this environment. It wouldn't kill me, but it would leave me paralyzed and in extreme agony. Forever.*

He couldn't leave me here.

Not like this, not after everything we'd been through.

Two thousand years of history.

This was just another one of his cruel tricks.

A fun game to see how much I could take.

But as time passed, I knew that wasn't true. He'd left me to suffer. Alone. In the darkness. Surrounded by unspeakable beings who would thrive on destroying my soul.

I shivered despite the fiery atmosphere. Sweat soaked my shirt and weighed down my shoes as I tried desperately to run in his general direction. But he was long gone.

My lips parted on an expletive, but no sound escaped. The thick, sulfur-infused air clouded my lungs, and I sagged against a burning wall. It singed my skin, but I couldn't feel enough to care.

Pain tore through my chest as Xai broke my heart once more and shattered the remainder of my resolve. If I found a way out of here, I'd retire. For good. No more working as an assassin for Hell. They could handle their own demon problems going forward. It was time I found some semblance of happiness before my soul fractured beyond repair.

Blackness overwhelmed my senses briefly, and I forced clarity through my thoughts just long enough to crawl to a nook off to the side. A brief nap might help me regain some strength. Or maybe it would knock me into a state of unconsciousness.

Anything to remove the agony flooding my veins.

"You don't belong here," someone said from above me.

I snorted at the obvious and tried to shift into a defensive stance, but my limbs refused to work. This was worse than Falling. I had no energy, no thoughts, nothing.

Something clamped around my arm. A hot brand that reminded me of melted steel. I wanted to fight, to yell, to do something, but my body fell limp.

And then I was flying. Not in the way I remembered, but in an abnormal shift of elements that cramped my stomach.

A Portal Dweller.

With bright emerald eyes.

Returning me to Earth.

My eyes snapped open as the dream fled. I'd suppressed that nightmare for so long that I'd forgotten a vital detail. The one about my escape.

I hadn't found a Portal Dweller that day; he had found me and propelled me back to Earth.

Why?

I looked for another door, one that might have an answer, and froze.

The white corridor was gone.

Instead, I was locked in a cage of sorts, lying on a lumpy old mattress. Cold iron bars decorated the walls, and a drop ceiling with missing patches of drywall rested above.

I shivered. My hallway of horrors had nothing on this very real place.

Terror lived here, and I'd arrived without backup. Because I had no doubt in my mind what that jaunt down memory lane had been about. A stark reminder that when I needed him most, Xai always disappeared. It would be up to me to get myself out of this mess, as well as the one created by Kalida's murder. The bastard probably set me up himself.

My hands curled into fists.

Just when I thought things had changed—again—Xai let me down.

And I only had myself to blame.

When would I learn to stop letting him in?

Never.

My heart beat in protest. Hope resided there. A treacherous, hurtful emotion that would one day destroy my soul. Because part of me wanted to believe he hadn't left me to die, that he'd finally changed for the better, that he did in fact love me.

Deep down I knew he did, but he always shoved me away in the most brutal of ways. And I never understood why.

He insisted on helping me with this case, and things had been different between us. More real than they had been in a long time, and genuine. Master manipulator or not, some feelings couldn't be faked.

Someone gave him a holy blade.

Fear had edged Xai's voice when he spoke those words. Not for himself, but for me. And I'd believed him.

But I'd also trusted him when he'd asked me to Fall. When he'd led me into Hell...

I shook my head.

Now wasn't the time to ponder Xai's motives. I'd spent an eternity trying to understand him. If he'd taught me one thing with all his callous decisions, it was that I needed to rely on myself, and I would.

I just had to get out of this cage first.

CHAPTER FOURTEEN

ASKING PERMISSION NEVER KILLED ANYONE, OR MAYBE IT DID

I PRETENDED TO sleep on my cot while cataloging the scents and sounds surrounding me. Three things occurred to me quickly.

First, I wasn't alone down here.

Second, I needed a key to escape.

And third, demons lurked nearby. At least six of them.

A dull thud repeated overhead, suggesting Streator had deposited me in the basement of a nightclub. He'd left me clothed with my jewelry, silver heels and hair sticks. Not my preferred weapons, but they'd make do whenever he or one of the hellish bodyguards showed up.

The presence of the underworld placated me a little

because it meant this plan hadn't been a complete waste of time. I'd questioned whether or not Streator's penchant for sex slavery was linked to the demon parade the other night, but this proved that, at the very least, he had several unusual ties to Hell. And that was worth exploring.

Soft cries and sniffles pricked at my conscience. There were seven other women down here, all in their own ten-by-ten cells. A parade of goose bumps marched down my arms at the thought of their fates. My angelic soul craved justice on their behalf, and I would seek retribution when the time came for it.

I withheld the urge to drum my fingers while I waited. If I woke too early from my drug-induced coma, the owners of this shithole would question my reaction. Given their confirmed association with Hell's minions, that could lead to some interesting theories I'd prefer to avoid.

The demonic auras above pulsed with menace, an indication that they were the types I enjoyed killing. I suspected the majority were Guardians. They would be the most useful to a mortal like Streator.

I tried to pinpoint their location in the club, but approaching footsteps distracted me from the task.

Three sets, all human.

A door at the far end of the room swung open to allow their entry.

I peeked at them through my eyelashes while remaining utterly still. The shadows in the cell would keep my face hidden until they stood outside the bars, but I could make out their features in the dull yellow lighting overhead. Several of the women scurried to the corners of their available spaces, while one curled into a defensive ball. She was stark naked with marks along her skin that revealed too much about her situation.

When the shorter, muscular man smirked at her, I knew who had caused her bruises.

Asshat One. He'd die first.

An invisible cloud of intimidation surrounded the

men as they moved with purpose toward my space. All wore expressions that suggested they did this far too often and *enjoyed* their work.

These were the kind of mortals I assassinated. The types that deserved a date with death.

"When did Scott say she'd wake?" The gravelly tone belonged to Asshat One.

Whatever Streator had shot into my veins had clearly been meant to fuck me up for quite some time. I suspected it also contained a narcotic—something addictive to keep me in line like a good pet. Good thing those types of drugs didn't work on my kind. At least not in the same way it would a human.

"Another hour or so," his fat buddy replied. Baldy seemed a fitting nickname for the round, hairless imbecile.

My eyes fell closed as they reached my cell, leaving the third with a sad nickname of Thing Three. He had thin brown hair and a lanky build. Nothing remarkable about him.

"Should be enough time, then," Asshat One replied as he jingled a set of keys.

"You can't touch this one," Thing Three said quickly, ruining my fun. I had hoped they would try to touch me so I could properly introduce them to the new toys Gleason gave me earlier this week.

"Yeah, Streator said she's intact," Baldy grumbled. "Gotta take her over to Becks for inspection."

Oh, that sounded fun.

"There are other ways to use her." Asshat One really wanted to die first. I'd happily oblige once he finished unlocking my fucking door.

"Compton said no touching." Thing Three appeared to be the voice of reason and, from the sound of it, also the one in charge of this trio. But the name he'd dropped captivated my interest most of all.

Who the fuck is Compton? I mentally reviewed all the notes on Streator and came up blank. *Tell me more, boys.*

The door swung open, and the urge to kick some ass

hit me hard, but patience held me still. I needed to play this out until I gathered all the intelligence I could.

These three were useless to me. I wanted their leader. One I suspected might be a demon. It was the only way to explain the underworld presence around this club and could also be related to the horror parade from the other night. Hell didn't mingle with humans, not unless they were useful.

A clammy hand slid up my leg to fondle my silk panties. It took considerable effort not to cringe when my violator drew a finger down the center.

"Mmm, I hope Scott's wrong." Apparently, Asshat One had a penchant for unconscious women. How charming. I hoped he enjoyed fucking sharp objects, because I had a few on my person that would happily make his acquaintance.

Thin, stick-like arms encircled my body and lifted me into the air. My limbs fell limp despite my heart's desire to fight. *Patience.*

I ignored the men's salacious comments as we moved, and focused on my changing surroundings.

No stairs. Just a long hallway leading to another area of the club that felt somewhat closer to the demonic presence above. There was a pause as the men unlocked a door, and then sterile, clean air tickled my nose. Better lighting, fresh paint, and a touch of coffee. An office area?

A snick of the door sounded, followed by a series of beeps as they secured the prison area, and then we were moving again.

Eleven steps.

Stop.

"Is this her?" a female voice asked. She sounded curious in a morbid way.

"Yep. Need proof of virginity for the auction," Thing Three explained as he dropped me unceremoniously onto a hard mattress. Bleach and cotton assaulted my senses, as did the underlying scent of fresh blood and another familiar scent.

Death.

Someone had recently departed this plane for another, in this room.

Great. Just what my soul needed.

"I'll get to work," the woman said with an excited hitch in her voice.

Now, I wasn't well versed in physician visits, as I didn't really need them, but her reaction did not strike me as normal. What kind of doctor looked forward to an intimate patient exam?

"Thanks, Becks. We'll be upstairs if you need us." The authority in Thing Three's voice confirmed my suspicion about him being in charge. Maybe he would be useful to me after all.

"I'll be fine," Becks replied as she secured my wrists with flimsy restraints. I almost laughed. If she thought those would hold me down, then she was in for quite a surprise.

The shuffle of feet followed by the closing of the door told me we were finally alone.

Time to work.

I held still while Becks positioned my legs on the bed. When her hands went to my underwear, I opened my eyes, but she was too focused on her task to notice. Brunette, creamy skin, frown lines, and delicate features. Nothing extraordinary, but not ugly either.

While she attempted to pull down my underwear, I examined the binds on my wrists. They were affixed to the bed railings. Rookie mistake. One sharp tug, and I'd not only be free but also wielding metal bars. To be fair, the woman's previous subjects probably didn't contain my strength.

Right, then. How about a little test to get this party started?

I closed my eyes and whimpered softly, pretending to stir. Becks blew out a breath and grumbled, "God damn it," under her breath. She left the black silk around my thighs and opened a cupboard to the left. "Never the right dose," she continued, irritation evident.

"Wha-what… ?" I cleared my throat and thrashed my

116

head as if trying to clear it. "I-I… ?" I forced a tremble and squinted at her.

The doctor set something on the counter and continued her shuffling, ignoring me.

"Who?" I feigned panic as my surroundings registered. "Wh-where?"

"Just stop. It won't do you any good." The doctor paused her search to watch me fake-struggle in my restraints. "Not as if you would be smart enough anyway, right? I mean, you let a man like Scott trick you."

She shook her head as if in pity, but then she laughed. Her dark amusement told me everything I needed to know. This was not a woman being forced into a profession that hurt people. Doctor Becks *liked* it.

I sighed. Damn. I should have expected it. Her dark soul practically sang to the grim reaper inside of me when I first looked at her, just like the three men who had taken me from my cell. As Azrael's daughter, I had certain lethal skills that applied in situations like this and a heavenly duty to carry out vengeance for the innocent.

I was literally born to protect and kill.

And dear old Becks was my ideal mark.

But I needed some answers first.

"Hold on, I have just what you need," she said. Given what I knew about trafficking from my days as an assassin, the doctor probably intended to shoot me full of addictive drugs.

The bitch flashed a vial at me not a second later and waggled her brows. If I had any doubts before, they were long gone now.

She returned to her task, presenting me with her back. *Playtime.*

I yanked my hands up at a calculated angle and smiled when the hinges popped. The doctor's head snapped around just in time for me to swing the new weapons up into my palms.

And then I moved.

Beck's back hit the wall with a thud as I pinned her with the bars against her throat.

"Would you mind pulling my underwear up, please?" I asked. "It's chafing my thighs, and I don't think we've quite made it that far in our relationship yet."

Her eyes rounded as her mouth formed on a silent scream.

I tsked and shook my head.

"Yelling requires oxygen. Surely, as a doctor, you understand that?" I paused, considering. "You are a real doctor, right?"

Despite her dire state, her eyes narrowed. That'd be a yes on the doctor front, then.

"Right. I'll let you breathe after you fix the panties you so rudely tried to remove. Then we'll have a chat. Female to female." She just gaped at me, so I applied pressure to the metal against her neck. "That wasn't a request, Becks. Fix it. Now." The threat in my voice propelled her into action.

Her fingers fluttered against my thighs as she struggled to pull the elastic up. Such a weird feeling having another woman dress me. A lot of immortals experimented with both sexes, as well as a variety of kink, but it never appealed to me.

I eased up on the bar to let her inhale after she haphazardly fixed my dress. "Now, let's start with the obvious. Whom do you work for?"

She wheezed and coughed in reply.

My eyebrow inched upward. "I'm sorry, Becks. That wasn't the answer I was looking for."

I shifted to pin her again, and she croaked out, "Wait." Another cough. In my haste to pin her, I'd damaged her windpipe. Xai had called me soft, but really, he meant "out of practice." Torture was a fine art. One wrong move, and the subject died. I'd have to be more careful with Streator later.

"A name, Doctor. You can mouth it."

Fuck you, was her response instead.

"How original." The least she could do was try to be inventive. I stepped back, lowered the bars, and slammed my fists into her stomach while still holding on to the metal rods. Before she could keel over, I caught her neck with the poles and shoved her back against the wall. "Try again, please."

Tears streamed down her face as true fear registered.

"Yes. I'm stronger than I look," I confirmed. "A name, Becks. Not difficult. Whom. Do. You. Work. For?"

Torturing humans never really appealed to me, even when I knew they deserved it. Hence the reason I barely hit her, yet it'd clearly been enough to loosen her tongue.

"C-comp-ton," she managed on a rough exhale.

Seemed to be the name of the day. "Does Streator work for him too?"

She huffed a broken laugh and tried to shake her head, which ended in a rough hack. "P-part-ners, and not…" More coughing cut off whatever she'd been about to add.

I frowned. The notes didn't say anything about Streator having a business partner. Maybe they were silent buddies in the trafficking industry?

"So, they procure and sell women together?" I asked.

She grimaced. "N-no. C-compton auction. St-streator f-finds girls."

Semantics. Streator acquired the product, and Compton auctioned it. Equally bad.

"And the demons? What can you tell me about them?"

The look she gave me was answer enough. She thought I'd lost my mind. Typical mortal reaction to the unknown, which meant she knew nothing useful about Streator outside of this fucked-up hobby. But there had to be a reason the demons were involved. Hell didn't need humans to run a scheme like this to engage in sin. Something else was going on here.

"Whom do Compton and Streator report to?" Because maybe she'd heard a name that could help me.

Confusion fluttered through her features. "Wh-what?"

Well, this had been a colossal waste of my time. "You've been very unhelpful, Becks, but I'll make do.

Thanks anyway."

I slammed the bars into the side of her head with the designed intent to kill instantly. A painless death. The only gift I could give a woman of her chosen fate. I inhaled deeply as her soul departed this plane for the next, and calmed as the sensation of justice served settled over me.

Peace. Understanding. Rightness.

Removing evil from Earth always granted me a feeling of satisfaction. I'd missed this.

A complication of my birthright was the ability to see the darkness in others. It left my lethal side eager to settle the balance, to help humanity thrive by removing those with vile intentions, but I'd ignored it lately. Mostly because I'd been hell-bent on retiring, but also because I needed a break.

I didn't enjoy killing, but I craved the act of punishment. And sometimes that craving was addictive. Today I would let that desire loose. It needed a good workout.

I slid the bars out of my restraints and went to work finding the key to remove the cuffs from my wrists. After freeing myself from the unfashionable accessories, I raided the cabinets for scalpels and anything else practicable.

My inherent ability to turn anything and everything into a deadly weapon was a useful trait since the man responsible for safeguarding my silver had disappeared.

I tucked a few items into my silk undergarments and used some medical tape from the cabinet to secure three drug-filled syringes to my thighs. A heroin overdose would be a horrible way to die, but the men in this club deserved it.

I snagged the set of keys I found on Doctor Becks and peeked out the door into the empty hallway. I probably had twenty to thirty minutes before the trio came back to check on the doctor. Plenty of time for a self-guided tour of the facility.

CHAPTER FIFTEEN

IF HELL OWNED A NIGHTCLUB,
IT WOULD LOOK SOMETHING LIKE THIS

NO SECURITY CAMERAS DOWN HERE.

The men in charge clearly didn't think their prisoners could escape or pose a threat—a misconception I would be rectifying very soon.

I moved down the hall, keeping my back to the wall. My heels were silent against the concrete, a skill I'd mastered in my assassin days. It helped that the dull, repetitive beat above drowned out all other noise. I used the bass to my advantage, moving in time with the rhythm. Each step took me closer to the demonic beacon above, which was my goal.

The roar from above had me wondering about the time. Streator and I had left the club close to midnight, and I'd likely been out an hour or two, which meant the party above had to be dying down soon. But the increasing level of noise almost seemed to negate that notion. I should have checked the doctor for a phone or a watch. Too late now.

I passed two vacant offices on my way to the door at the end of the hall. It hung slightly ajar, and I gave it a tentative push.

Stairs, and from the sound of it, they led into the club.

A sharp crack from the dungeon at the other end of the corridor caused me to pause. It reminded me of a gunshot. Two more in quick succession had me freezing with a foot on the first step.

Fuck.

I'd intended to go back for the victims later, but their fear tugged at my heart.

You don't have the door code.

That hasn't stopped me before.

Silence fell as logic worked through my brain.

Only three shots fired. Not nearly enough to kill all the women. It was more likely one of the guards trying to scare them into submission. From what I had observed, the girls were all healthy and relatively new. Like me. Harming them before the auction would be counterproductive to the organization's goals.

My pulse thrummed with the need for vengeance. Those women didn't deserve this fate, and I would see to it that their captors served a worse one. And then I'd free the innocents locked up in the other room.

Eyes narrowed, I started upward with a newfound purpose.

The stench of demon thickened with each step, telling me I'd stumbled upon their lair. I sensed at least eight of them now. By the time I reached the top stair, my head was spinning. The pure essence of sin on this level reminded me of Hell.

So cruel, thick, and unexpected.

I blinked to clear the fog from my brain, but it lingered.

My instincts flared. *Danger.*

Something powerful lurked up here.

A being that oozed cruelty and pain.

Wrongness settled over me, much like at the shipping yard, only worse.

Whatever monstrosity existed in this club did not belong on Earth. It contained too many hellish qualities.

I need to get the fuck out of here.

My feet were moving before I could think, and I found myself staring out into the club. Humans, mostly men, surrounded scandalously dressed women who were clearly unwilling participants in this room. Most danced in cages, but a few seemed to be servicing men on the couches along the back wall. Their dead gazes claimed them as the veterans of this club, while those gyrating in the wired cages boasted freshly terrified expressions.

I understood dominance in the bedroom, but this took power to a whole new level. And it infuriated me. I wanted to burn this place to the ground with all the perpetrators inside of it.

"You're new," a deep voice murmured from my left. His gold cuff links and crisp suit demonstrated wealth, as did the crystal glass in his hand.

All the males in attendance boasted money.

Buyers.

Bastards.

Cutting through the crowd unnoticed would be impossible in my skimpy purple dress and heels. If I had my blades, I'd slice my way through, taking down as many of these jackasses as possible on my way out the door.

A hand on my shoulder had me reacting on instinct. I grabbed the thick fingers and twisted until they snapped. The man with the gold cuff links crumpled to the ground, and I kneed him in the face along the way. Any person who could use wealth to procure an unwilling slave deserved pain.

"Oh, I'm sorry. That was rude of me." I placed my foot on his crotch and didn't hesitate to introduce his manhood to the floor. His agony was music to my ears. "Maybe you'll think twice about touching a woman without her permission next time."

My smile was short-lived as I realized I'd caught the attention of several partygoers. Great. Not what I needed.

I stepped backward into the sulfur-ridden hallway behind me and looked for another way out, but I only spotted the stairwell and a single door. The source of the un-Earthly presence.

That overwhelming sense of the underworld surrounded me again, leaving me breathless. I'd sensed the demons from downstairs, but this felt different.

More powerful.

Deadly.

Wrong.

"What the fuck?" A bulky human stepped into the darkened corridor after me, his expression furious.

I batted my eyes innocently at him. "Sorry, did I handle that situation incorrectly?" I cocked my head to the side and ignored the bile surging in my throat. "Was I supposed to lie down and take it?"

"You think this is funny?" His expression and tone stated that he didn't find me very amusing. How sad for him. "I'll show you what we do with *funny* girls."

He came at me with his size in mind and completely underestimated my skills despite seeing me take out his buddy. Idiot.

I ripped off the scalpel taped to my thigh and cut his shoulder at a calculated angle when he tried to grab me.

"Fuck!" he cried as his hand fell limp at his side.

"No, thanks." I sliced the tendon of his opposite shoulder, leaving him defenseless, and brought my foot up to kick him square in the abdomen. He fell on his ass with a heavy thud and a shout. "Well, that wasn't entertaining at all."

Not even twenty seconds, and he'd given up. Figures. I started to wipe off the blade on my dress, when the door down the hall flew open. The stench slammed into my gut, knocking me off-kilter. I dropped the weapon and reached out to the wall to steady myself, but it did little to dispel the nausea.

What fresh hell is this? I'd hunted and slaughtered countless demons, but whatever or whoever sat in that room was something horrible. The vilest of Hell's creations. It literally burned the goodness inside of me.

Brimstone and fire...

I swore I smelled fresh flames, but the source confused me.

Heat and disgust boiled over my skin, and it took me a moment to realize the source.

The demon's beady red eyes blazed as he held me captive with one hand around my throat and the other trailing down my exposed arm. I'd been so out of it that I hadn't even noticed his approach, let alone his touch.

"T-tassste sssweet," he hissed. His tongue darted between his thick lips just like a snake, and I realized this was one of those *things* I saw slither out of the crate. Shit. I brought my knee up between his legs and connected with nothing.

Gross.

Plan B.

I swung my arm around and connected with his, but his boneless elbow merely bent and straightened again. Solid muscle. Like a snake. Not humanoid in form at all, yet residing on Earth.

Logic rebelled inside me. This should not be happening. It broke so many underworld laws.

Not the time, Eve.

When his too-long tongue snuck out to lick my cheek, I reacted. Even snakes had hearts, and I'd find his.

Ignoring the confusion and hysteria bubbling up inside me, I snatched my hair sticks and slammed them into the center of his chest before swiping down as hard and as fast as I could.

His scream was bone chilling and grabbed the attention of all his un-Earthly friends. Including the one so evil that it left me sick to my stomach.

A Pestilence demon.

No wonder I felt ill.

Fuck.

Six to one.

I could not take them all out with a pair of silver shoes and two sticks, but they left me no choice. The two Guardians attacked as one, but their moves were predictable. I took one out with a well-placed heel kick and the other with a hair stick, but then the others were on me.

Another one of those snake things and two unknown humanoid-looking fuckers.

But it was the Pestilence demon that held my wary interest as he spun a thick yellow cloud of *something* with his hand.

This would not end well.

I rammed the three heroin-filled syringes into a meaty arm, but it did nothing. Not surprising.

That left me with my necklace, one stick, and a single shoe. My dress hung in tatters around me. It all happened so fast. In seconds. But I refused to go down without a fight.

I ducked a blast of mist from the disease-wielding demon and ended up on my back with the snake-man on top of me. His fury was a very real thing. The first dude must have been his brother or lover. My bad. He hissed in a language I didn't understand while the others all scratched at me with clawed fingers.

I fought hard from the floor, trying to climb to my feet, and managed to take one of them down with my final stick.

Blood and other unmentionables coated my skin, and the stench from the Pestilence demon made it impossible to breathe. Nothing he could give me would kill me, but it would no doubt incapacitate me, which was a fate worse than death.

To be held prisoner by Hell?

No, thank you.

My final heel went into the other humanoid while I continued to wrestle with snake-boy on the floor. I shoved him off me just as another gruesome cloud shifted my way. Who knew what disease he was unleashing in this club. The men deserved it, but not the imprisoned women.

I kicked off what was left of my tattered shoes and stumbled to my feet.

Arms locked around me from behind. They were thick and unyielding, and I glanced up into a single eye.

"Oh, for crying out loud!" I snapped.

A fucking Cyclops.

In the club.

Fifteen feet tall and five feet wide.

"How the hell did they even get you through the fucking door?" I started to squirm, but his strength crippled mine. All I had left on me was the necklace and that...

A silver blade landed square in his pupil, causing it to explode with a loud pop. The muck landed on top of my head, but then I was free. He stumbled backward, and I wiped the goop from my eyes just in time to see another blade land directly in the giant's chest.

My head whipped around to see the last person I expected to come to my aid.

Xai.

He wasted no time handling the snakelike creature, and the Pestilence demon fled. I started after him but tripped over my own feet and landed hard against the wall. My limbs shook with exertion, so much so that my toes felt numb.

Xai's hands were suddenly on my face as he forced me to meet his gleaming gaze. I couldn't help the gasp of surprise, or the whimper of relief. So uncharacteristic, but warranted in this insane situation.

A nightclub of immoral humans I could understand, but this fresh batch of Hell's worst creations? No. They had nothing to gain by being here—not the way a humanoid male did, anyway.

I tried again to go after the last demon, but my body refused to work.

"Eve." The urgency in Xai's voice drew my focus

back to him. He'd been talking, and I hadn't heard a word. The look he gave me said it concerned him.

"Yeah?" The raspiness of my voice sounded wrong. I tried to clear it but failed.

Xai swung me up into his arms and started moving while the lights dimmed and brightened overhead. I squinted and smacked my numb lips. Right. That couldn't be good. I finally took in what was left of my dress. Not much. But most of my skin was covered in a black ooze that triggered my gag reflex.

"It's from the Slither demon," Xai explained. "A paralyzing toxin."

Great. The dude had ejaculated venom all over me.

Sunshine blinded me a second later, causing me to flinch.

"A shower, love. That's all you need. And then we'll talk."

I nodded—or tried to, anyway—against his shoulder.

We'd be talking all right.

Starting with what the fuck had taken him so long and ending with me kissing the hell out of him.

Because he hadn't left me.

For once in our very fucked-up existence, he'd followed through on his word.

And he'd just saved me from an unspeakable fate.

"They're all secure," a deep voice said. "Where to now?"

"The hotel," Xai replied. "Then I want you and Tax to burn it down."

"Yes, sir."

Burn what down?

And why is he addressing Xai formally?

My eyes refused to open, as did my mouth.

Fucking demon venom.

What had Xai called it—a Slither demon? How did he know that? And why wasn't the toxin paralyzing him?

All questions I'd voice once my mouth worked again.

CHAPTER SIXTEEN

SO MAYBE XAI'S COCKINESS IS WARRANTED...

I WANTED TO KILL SOMETHING.

Preferably a demon.

One with a slithering tongue and a penchant for oozing on people.

The toxin made me immobile, yet I felt everything. A nasty little nuisance that left me completely at Xai's mercy. I refused to think about what would have happened had he not shown up.

Water trickled over my thighs and stomach, followed by Xai's hot palm. He'd laid me naked in the bathtub with a towel beneath my head and gone to work removing the grime from my torso.

Fury mingled with mortification inside.

That thing had left me helpless.

I didn't do helpless.

Nor did I require backup.

Until tonight.

Because those beings from Hell played outside my field. A rarity, one that churned my gut and shot fire through my veins. Had I been properly armed, I could have taken them all down with a few well-aimed throwing blades.

But no. I'd been without my weapons and outnumbered.

An excuse, I thought with a mental sigh.

I knew better than to go unprepared into battle and had to rely on someone to save me as a result. It grated on my nerves and created a maelstrom of emotions that required an outlet, but I couldn't fucking move.

"It's a topical poison," Xai said as he drew a finger down my sternum to my belly button. "The effect on a mortal is instantaneous, but we're built differently, so it required a hell of a lot more effort from the Slither demon to take you down. I wouldn't be surprised if he expunged his entire venom supply on your breasts."

He sounded far more amused than I felt. Bastard.

"Always so stubborn." He tsked. "You should have waited, love."

As if I needed his admonishment. I was doing a fine job of scolding myself for that mess back there.

"There." He shut off the water but left his palm on my lower belly. "You still need a shower, but the paralyzing toxin is gone. I suggest you start slow."

I tried to furrow my brow but failed.

Nothing.

I felt nothing.

My heart kicked up a beat as adrenaline shot through my veins.

What if…

Wait…

That's…

It tingled. First in my fingers and toes before inching up my limbs. I licked my lips on a sigh and fluttered my lashes.

Finally.

Xai's black gaze met mine, causing my heart rate to speed up for an entirely different reason. Desire, love, and something darker all mingled together in his dilated pupils. I couldn't tell if he wanted to fuck me, kill me, or spend eternity with me. Maybe a touch of all three.

"I'm going to help you stand." He didn't wait for me to reply, just grabbed my hips and lifted me out of the tub. My legs wobbled beneath me, but I managed to stand with his assistance. "As much as I adore the warrior look, you need a shower."

A glance in the mirror had me agreeing with him. Blood and demon gore mingled with my blonde hair, lending a zombie-like appearance. Not my most attractive look.

Xai guided me into the oversized standing shower, where I leaned against the marble wall for support. I grimaced at my display of unwanted weakness. It went against the grain, especially when in the presence of a stripping predator. His soiled button-down shirt hit the floor first, followed by his black dress pants.

No boxers or briefs.

The man was fuck-me gorgeous in clothes, but out of them, he resembled a god.

Perfection.

Revered.

Unworldly.

Deserving of worship.

"I do love it when you look at me like that," he mused as he joined me. "Brace your hands against the wall, love."

My usual retort sat unused on my tongue. The fury from minutes ago had been replaced by exhaustion. I didn't want to fight him. Not over this.

I turned around and pressed my palms against the cool tiles. His finger slid over the curve of my back as he placed a kiss on my shoulder. Such a tender, unexpected move, as was the exhale that followed. He seemed almost relieved by my compliance. Thankful, even.

Water trickled nearby as Xai adjusted the temperature. My skin basked in the heat from his naked body, so near, but too far to touch.

I yearned to fall backward into him and rest. An insane notion considering our history, but he boasted an air of protection that called to my soul. After everything he'd put me through, the most important part of me still trusted him. I both loved and hated it.

Warmth met my scalp as Xai began washing the gore from my hair. He held the showerhead in one hand while he used the other to comb through my tangled strands. The sensual assault sent a shiver down my spine.

Xai never took care of me. Not like this. But each measured stroke exuded a tenderness I couldn't ignore. He lathered shampoo into my hair, followed by a eucalyptus-scented conditioner, and then he began soaping every inch of my body.

My emotional walls crumbled with each touch.

I couldn't handle it.

He left me, then came back for me.

He cherished me while pretending to hate me.

And then sometimes, he loved me.

A tear fell, followed by a second.

I wanted to loathe him, but this attentive side of him burned through all my defenses. If he were anyone else, I would have killed him centuries ago. But he had stolen my heart, and no matter how hard I fought to yank it back from his grasp, I failed.

And now this… I didn't know how to handle this.

He turned me to face him so he could have better access to my breasts, and I gazed up at him through my damp lashes. His lips feathered over my cheeks, catching the tears and licking them away. I shuddered beneath his warmth, and a fundamental part of me shattered, leaving me vulnerable and broken.

"You didn't leave me," I whispered.

"You're never alone, Evangeline." His words were an exhale in my ear as he grabbed my hips. "I'm always there."

I shook my head against him, denying his words. "Liar."

His teeth sank into the pulse point at my neck, sending a jolt to the sweet spot between my legs. He bit just hard enough to pinch in a delicious way that didn't evoke pain.

"Accuse me again, darling." A dare underlined with threat.

"Not an accusation," I breathed, arching my neck to grant him better access. "A fact."

He lifted me into the air, and I wrapped my legs around his waist on instinct. His cock settled between my slick folds as he pinned me against the wall with a hard thrust. An expert move meant to tease and punish at the same time. My clit throbbed against his hot length, begging him to move while he held me in place and scraped his teeth along my tender throat.

"When will you understand?" Another nip, this one sharp enough to draw blood. His tongue soothed the sting, sending pleasure zipping down my spine. I loved this game, and only Xai knew the way I liked to play.

I threaded my fingers through his thick hair and tugged hard to force his smoldering gaze to meet mine. "I'll understand whenever you stop being so fucking cryptic."

His grin lit a flame deep inside me, one only he could light. "What you call 'cryptic,' I refer to as 'obvious.'"

I tightened my grip on his silky strands just enough for him to flinch. "You're an asshole."

"And you love it," he growled before he captured my lips in a soul-binding kiss. His tongue dominated mine in a single swipe, but that didn't keep me from putting up a fight of my own.

He infuriated me like no other and made me hotter than anyone ever had. My nipples hardened to painful peaks as my sex pulsed with need.

Fuck.

I couldn't remember the last man I'd been with, or when. Nor did I care. In these moments, only one person mattered.

Xai.

My thighs tightened around him, begging him to take me in the way I knew only he could. But he held me captive against the wall while he devastated me with his mouth.

I moaned his name over and over, giving in to the silent demands of his tongue and declaring him the winner, but it wasn't enough. He wanted more and seemed hell-bent on taking it.

His hard length felt like a brand between my legs.

Hot, thick, and all mine.

I tried to arch against him, but those hands on my hips didn't budge. I scored my nails down his back in protest, eliciting a chuckle from deep in his chest. The rumble vibrated my aching breasts, sending goose bumps down my limbs.

I captured his tongue between my teeth to grab his attention. "Fuck me, Xai."

"Mmm." He tossed me onto the marble bench, and I landed with a thud. It placed my head at his groin, which was not what I had in mind, but it wasn't as if I'd been clear on how I wanted to be fucked.

I wet my lips in anticipation. The man hadn't been wrong when he referred to his cock as his best feature.

He fisted himself and pressed the tip to my mouth as a tease. My tongue darted out to catch the drop of pre-cum before it fell, and I moaned.

Fuck, I had missed the spicy taste of him.

So addicting.

I needed more.

But he had another idea in mind as he went to his knees before me and shouldered his way between my legs.

"Just relax, love. This is about you," he whispered against my inner thigh.

"What are you doing to me?" I asked on a groan, because none of this added up to his usual motives. We should be fucking right now.

"I think that should be obvious." The response vibrated my damp flesh, sending a shiver up my spine. "I've missed you, Evangeline. More than you'll ever know."

"Xai…" I trailed off on a curse as he wasted no time reacquainting his tongue with my sensitive center.

The man's mouth redefined the meaning of sin. Water and soap suds streamed around us, reminding me of how this all started. He'd been cleaning me thoroughly, and now he was bathing my clit with his tongue.

My head fell back against the glass as he pulled my hips forward and draped my legs over his shoulders. Being manhandled should have bothered me, but I didn't have it in me to stop him now.

Sensation burned over my skin, sprouting a flourish of gooseflesh up and down my arms. I was a trembling mess of nerves, and those hot hands on my hips were not helping matters. He held me steady when I wanted to move, and controlled every upward stroke against my core.

Xai's subtle domination set my blood on fire.

This was what I craved.

That moment where I gave someone else total authority over me.

No decisions.

No worries.

No thinking.

Only pleasure.

The release I didn't know I needed built up inside me with a flurry of hot sensations. My limbs began to shake as my thighs clenched.

"Come, Evangeline. I need to taste your pleasure. Now." Xai nipped my swollen bud and stared up at me through his thick lashes. The wickedness lurking in his dark depths was what pushed me over the edge. It was a look of promise for what would come next, and I needed his brand of fucking more than I required air.

I came apart on a scream that had built up inside me over the last few days. Pleasure mingled with pain and regret and, most of all, fury. Both at him and myself, and this entire fucked-up situation.

But above all else, I felt peace. A sense of belonging and rightness that only Xai provided, and for a moment, I remembered why I loved him.

"I'm going to fuck you until you can't walk." Xai placed an open-mouthed kiss against my inner thigh and stood. "But first, I want you to return the favor."

He held out a bar of soap, indicating what he meant, and presented me with his muscular back. Two thin white scars marred his otherwise flawless skin. I had the same markings on my shoulder blades.

A reminder of our past.

One I ignored as I slid off the bench.

"Delayed gratification?" I asked. "That's not usually your style."

His wide shoulders lifted and fell. "Maybe I'm trying something new."

"New?" I repeated while creating suds against his tanned skin. "Is that even possible for us?"

"I hope so," he replied softly. "More than you know."

I paused at his words. "What do you mean?"

He turned to arch an eyebrow at me. "Did I give you permission to stop?"

"Don't," I said. "Don't change the subject."

"There's nothing else to say." He wrapped his fingers around my wrists and placed the soap-holding palm against his abdomen and the other on his cock. "My patience is waning, Evangeline."

"You're the one who demanded I return the favor." I stroked his arousal because I could, and luxuriated in the hiss that escaped his lips. "Should I wash you slowly, Xai? Would that be *new* enough for you?"

His shaft pulsed against my hand.

I continued lathering his abdomen and chest while sliding my opposite palm up and down his impressive length. The job really required both hands, but he'd insisted on this approach.

"Evangeline…" A warning lurked in his growl.

I ignored it.

"Sorry, did you require slower?" I demonstrated with the fingers wrapped around his erection, shifting slowly upward and squeezing the tender head just a little too hard. "How's that for *new*?"

He slammed me against the wall and captured my yelp with his mouth. The bar of soap fell from my grasp as I fought for stability. His fingers were wrapped around the back of my neck in a bruising hold while his opposite hand gripped my hip.

This was going to hurt.

And I couldn't wait.

I grabbed Xai's shoulders as he lifted me into the air single-handed, but unlike last time, he didn't rest his arousal against mine. No, he slid home in a single thrust that elicited a scream from my throat.

Too much, too fast.

And he knew it too.

His version of a punishment, or a loss of control—I wasn't sure. Probably a mix of both.

Fuck.

My head fell to his neck as I panted from his assault. It didn't matter how prepared I was, it always hurt the first time. Mostly because we went so long without seeing each other, and I rarely took other partners to bed. There was never any point. No one satisfied me the way Xai did.

His lips feathered over my temple and ear. Not a vocal apology, but his version nonetheless. I squeezed his shoulders as an indication of forgiveness, because my mouth refused to work.

Xai would break a mortal with his roughness, but never me. Because I not only accepted this part of him but also enjoyed it.

I tilted my hips upward and shivered at the overwhelming sensation of fullness. It felt right. Perfect. Like home.

My lips found his as I mouthed the words I knew he wanted: "Fuck me."

But he startled me by replying, "No."

His tongue slipped into my mouth, muting my reply and confusing the hell out of me. Again. This was the part where he took his pleasure and gifted me the same, but instead, he moved slowly against me.

Taunting.

Loving.

And he replicated the actions with his mouth.

He used his grip on the back of my neck to tilt my head for better access and deepened our kiss while continuing that sensuous assault below.

So deep.

Hitting that special spot inside me with each measured thrust.

It created a slow burn between my legs, all centered on that pleasurable point.

My hips rose to meet his as he picked up the pace.

"I need more, Xai."

"I know you do," he replied. "But not yet."

My teeth clamped down on his bottom lip, drawing blood.

He merely smiled. "Trying to provoke me, darling?"

"Trying to *encourage* you," I corrected.

"Maybe I like this pace."

I dug my nails into his shoulders. "I know you don't."

"Mmm, I would argue that you don't know as much as you think, Evangeline." He smeared his bloody lip against mine before returning the favor with his own teeth. "Is that what you wanted?"

"It's a start," I whispered as he licked the wound he created. It would heal in seconds, but the sting fueled the fire brewing inside me. "Take me, Xai. Please."

"Begging," he murmured, approval in his voice. "Again."

"I need you," I moaned as he slid home with more force than before. "Yes, hard and fast. Please, Xai." My head fell back against the wall as he shoved into me again with even more power. "Like that, but faster."

"You'll bruise." The words were a whisper against my

throat.

"I'll heal."

"Mmm, indeed." He kissed my pulse before adding, "I never could deny you, Evangeline. Even when I tried."

I clung to him as he thrust hard and deep, my back scraping against the wall with his violent invasion. The Archangel in his soul came out to play, and the angel in me thrived.

This was what I needed, what I missed most.

Only Xai.

Always Xai.

Our mingled pleasure pushed beyond ecstasy to a place where another world existed.

A land bathed in white lights and warmth.

Memories and centuries flooded my thoughts, bringing tears to my eyes.

And I loved every single minute.

My limbs quivered, my back ached, and my heart soared.

Bliss unlike anything on this plane penetrated me from within as I shattered around him, and he followed me over the precipice, my name a benediction on his tongue.

And I knew this was only the beginning. Because once we started down this path, we couldn't stop.

It was an addiction that crippled us both.

One we couldn't fight.

"More," he demanded.

"Yes."

CHAPTER SEVENTEEN

EVEN ASSHOLES DESERVE A
THANK-YOU EVERY NOW AND THEN

I WOKE TO XAI tracing the scar along my shoulder blade. Despite millennia of healing, it still felt sensitive to the touch. Goose bumps pebbled down my arms, not from his reverent stroking but from past experience.

This was how it always started.

A reminder of our history that ended in Xai being an ass.

He placed a kiss on the back of my neck and nuzzled the tender skin.

"I've missed you, Evangeline," he whispered.

I frowned. "Have you?"

Another kiss, this time beneath my ear.

"Yes," he breathed and pressed his growing erection into my backside. "I'm not nearly done reacquainting our bodies, but we have work to do."

His words were unexpected but welcome. I arched back into him and rubbed my ass against his hardening length.

"What did you have in mind, dear?" I asked with mock innocence.

He rolled me onto my back and slid a muscular leg between mine. Embers smoldered down at me through his aroused gaze. "Tax messaged me a few minutes ago. Streator is back in the hotel."

I grinned. "Are you thinking it's my turn to take him on a date?"

"Only if you invite me, love. You know how I enjoy watching you work."

"A threesome, then?" I pretended to think about it. "I suppose I can oblige, but I'll need my toys this time."

"I had your weapons last time, but you went to work without me."

"I thought you'd left me again." And he'd taught me a long time ago not to wait for him.

Something flashed in his eyes, but it was too quick for me to catch. "Just because you can't see someone doesn't mean he isn't there." He brushed his mouth over mine. "I'll order some room service while you prepare. Something tells me it's going to be a long night."

Xai slipped out of bed and stretched his arms over his head. The ripple of muscles dancing along his abdomen had my lips quirking up at the corners. He appeared relaxed and well sated, yet more than ready to take me again.

"I've missed this view."

"Likewise, love." His ebony eyes traced over every inch of my naked form before he bent to take my mouth in a kiss filled with dark promise. "Mmm, exonerating you takes precedence at the moment, as we only have four days left. But after… ?" He captured my gaze with his and held it. "Afterward, Evangeline, you're mine. And this time, I won't be letting you go."

He straightened and sauntered to the bathroom to grab a robe, then disappeared through the bedroom door, presumably to order food.

I gaped after him, unsure of what to say or do.

The promise in his tone had been far too real, but the words were what held me captive in his bed. Because it'd sounded a lot like he'd just laid claim to me for the long term. Which, for us, meant eternity.

Hope unfurled in my heart while my brain attempted to see through this trick. Xai loved a good game, but this didn't feel like a taunt.

All his actions this week didn't match up to his antics of the past, and his abstruse comments about always being there had me questioning my memories. Either he meant it and I'd missed something obvious or he was planning the backstabbing of a lifetime.

Because if he kept this up, all the barriers would fall, and he'd have the ability to well and truly shatter my heart.

I combed my fingers through my hair and sighed. Now wasn't the time, not when we had more important things to focus on, such as Streator.

Nothing better to motivate a girl out of bed than the thought of torturing an immoral being.

I slipped on a pair of jeans, boots, and a black tank top and snuck off to my original bedroom to collect a few tools. Xai met me in the living area. He'd traded the robe for a pair of trousers and a navy button-down rolled to the elbows. Not the most appropriate outfit for our mission, but I'd be the one doing all the work.

Because Streator was mine to maim and kill.

Xai laid my hair sticks and three daggers on the kitchen counter. "Remy retrieved these from the club, and I deep cleaned them while you were sleeping earlier."

"Remy?" I repeated as I caressed the pretty silver. They looked brand new.

"Portal Dweller. Friends with Tax." He left my side for the door and opened it just as a hotel employee had been about to knock. "You can set it over there." Xai gestured toward the table, but the short blonde pixie couldn't seem to tear her glassy eyes away from my dark angel's profile. Her lips parted in unconcealed awe as her legs forgot how to function.

"Yes, he's gorgeous," I agreed. "But I'm starving. So, if you wouldn't mind?"

Xai smirked at the impatience in my tone that he no doubt mistook as jealousy. Hardly. I was more than used to women ogling him.

The pixie snapped into action, her cheeks burning pink.

Tax walked through the open door, lifted his chin at Xai in acknowledgment, and plucked a piece of toast off the blonde's cart. He gave her a wink as he relaxed into one of the chairs.

"Remy's busy dealing with the mess you left at his house," he said around a mouthful of bread. "He's fucking pissed, by the way."

"It had to be done." Xai handed the woman a large tip as she ducked under his arm to leave. "Thank you, darling."

"A-anytime," she stuttered with a glance back at me. I gave her a finger wave before selecting an apple and taking a bite. Seemed appropriate given my namesake.

I held it out toward my dark lover and cocked a brow. "Want some?"

He closed the door and sauntered over to sample the item in my hand. Only he could make something as simple as biting an apple sexy.

"Delicious as always, Eve," he murmured, eyes wicked.

"Kill me," Tax deadpanned as he kicked his chair back to balance against the wall.

"Happily." I swapped my apple for one of the freshly cleaned sticks and twirled it tauntingly before using it to secure my hair with its partner. He didn't even flinch.

Confident for a scrawny demon.

"But seriously, Remy says this is the last time." Tax uncovered one of the plates and turned up his nose. "Omelet. No, thank you."

"Good, because that's for Evangeline and not you."

Xai pushed the plate my way before taking the seat beside Tax. "And I'll deal with Remy."

I took the plate and silverware and hopped up onto the counter beside my pretties. Ham, cheese, and tomatoes taunted my senses. I didn't know how he convinced the kitchen to make breakfast at eleven o'clock at night, but I was damn grateful. Unlike the Tracker demon, I loved all things egg.

"I still don't get it, though, dude." Tax stared down Xai. "Why save them all?"

"Because it was the right thing to do," he answered as he started cutting his steak. He always did enjoy a good filet, and that one appeared to be cooked to his liking.

"What will you do with them all?" The Tracker pressed, curiosity evident in his voice. "Build a harem?"

My eyebrows shot up at the sincerity in his voice. "What the hell are you two going on about?"

Tax's brow furrowed as he looked between me and Xai. "You didn't tell her?"

"We didn't do a lot of talking today," Xai murmured before taking a bite and relaxing into his chair. "He's talking about the human women from the club. I sequestered them all at Remy's apartment, and apparently, he's displeased."

Wait, what?

Tax spoke before that thought fully registered. "Oh, he's more than displeased. They're hysterical," he said.

Xai shrugged. "At least they're safe."

"Until he portals them to Hell, which, by the way, he's threatening to do."

Xai arched a brow and pulled a phone from his pocket. "One moment." He hit the speed dial and listened while someone spoke loudly over the line.

Well, that's an enjoyable greeting.

"If you're quite finished, I merely called to ask if you remember that time Lord Zebulon introduced you to his pet Dargarians?" He waited, and the voice was notably quieter this time. "Yes, I see you do. If you could bear with me another twenty-four mortal hours..." He trailed off as the man started speaking again. His expression told me whatever the man was saying satisfied him.

"Excellent. Thank you, Remy." He set the phone aside and continued eating as if nothing had happened. "He will not be depositing the girls in Hell."

"Great," I replied. "And also, how exactly did you *sequester* the women from the club?"

"Not all of them, unfortunately." He used the napkin to dab at his mouth and gestured to my mostly full plate. "Eat, and I'll explain."

A demand. Wonderful.

But my stomach agreed with him, so I played along.

"I followed you and Streator to that cheesy place on the beach and then to the underground club. It took considerable effort not to kill the human, especially after he knocked you out and took certain liberties..." His hand curled into a fist as my lips parted.

You're never alone, Evangeline.

My angelic soul smiled gloatingly. *He means it.*

"Anyway," he continued, "I scoped out the interior, noted the demonic presence, and called Remy for a favor. By the time he arrived to portal me into the cells, you were gone. So I took out the guards and instructed him to handle the women while I went after you. And thank fuck I arrived when I did."

"Don't forget the part about torching the building with all those humans inside," Tax added rather gleefully. "For which, by the way, you're welcome."

Xai gave the demon a doubtful look. "You're requesting thanks for my granting you permission to destroy something?"

"I'm just sayin' that took skill and effort," he replied. "Not that I didn't enjoy it, because I most certainly did."

I ignored the demonic creature's babbling about mayhem and focused on the pertinent details. "You saved the mortal women and then burned down the club."

"With all the buyers inside," Xai clarified. "Yes."

"Why?" I asked.

"Quarantine, Evangeline. The Pestilence demon unleashed a disease in that club, and I didn't want to risk it spreading to the human population. So, although it was too polite a death, I burned them all alive."

My heart skipped a beat. His explanation insinuated that he had tried to protect Earth from an outbreak.

I shook my head to clear it. The fire wasn't what I meant to inquire about. "Sorry, I was referring to the innocents in the basement. Why did you save them?"

"See!" Tax exclaimed. "*That* is what I want to know. I understood the mass slaughter, but what purpose do a bunch of damaged mortals serve?"

Okay, not what I'd meant to imply at all, but exactly how I expected Xai to react in the situation. Yet he'd saved all the girls in that basement.

"Why?" I repeated. Because there had to be a selfish reason for his behavior. The man had lost his humanity eons ago.

He clasped his hands over a knee and studied me. "Would you rather I had left them there to die?"

"Of course not."

"Then why even ask me that, Evangeline?"

"Because it's not logical?" Tax suggested.

I held Xai's gaze as I gave him the truth. "Because I've never known you to go out of your way to help anyone but yourself."

His eyes burned impossibly darker. "Yet here I sit putting my life on the line to assist you. Tell me—what exactly do I gain by doing that? Other than the pleasure of enduring your endless accusations and attacks on my personal character, I mean."

I scoffed at that last bit. "What did you expect, Xai? Me to fawn all over you? To worship the ground you walk on?"

"No, but an inkling of gratitude would go a long way. You seem to think we're playing a game of chess, but you fail to realize I'm not your opponent. I'm your ally." He pushed away from the table and grabbed his phone. "I need to make a call to an old friend in law enforcement about the mortals I apparently should have left to burn. Then you and I will be having a nice chat with Streator. Do try to remember he is the one you want to torture and kill, love. It'll save us both time and effort."

My voice failed me.

As did my breathing.

Because wow.

I'd angered Xai. No, that wasn't quite right. I'd *hurt* him. I didn't even know that was possible.

Tax whistled and gave me a cursory glance. "I'd heard rumors, but he really is different with you."

I eyed him back from my perch on the counter. "You have a death wish, don't you, demon?"

He seemed amused by that. "Funny coming from the woman with only four days left to live on this plane. I'd say you're the one with a death wish, considering you keep disrespecting the only being who wants to help you." He paused to give me a thoughtful look. "You must be a fantastic fuck for all the shit he's gone through on your behalf."

Okay. I liked the Tracker before. Now, however, I wanted to practice my throwing skills with the blades by my elbow.

"What?" he asked, arching a thin blond brow. "Did that piss you off? I'm sorry." The fucker didn't sound very apologetic. "But Xai is right. You could be a little more thankful."

I palmed one of my knives and twirled it between my fingers in warning. "Dangerous words for a man who knows nothing about our past."

He snorted. "Man, you've been hangin' with the mortals too long. Look beyond the history, angel."

"Keep talking," I dared.

And the idiot took that as an invitation rather than a warning.

"All I'm saying is, that man has been through hell for you, literally, and I've yet to hear one ounce of appreciation from your ungrateful ass. When he returned empty-handed last week after Lord Zebulon had demanded your immediate presence, I thought my lord was going to kill Xai. But he took the punishment—for you, I might add—and eventually convinced the lord to see reason." He shook his head. "Xai's a far more tolerant man than I am."

The metal stilled in my hand, as did my heart. "Go back to that part about Zeb punishing Xai. What did he do?"

Tax's light eyes narrowed. "What do you think he did? He took him to Hell and unleashed on him. Nearly killed him with that blade, too, but somehow Xai talked him out of it. Took a few weeks, though."

A chill slithered down my spine as fresh images of the devil's plane flashed behind my eyes. Heat. Torture. And with a weapon designed to assassinate a Heavenly being.

"How long?" I asked because time functioned differently between planes. A year in Hell equated to a day on Earth. And the Tracker had already mentioned *weeks*... "How long was he in the underworld?"

"Two months," he replied quietly.

It took me a moment to do the math because the time differences always boggled my mind.

Two months would only be four hours on Earth, but it wouldn't have felt like that to him. Heavenly beings surrounded by evil for any length of time increased the risk of insanity, but not for Xai. His soul thrived in chaotic environments, while mine wilted.

The dark to my light...

"Lord Zebulon forced him to heal in Hell as well," Tax added. "Which, as you can imagine, took a while."

Xai chose that moment to reenter the room, and the look he gave the Tracker said he did not appreciate our conversation.

I slipped off the counter to stand between them. A protective instinct for the demon at my back. I knew that expression on my dark angel's face. Tax's story had put Xai in a destructive mood, and the Tracker was the source of his irritation.

"You were supposed to take me to Zeb, and you

didn't," I whispered.

Xai crossed his arms. "Am I supposed to confirm that redundant statement?"

"You told me he wanted a meeting."

He shrugged. "I scheduled one, and here we are. There's nothing else to say."

Wrong. There was so much more to say.

"Why didn't you tell me?" I asked softly.

"What good would it have done?" he countered. "It holds no relevance to the task at hand, nor would you have believed me."

This enigma of a man.

This dangerous, impossible, arrogant angel had gone to Hell for me. Literally.

He was cruel, overbearing, and sadistic, yet when I needed him most, he always appeared. And then pushed me away when he finished helping me.

Every.

Single.

Time.

"Walk away from me this time, and I will kill you," I threatened as I stalked toward him. "We've danced around this for millennia, Xai. I'm tired. I'm old. And I'm done."

My patience was gone.

And the walls around my heart had crumbled to the ground.

He caught my hips as I stepped into his personal space. "You still have so much to learn, Eve."

I gripped his collar to yank him closer. "Shut up and kiss me."

"We have a misbehaving human to torture first, love." His lips brushed mine with each word, the tease. "Consider it foreplay."

"You're punishing me." And, according to Tax, I more than deserved it. But then again, so did Xai. All his previous actions earned my inherent doubt of his character, even if I had been a bit of a brat about it.

"I'm prioritizing," he corrected with a small smile.

I pressed my mouth to his in a soft kiss that belied the electricity firing between us. He wanted me just as much as I did him, but his restraint was stronger. "Xai?"

"Yes, Eve?"

I touched my lips to his once more before pulling back to study his expression as I debated uttering a phrase I'd never said out loud in his presence. Not with sincerity, anyway.

But as I stared deep into his eyes, I finally saw it. The concern, wariness, and overall sincerity that he shielded so well behind his wall of indifference.

Love.

My heart skipped a beat as warmth fluttered deep inside.

I swore my angelic soul smiled with recognition. She always knew how Xai felt, even when every other part of me doubted him. We still had a hell of a lot of issues to work through, and he owed me several explanations, but maybe this time would be different.

Hope.

A lethal emotion designed to kill, and it just might eventually. But fuck if I cared anymore.

The damn Tracker had been right. Not that it mattered right now.

Xai was the only one worthy of my thoughts and, most of all, my gratitude.

"Thank you."

CHAPTER EIGHTEEN

HOW TO INVITE AN ASSASSIN INSIDE 101: LEAVE YOUR DOORS UNLOCKED

"HE'S IN THERE," Tax confirmed. "And he reeks of demon."

I cocked my head to the side from my perch on the balcony's railing. "Isn't that a bit like the pot calling the kettle black?"

The Tracker frowned. "Did you hit your head on the way up here?"

"It's a humanism, recent too," Xai explained. "She's teasing you for criticizing your own kind."

"By referring to me as a..." He trailed off with a shake of his blond head. "Never mind. Do you two need me for anything else, or can I take the rest of the night off?"

"Can you tell which demon aura clouds him?" Xai asked.

LEXI C. FOSS

"No, but it's fresh from Hell and unfamiliar."

"Then enjoy your night off," Xai replied.

Tax gave us a mock salute and fell backward off the balcony into a somersault. When he landed on his feet, two stories below, I smirked. "The demon actually has some skill."

"Why do you think we're friends?" Xai combed his fingers through his windswept hair and gave me an amused look. "How do you want to play this, darling?"

I thought he'd never ask. "Surprise party."

"Through the glass?"

"Absolutely."

He gestured at the veranda overhead. "Ladies first."

I stood on the railing's ledge of our room's balcony and jumped up to grab the landing above me before pulling myself upward. Xai joined me a half a second later, pleasure evident in his expression.

"Enjoying the view?" I whispered.

"Always."

"Then you're going to love this." I brushed a kiss over his stubbled jaw and sauntered over the marble surface toward the glass doors.

The bright interior lights cast me in shadows outside, something that worked to my advantage. Streator sat at the table with an expensively dressed businessman to his right. They appeared to be engaged in a heated discussion, while Streator's oblivious bodyguards watched television from the couch several feet away.

I sighed when I realized the door wasn't even locked.

No challenge whatsoever.

How boring.

I wandered over to the opposite side of the oversized patio and peered into the darkened bedroom. Empty, and another unsecured entry.

I shook my head in disgust.

Streator needed to hire more-efficient henchmen. Being on the twenty-fifth floor did not translate to security. Even scrawny mortals could scale balconies. Idiots.

I slid the door open and stepped inside, while Xai leaned against the brick banister of the balcony with his legs crossed at the ankles and his hands in his pockets. He winked as I closed the glass. A way of reminding me he was there if I needed him, but we both knew I didn't.

The master suite rivaled the one Xai and I shared last night, but the stench of cigar smoke spoiled the elegant atmosphere. Sex mingled in the air, suggesting Streator had taken a woman to bed last night, or perhaps even today.

Something spicy and familiar taunted my senses, but I couldn't place it—a feminine perfume of sorts, overbearing and flowery.

I explored the other two bedrooms in the suite and found an array of weapons that I disabled. The bodyguards would never have a chance to go for them, but precautions never hurt anyone.

Once everything was secure, I grabbed a few plush towels from the master suite and sauntered down the hall toward my prey. No one saw or heard my approach because their backs were to the bedrooms and the television drowned out my steps.

Pity. I always enjoyed a dramatic entrance.

I set the towels down on the counter and leaned against it. "You're killing my excitement here, boys."

Streator's and his business associate's heads snapped around as the two bodyguards glanced up dumbly from the couch. It took several seconds for recognition to dawn, and then they were on their feet, weapons drawn and aimed my way.

"Excellent," I murmured. "Who wants to die first?" I glanced at the now-standing Streator and his fancy friend. "That's not a question for you two, by the way. So you stay put."

"Violet?" Streator's hazel gaze ran over my body with interest. "What the fuck are you doing here?" The jackass didn't even sound concerned, just confused.

Okay. Maybe this would be fun after all.

"I'd like to file a complaint about our date. It sucked."

153

"Your accent—"

"Was all part of the act," I said before considering Mister Fancy Pants beside him. "I don't suppose you're Compton?" Because that would be fantastic.

The bastard laughed and looked at me as if I'd lost my mind. "Do I look like a bitch to you?"

A simple no would have sufficed, but the additional information proved fruitful. Referring to Compton as a bitch suggested the infamous auctioneer might be a woman, not a man as I had originally assumed.

Interesting.

Both bodyguards had moved around the couch during my little introduction and seemed to be considering how they wanted to handle me. Eagerness shone bright in their gazes. They thought this would be enjoyable. How cute.

"You never answered my question, boys. Which one of you would like to die first? I promise to make it mostly painless." Evil lurked in each of their auras, warranting their deaths, but their darkness had nothing on my mark for the evening.

"Okay, little one." The blond brute handed his weapon to the opposite bodyguard with a smirk. "I call dibs."

His bald counterpart merely shrugged as he holstered his own gun and held the other to his side. "Be my guest."

"Hasn't anyone ever told you not to judge a book by its cover?" I asked as I relaxed my elbows on the counter behind me.

The weaponless imbecile ran his eyes over me. "Oh, I'm judging, and liking my odds."

"How did you get in here?" Streator demanded.

"Finally, an intelligent question." I considered applauding him, but his ego didn't require additional stroking.

Bodyguard One must have assumed I was distracted, because he chose that moment to pounce. His long legs ate up the space between us in four steps, giving me plenty of time to palm one of my knives and dance out of his grasp.

I threw the blade at his chest with perfect aim. Nothing fancy or exciting, but an instant kill that brought the first giant to his knees.

"What the—" Bodyguard Two clasped his throat and wrapped his hand around the dagger I'd just landed there while he'd been reacting to his buddy's timely demise.

My third knife landed in Mister Fancy Pants's arm as he went for his weapon. I kicked it out of his hand before introducing my foot to his gut. He went sailing into the back of the couch and fell to the floor with a thud.

Streator tried to go for his own gun, but he was too late. Xai had slipped into the room through the unlocked door while I was taking care of the business associate, and stepped up behind the overconfident human.

"Fuck!" Streator yelled as Xai snapped his wrist and procured the firearm.

"That is something we won't be doing," I replied as Xai shoved the jackass back into the chair at the table.

"Do you require any bondage tools, darling?" Xai asked while disassembling the firearm. He secured the weapons from the unconscious businessman and dead bodyguards, then took them apart with the ease of a man who cleaned guns frequently.

I grinned. "You know I prefer it when they fight."

He shrugged. "The gentleman in me had to offer."

"Who the fuck are you people?" Streator snapped while cradling his hand. No fear, only anger. I ran my gaze over him for more weapons. Only a man confident with his position would glower at me like that.

Xai relaxed into the oversized recliner with the television remote and started searching for something more suitable to watch while I retrieved my freshly used blades. After laying them on the towels, I turned to face Streator.

"Ever heard of Azrael?" I asked, genuinely curious.

"What?" He sounded irritated. Another intriguing reaction.

Why are you so calm, Scott Streator?

"Angel of Death," I murmured. "Ring a bell?"

His gaze narrowed. "Are you high?"

I laughed. "You consort with demons daily and question whether angels exist?" I tsked. "But, seeing as you asked, I'm Evangeline. Daughter of Death, and I do mean that literally. And that"—I gestured to my gorgeous counterpart—"is Xai. Son of Chaos."

Streator *finally* faltered.

"Ah, so you've heard of us. Excellent." That would make this far easier. I pulled up a chair, flipped it around, and straddled it. "Who's the monkey in the suit?" I nodded my chin toward said monkey on the floor. If he didn't answer, I'd just search the man for a wallet.

"Carl DeFleur," Streator replied.

"The club owner," Xai added. He had one arm tucked behind his head and his legs kicked up on the footrest, his gaze on the television. He seemed to be scanning the movie channel. "I imagine they were meeting about last night's fire."

"That was you?" Streator sounded furious. "*Fuck.*"

"That's what happens when you don't run a thorough background check on your dates, Streator," I chastised lightly. "They might end up being a hell of a lot more trouble than you realize. And in this case, I guarantee it."

I popped up from my chair and knelt by DeFleur. His salt-and-pepper hair and age lines suggested he was nearing sixty mortal years.

"Do we need him alive?" I asked, my blade at the bastard's throat.

"He merely owned the property," Xai replied. "I doubt he'll be much more useful than that."

"But he knew what they were using the club for." Not so much a question as a statement. My affinity for sensing the menace in others rang high with this one. Carl DeFleur was not a good man.

"He not only knew but also partook in the activities." Xai selected one of those cheesy horror movies and set the remote on the table. "I saw his name on the client list.

He had a preference for girls under sixteen, if I recall correctly."

Streator's grimace confirmed that to be true.

"Well, that's good enough for me." I sliced through Carl's tender skin and allowed myself one second to enjoy the rightness of his death. A gift to humanity, and one less vile soul on Earth. Too bad the one sitting five feet from me was more heinous than all the others combined.

I placed the bloody tool beside the others on the counter and sat in front of Streator again. He met my gaze without flinching. Still so self-assured.

"Whom are you expecting?" I asked.

His responding grin confirmed my suspicions. "Wait and find out."

"Oh, we will. But what makes you think they'll make it in time to save you?" I glanced over him again. "You mortals wound so easily. Just ask Becks. I was a little too eager and destroyed her windpipe by accident. Might do the same with you."

He shrugged. "Then you'll get nothing from me."

"Like the name of your employer?" I suggested.

Another grin. "Go to Hell and find out."

"Oh, this is going to be such fun." I reached around my back to retrieve the pouch I'd stashed in my pocket and showed him. "Looks pretty unassuming, right? Three inches by three inches, and velvet."

I flipped the flap open to reveal the sharp items inside. Over a dozen slivers of silver, similar to sewing needles, and drenched in a toxin not of this Earth.

A gift from Xai several centuries ago.

"Those bring back delicious memories," he murmured from the chair, surprise evident in his tone. Apparently, he didn't know I still had these and probably assumed I'd discarded them long ago. As if I could ever destroy something so precious.

I slid one from the package and rolled it between my fingers. Streator didn't appear at all impressed, something I would rectify shortly.

"Dargarians are evil little fuckers," I said more to myself than to my prey. "They're fire-breathers, in case you're unfamiliar, but it's their blood that's particularly potent. When it comes in touch with, say, mortal blood, it sets the stream on fire. Or so I hear."

I left the chair to stand behind Streator and traced his neck with the tiny pin.

"These might look innocent at first glance, but I assure you, they're not. Care for a demonstration?"

I didn't wait for confirmation to stick him. Men like Streator didn't break without proper motivation. And these little babies would provide just that.

Seven seconds.

Sweat started beading on Streator's hairline.

Twenty seconds.

His knuckles turned white.

Thirty seconds.

The screaming started, so I added another dagger and watched as he crumpled to the floor at my feet.

Not so confident now.

"I'm going to ask you a few questions. Answer them all to my satisfaction, and I'll give you the antidote." I slipped the pouch back into my pocket and knelt beside him. "Whom do you work for?"

"Myself," he wheezed. It pleased me to no end to see him in pain, but his one-word answer didn't do it for me.

"That's not the response I'm looking for, Streator." Threatening him with more needles would be a waste of material. Two would do the trick just fine. I massaged the sliver in his neck, eliciting a scream that was drowned out by Xai's movie choice. "Try again."

"It's the truth, you fucking bitch!" he shouted as he tried to curl into a smaller ball. As if that would save him.

I removed my hand from his neck. "So, you and Compton are partners?"

"Yes."

"And you don't report to anyone else?"

"No," he growled with a violent shudder. Dargarian blood burned like a son of a bitch. I knew because I'd been tortured with these on several occasions. But unlike Streator, I never caved. My body was built to sustain torture of the highest degrees. Both a blessing and a curse.

"Then whom are you procuring demons for?"

"One of her associates," he said, confirming Compton was a female.

"Which associate?" I asked, though I already suspected the answer.

"Geier," he growled.

And there it was.

"Is Geier a demon?"

He huffed a laugh that sounded more painful than humorous. "No."

Not what I expected to hear, unless Geier hadn't outed himself as a Demonic Lord. Zeb resembled a human on the exterior—typical humanoid with an unnaturally beautiful appearance. He passed as mortal to the average person. Geier could do the same.

"Describe Geier."

Streator clenched his jaw as a tremor shook his entire body. "Never saw him."

"So how do you know he's not a demon?"

"She wouldn't work with one," he gritted out. "Hates them. That's why..." He squeezed his eyes closed as another tremble rocked through him. "F-fuck." His teeth started to chatter, which I recognized as stage two of his torture. The venom heated foreign blood to the point where the victim felt cold. A miserable sensation I didn't regret inflicting on him.

"She t-took the demon j-job because she h-hates them."

"How does she even know about them?" I wondered aloud.

"K-killed her mom."

I sighed. That would do it, then. "I assume the *she* you are referring to is Compton?"

"Y-yes."

I met Xai's curious gaze. "I think we need to have a

discussion with Ms. Compton."

"I haven't seen anything about her in the files," Xai replied. "I assume you heard about her while gallivanting about the club unarmed."

Oh, right. We hadn't debriefed each other after the incident. I couldn't bring myself to feel all that bad about it, not with the reminder of Xai's thorough loving still thrumming through my veins.

"The three stooges who dropped me off with the doctor to have my virginity examined were kind enough to give me her name," I explained before refocusing on my shaking prey. Amazing what two tiny needles could do to an arrogant man's confidence. "Where can we find her?"

His lips set in a firm line even as he grimaced through the pain.

No response.

That piqued my interest.

Everything else he opened up about, but he chose to remain quiet about how to locate Compton.

"You don't want us to find her," I murmured, studying his reaction. The clench of his jaw told me all I needed to know. I recognized that look. Xai wore the same one when anyone threatened me.

Protective.

Streator and Compton were definitely more than business associates. Likely lovers, yet he had also been fucking Kalida. Which would infuriate most women. Mortal or not, we liked our men to remain faithful.

But Compton was no average mortal. She had ties to demons and potentially a former Demonic Lord.

And so, she had made an agreement.

Trafficking services in exchange for removing Kalida—the competition.

Something only a powerful demon could truly accomplish, as Kalida's bloodline made her difficult to kill.

But how did Compton obtain a partnership with the underworld? Hell didn't mingle with humans unless they were useful, and the ability to procure and sell innocents didn't qualify her capability to handle evil creatures.

Zeb's compulsion suggestion tickled my thoughts. He wondered if Streator possessed an ability to compel, but perhaps it was Compton all along.

"I think we have our lead," I said, meeting Xai's knowing gaze. He'd come to the same conclusion.

"Yes." He stood. "But there's still something I'd like clarification on, if I may."

I waved him forward. "Be my guest."

He brushed a kiss against my temple as he passed. "Thank you, love." He crouched beside Streator's convulsing form. "Tell me, Scott—why were there demons in the nightclub?"

A good question. They weren't imprisoned like the women in the basement, and the snakelike demon had only seemed curious, not necessarily concerned, by my presence. And his buddies didn't react until after I killed him.

"Fuck. You," Streator spit out.

Ouch. Wrong answer.

Xai picked up the idiot's wounded hand and toggled the broken wrist. A shrill scream rent the air, sending a shiver down my spine. It would worsen if the asshat on the floor didn't start talking, and fast.

"I'm a possessive man, Scott, and you hurt the one being in existence that I actually care about." Xai's cool tones could barely be heard over the other man's whimpering. "You cannot even begin to fathom the many ways in which I would like to punish your transgressions."

He didn't give the jackass a chance to speak further before he snapped one of his bones like a twig. Streator howled in reply. I knew from experience that my lover was ruthless, especially against those who pissed him off. And this human had more than done that.

"You have four more," Xai informed in a dark whisper. "And that was only your pinky. Imagine what the thumb will feel like?"

"Meeting!" Streator shouted. "A fu-fucking meeting!"

I frowned. What could a bunch of illegally trafficked demons be meeting about in a public nightclub? And why?

"A meeting implies freedom," Xai murmured. "Which seems rather strange considering you stated the demons were all procured for Geier."

"Not all," Streator wheezed. "S-some were f-friends."

"Of Compton?" I asked, clarifying.

"Y-yes."

"Earlier you stated she hates demons," Xai said before I had a chance. "Explain."

"Most," Streator grumbled. "She hates... most."

"And the others were friends." Not so much a question as a retrospective statement. Uncertainty nagged at the back of my mind. Demons did not befriend humans.

Xai glanced up at me with a similar question in his eyes, as if the thought had hit him at the same time. Then his gaze widened with understanding, and his focus snapped back to the human on the floor.

"What's her first name?" he demanded.

Oh, shit. How had I missed the obvious connection?

I'd assumed Compton was a scorned lover seeking to eliminate the competition through her inexplicable demonic connections. But that theory no longer held merit.

A working partnership I could maybe believe, but not a friendship. Even those who had lived on this plane for centuries preferred mingling with their own kind. No way would a being fresh from the underworld *friend* a mortal.

Which meant Compton wasn't human at all.

But a demon who hated most of the others from her realm.

Because they had killed her mom.

"Kalida," I breathed.

The color drained from Streator's face, confirming my suspicions.

Well, fuck. The bitch was alive.

CHAPTER NINETEEN

PORTAL DWELLERS
ARE USEFUL LITTLE FUCKERS

"IT'S IMPOSSIBLE TO KNOW FOR SURE," Tax said as he paced the living area. "If Kalida killed the demon, then her essence would mingle with the ashes and could give a false-positive identity of the remains. But I should have picked up on the other aura."

A bone-chilling crunch sounded from the dining area. Xai had called in a few Ghouls to take care of the dead bodies, and they were openly enjoying their job.

"For fuck's sake, man." The Tracker stopped pacing to look imploringly at Xai. "Can we *please* go upstairs?"

Xai checked Streator's pulse. "Nope. Still beating."

Tax threw his hands in the air. "Then fucking kill him already!"

The soon-to-be-dead man's eyes had rolled back into his head after he lost consciousness. The only way to survive Dargarian poison was to undergo a complete blood transfusion; otherwise, the venom ate through the body slowly and painfully until all the organs failed.

A fitting end to a miserable life, but I supposed he had suffered enough. Chances were he couldn't feel anything given his comatose state.

I plucked one of my freshly cleaned blades from the counter and raised an eyebrow at Xai. *May I?*

He responded with a nod. *All yours.*

"Streator, may you rest in Hell." I swiped the blade across his throat. The slight gargle was the only indication that he struggled to breathe, and then relief settled over my shoulders. Another evil being removed.

Xai wrapped his arm around my upper back, and I folded into him. He understood my plight better than anyone.

"Don't eat that one," Xai warned over my shoulder. "He's full of Dargarian venom."

"Gross," the Ghouls replied in unison.

"Right, but devouring that old man's thigh is perfectly appetizing," Tax deadpanned.

"It's meaty," one of them said.

"Juicy too," the other added.

Tax gagged and stalked over to the foyer. "I'll be downstairs when you're ready to resume." He didn't wait for permission to leave and slammed the door behind him on the way out.

"Rude," one of the Ghoul's grumbled.

Xai's leg started to vibrate against mine. He kept one arm around me while he fished the phone from his pocket and answered with his opposite hand.

"Who is this?" he demanded.

"You damn well know who this is, you dark bastard. Now, where the fuck is Eve?"

My eyebrows shot up at the familiar tone of my best friend coming loudly through the speaker. *Where did she find his number?*

"Guinevere, charming as always," Xai replied dryly.

"Fuck you."

"Is that an offer, love? Because I'm afraid I need to decline out of respect for Evangeline." He hugged me closer as he spoke the words while I rolled my eyes. I opened my mouth to reply, but Gwen beat me to it.

"First, you couldn't handle me. Second, put Eve on the phone."

I held out my palm, but he ignored me with a laugh. "Dear Guinevere, you seem to be under the false impression that I consider you a higher authority, which, to be frank, I don't."

Gwen's growl came through the line. "I will put your balls in a vise the next time I see you if anything has happened to Eve."

"When have I ever allowed anything or anyone to harm her?"

"Oh, I don't know—how about that time you left her in the underworld?"

His amusement disappeared, replaced by a dark emotion that sent a chill down my spine. My best friend had struck a nerve. "She escaped unharmed."

"Did she, though? You weren't the one who had to nurse her back to health for three fucking weeks afterward."

"Okay, give me the phone," I demanded, but Gwen was already on a roll.

"And that was only the physical healing, jackass. She talks a big game, but I know your behavior haunts her. As do the nightmares of all the shit you've put her through over the last millennium. I swear to all that is holy, if I had the right weapon, I'd drive it through your shriveled, black heart just to protect her from you and your fucked-up games. Now, put her on the fucking phone!"

Xai's body had gone rigid during Gwen's rant, and danger emanated from him. So much so that the Ghouls had stopped eating.

"Xai," I whispered.

"You really ought to be careful whom you threaten, little demon," he replied. "Not everyone will be as forgiving."

"I'm not afraid of you," Gwen snapped.

"That's not your first mistake," he replied quietly.

"Just tell me she's okay." The worry in Gwen's tone knotted my stomach. I'd forgotten to call her earlier, and she'd clearly thought something bad had happened. Otherwise, she never would have called Xai.

"The fact that you have to ask tells me you know nothing about her skill set or mine."

"On the contrary, I'm far too familiar with your ability to torture Eve, which is why I'm worried. She might be indestructible on the outside, but she's vulnerable on the inside, and that's where you attack her most."

I squeezed the bridge of my nose. Apparently, I needed to have a discussion with my best friend about what constitutes appropriate conversation.

"I'm sorry you feel that way, Guinevere," Xai murmured. "One moment."

He handed me the phone and walked outside to stand on the balcony to admire the night sky. Longing filled his features for a brief second before his expression clouded over. Then he leaned his back against the railing with his hands in his pockets. Those dark eyes burned into mine as I raised the phone to my ear.

"We're having a long chat when I get home," I grumbled. Her intentions came from the right place, but her delivery left a lot to be desired.

"You promised to check in, Eve." Relief mingled with fury in her tone. "When you didn't answer your phone all day, I thought he had abandoned you somewhere again!"

My shoulders fell at her words. "I'm sorry. The hours have gotten away from me, and I left my phone in the room." I hadn't even checked it since before my date with Streator.

"Danny called me after he couldn't reach you, which scared the shit out of me. I know how much that mortal means to you." She sounded frustrated.

Xai cocked an eyebrow at that. Always eavesdropping. He hadn't stepped out so much to grant me privacy as to cool off. It seemed to have worked, as he appeared more curious now than irritated.

"I haven't had my phone on me," I told Gwen. "Tell Gleason I'll call him after this case is done and to enjoy his vacation."

"What case?" she pressed. "What does Lord Zebulon have you doing, exactly?"

I palmed the back of my neck and blew out a breath. "I can't go into it right now." Not with the corpse at my feet and the two Ghouls sawing up body parts behind me. They'd started bagging "food" for later.

"Talk to me," she whispered. "Please. I need to know you're okay."

The words *I can take care of myself* tickled my tongue, but I swallowed them. We both know when it came to Xai, my senses didn't function at sane levels. But this time was different. And the intense look coming from him now confirmed that.

"I'm okay," I promised. "Xai's helping me, Gwen. And I trust him with this."

Silence came over the line for too long.

"He's gotten to you again," she finally said, and the disappointment in her tone hurt a little.

"Yes." No sense in denying it.

She blew a raspberry over the line—the first indication that she was calming down. "You know I don't like it or him."

"I do."

"And I'm tempted to fly down to Miami to kick his ass."

I smiled both at Xai's answering snort from the balcony and the vehemence in her tone. "I know."

"But I trust you," she added. "Even if I think you've lost your mind."

"And I love you for that." I meant it.

"Good. I'll let Danny know to stay abroad."

Xai's eyebrow inched up again. He'd definitely be asking about Gleason now. Great.

I cleared my throat. "Thank you."

"Stay sane, Eve. And call me."

"I will," I whispered.

"Love you."

"Love you too," I replied and ended the call.

Xai held my gaze for a long moment before pushing himself away from the balcony to saunter back inside. I handed him the phone and shivered as he drew a finger over my inner wrist. A sweet, seductive touch that held so much promise, as did the look in his eyes.

But his words were all business.

"We need to discuss next steps."

I nodded in agreement. We were running out of time. Zeb would never believe his daughter was still alive without sufficient proof, and a hunch wouldn't cut it. To exonerate me, we needed to find Kalida.

"I expect this room to be spotless when you're finished," Xai said, addressing the Ghouls.

The one with dreads grinned. "That won't be an issue."

"Good." Xai met my gaze and gestured toward the door. "Let's go."

He had already hired a technical friend to erase the hotel security footage, which meant we could take the elevator down rather than scale the balconies. Xai might be an ass, but he was efficient.

I took a detour to the kitchen to retrieve my precious silver. The blade that killed Streator washed off easily. I dried it with a towel before picking up the others and storing them in their appropriate places.

Xai stood off to the side, his amusement palpable. I winked as I passed him and led the way down the hall, all the while feeling his gaze on my ass.

Electricity zipped down my spine as we entered the elevator—a sensation caused not only by the tension rolling off Xai but also by the hungry look he gave me as he punched the button to close the doors.

"Xai... ," I warned.

But he didn't care.

His fingers threaded through my hair as he backed me

into the mirrored wall and took my mouth in a brutal kiss. He led with his teeth, nipping my bottom lip hard and laving at it with his tongue. A not-so-subtle way of marking me as his. I returned the favor by digging my nails into the back of his neck. He didn't flinch, but he yanked my hair backward to expose my throat to his mouth.

"Gleason isn't a lover," I whispered as Xai traced my pulse with his tongue.

"I know," he replied. "This isn't about your silver supplier."

My heart skipped a beat. "You know about Gleason?"

He nuzzled my tender skin and hummed in approval. "Don't worry. Your secret is safe with me, love."

He silenced me with another demanding kiss. His tongue tried to dominate mine, but I fought back until both of us were panting messes in the immobile elevator. I had no idea what button he pushed to hold it there, or why he decided on here, of all places, but I was thankful for the short reprieve from reality.

"You're my only weakness and my greatest strength," he whispered against my lips. "I've never been able to resist you, Evangeline, no matter how hard I've tried."

"Then stop trying." It seemed so simple to me. We were a match made in Heaven, literally. Why fight it?

He reached past me to press a button that caused the elevator to move. "I'll take you up on that offer after we finish exonerating you."

Xai punctuated his promise with his mouth. I looped my arms around his neck and let him guide me backward onto our floor after the doors opened. He didn't stop devouring me until we hit the door.

Combustible.

Insatiable.

Powerful.

If we didn't have a demon to hunt down, I would have forced him to take me here and now. Xai always did enjoy a good bout of exhibitionism, but we would have to play later.

His breath feathered over my ear, causing goose bumps to pebble down my neck. I arched into him, craving a closer embrace, but he pulled away with a sharp nip against my neck.

"Behave, love."

I gazed up at him through hooded eyes. "Now that just sounds like an invitation to be bad."

"You know it is," he murmured before opening the door. I followed him inside to the living area, where Tax had sprawled out on the oversized couch. His hand was in a basket of popcorn, his eyes on the television.

I raised an eyebrow at his movie choice of a giggling woman observing a man struggling with cutting bell peppers in her kitchen. "Romantic comedy?"

"Yep." No shame or concern, just a straight answer. He paused the film and looked up at Xai.

"Right, as I was saying earlier, it's possible she's alive and I sensed her essence on those ashes because she killed the demon. But with all the prowling I've done around Streator and his gang, I should have picked up fresh traces of her aura and haven't. Which means one of three things: someone is helping her hide, she's really dead, or I'm losing my touch. As that last option isn't feasible, it's one of the others, and I'm betting on the first one, especially if she's hangin' with Geier."

He planted his feet on the ground and set the popcorn aside before resting his forearms on his thighs. "Which brings me to the obvious part, where I tell you this isn't nearly enough information to convince Lord Zebulon. Hell, I'm not even convinced yet."

"She's alive," I said, certain. Not just because Streator had reacted to the name, but because it glued all the puzzle pieces together. "She took on an alias, or perhaps adopted a last name, and went into the trafficking business with Streator. It provided her with ample finances and an endless supply of sustenance. It's the perfect ploy for a Succubus."

"I agree, but that doesn't mean she's still alive," Tax replied. "Maybe someone realized what she was up to and killed her for it."

"Then why continue trafficking demons?" I asked, playing devil's advocate. "Which, by the way, is my second point. Hell doesn't mingle with humans, thus implying that Compton has to be a demon herself to arrange a deal with someone like Geier."

"Assuming he's the former lord," the Tracker argued. "A fact we also haven't confirmed."

Xai relaxed against the wall, arms casually folded. "Proving Kalida and Compton are one and the same is an easily testable theory. We may also be able to verify that she's very much alive."

I met his black gaze and sensed I wouldn't like what came next, but I asked him anyway. "How?"

"Remy has an apartment full of witnesses. One of them likely met Streator's partner at some point."

His words pierced the hope floating around in my heart. I knew there had to have been a logical reason he saved those women, and now I had it. "You kept them alive for information."

Emotion swirled in the depths of his eyes. "Acknowledging their practical use may suggest motive on my part, but that doesn't detract from my decision being the right course of action."

Tax hopped to his feet between us. "I'll call Remy and ask for a pickup."

I ignored the Tracker and focused on Xai. "You saved them because it was the right thing to do, correct?"

"Ridicule has never flattered you, Evangeline," he chided. "But as you seem hell-bent on questioning my character, consider, Why not a patron or two? Surely they would hold the same informational value?"

I shook my head. "The Pestilence demon rendered all of them useless."

He grinned, but it wasn't friendly. "Perhaps, but I cleared out the basement well before he unleashed his essence in the club. I could have just as easily grabbed the guards downstairs and been done with it."

Sincerity radiated from him, as did a touch of

irritation. Because I had questioned his integrity again.

"This game is old, Evangeline. Either see me for who I am or don't."

"I'm trying," I admitted softly. But our history skewed everything. Forgiving and forgetting that past seemed impossible given all the crap he'd put me through, and his penchant for tricking me didn't help matters either. "I want to believe in you, but I don't know how."

He cupped my cheek. "Your heart knows the truth, love. It's your mind that requires convincing."

"Thank fuck, I need a nap," a deep voice announced, startling us from our embrace. "I'll drop you all at my place, then I'm crashing here. Where it's quiet. No crying."

A muscular demon had appeared in the middle of the living area wearing a pair of gym shorts and nothing else. With a body like that, I couldn't blame the guy for walking around shirtless. He wasn't Xai, but the tall demon could certainly turn heads. His chiseled jaw, sculpted cheekbones, and emerald gaze…

"I know you." The words tumbled out of my mouth without thought, but I couldn't help it.

"You don't belong here."

No wonder I recognized his voice… I heard it every time I dreamed of the underworld.

And those eyes… Two shining green orbs that had appeared in the darkest corners of the underworld when I least expected them and propelled me back to Earth.

"No shit." The Portal Dweller smirked and shook his head as if admonishing me. "You seem to have a knack for trouble, angel, but it's good to see you coherent for once. Or at least slightly more than the last two times I saw you." He cocked an eyebrow at Xai. "Perhaps you need to take it easy in the bedroom, mate. I think you've fucked her brains out a little too literally."

"It's a good thing you're useful to me, or I would have killed you a long time ago," Xai replied dryly.

"How do you two know each other?" I demanded.

The Portal Dweller palmed the back of his neck,

looking sheepish. "I found myself in a bind a few centuries back, and Xai helped me out."

"Understatement," Tax grumbled. "He pissed off Lord Zebulon and found himself bound to a rock in Hell. Xai bargained for his life."

"Why?" I asked, curious.

"Because he was innocent," Xai replied simply. "In case you've all forgotten, we're on a deadline. Shall we get moving?"

I studied his profile and the clench of his jaw as understanding hit me square in the chest. It knocked the air from my lungs and left me dizzy.

Centuries back...

They knew each other when Xai left me defenseless in the underworld.

But he didn't leave me.

"You're never alone, Evangeline."

"I'm always there."

"You're the reason the Portal Dweller came for me," I whispered.

Those dazzling irises burned into mine in answer. *Obviously I am*, they said.

"That Portal Dweller has a name," the shirtless man stated flatly. "Remy, in case you were wondering. And yeah, he sent me. Are we going? Because who knows what those girls are doing in my flat right now."

"Yes," Xai replied, his gaze on mine. Whether he meant to confirm my statement or agree with Remy, I didn't know.

Not that it mattered.

I had the answer in my heart.

He may have left me that day, but I was never alone.

Because just as he said...

Xai was always there.

CHAPTER TWENTY

APPARENTLY, HELL ISN'T
THE ONLY REALM WITH SECRETS

ELEVEN GIRLS HUDDLED together in Remy's guest room, dressed in various male outfits. He'd given them free rein to access his wardrobe. Most of them had donned sweatshirts and sweatpants. Not exactly Miami Beach attire.

I sat on the middle of the bed, legs folded beneath me, and waited for the humans to finish the cheeseburgers and fries I'd brought them.

Xai had suggested the detour to a fast-food restaurant.

"Consider it an interrogation tactic," he'd said in that dry way of his. But I saw through it. Beneath the cold veneer was a man who cared enough to consider human comfort.

"Thank you," one of the girls whispered. Several others piped up as well, but the one in the corner remained silent. Her knees were tucked to her chest, eyes downcast. This was the naked girl who had been curled into a ball in the middle of her cell. She didn't look much healthier in the clothes.

My heart burned in anger at the sight of her.

To see someone's innocence so cruelly removed...

"I'm sorry I couldn't do more," I murmured, meaning it. "But I promise you all that those men won't hurt you again."

I had already introduced myself as one of the good guys when I entered the room. They thought I was Agent O'Hara with the FBI. A white lie to keep them calm. The real authorities would be arriving soon, according to Xai. He also said there would be qualified female agents to take over after I left.

"Did you arrest them?" A petite brunette asked, her big hazel eyes curious. She couldn't have been more than fourteen years old. Her naïveté provided a beacon of hope in the otherwise dark room. No one had harmed this little one.

"There was a fire at the club." I kept my voice soft and comforting. "All the men inside died, including the blond one in charge. Scott Streator."

Only one of the girls reacted to my description and his name—the girl in the corner.

"We have reason to believe a woman was involved," I added, watching their reactions. "But we don't know much about her. Does anyone recognize the name Compton or remember seeing a woman other than the doctor?"

Most gave me blank stares, but the one in the corner paled. When she started to shake, I slid from the bed to join her on the ground. I positioned myself several inches away from her against the wall and made sure she had plenty of space to escape if needed. Crowding or touching a victim never helped in this type of situation.

"They'll tell you talking about it helps, but it won't feel that way. Not at first, anyway." I spoke loudly enough for all the girls to hear me, while maintaining a low tone intended to soothe. A trick my mother taught me at a young age. *The voice of an angel*, she had said. Most of my traits came from my dad's genetic tree, but my deep-seated need to save innocents came from my mom's healing nature.

"I don't expect you to trust me or tell me what they did to you, but I do need to know more about Compton. It's the only way I'll catch her and stop her from hurting others." Sincerity underlined my words, as did the truth. I needed the girl to hear me, to believe me, and to confide in me. "Anything you can tell me about her will help."

"She has thick brown hair," one of the others whispered. "To the middle of her back."

"And creepy eyes," another added, shuddering. "They *glow*."

"I thought we were friends."

"Me too."

"She invited me to the club. I thought we were going dancing."

"She laughed…"

"It was a cackle."

"I hate her."

"Bitch."

Four of the girls went back and forth, sharing their stories in hushed tones that grew with each word. Until, finally, the girl in the corner added her experience.

"She watched." She paused to swallow and closed her eyes as if it was too hard to hold them open. "The b-blond… he d-did things to me, and… and she liked it. Made him c-call her name."

"Compton?" I asked softly.

Her tangled hair waved back and forth as she shook her head. "N-no." Another swallow. "K-Kalida." A tear streaked down her cheek. "O-over and over. I'll n-never forget that n-name." She flicked the tear away angrily before opening her eyes. "I felt s-so weak…"

The confusion in that last word confirmed everything. A Succubus drained her victim's energy. Even if it was Streator's lust she fed off of, she would have exhausted the girl, too, by proxy.

This confirmed my theory that Kalida had gone into business with Streator to feed her Succubus appetite. As a hybrid demon, she could live off lust alone, hence her penchant for auctioning off innocents. The male audience would have provided ample sexual energy that could please her for weeks on end.

Gwen, as a purebred, needed the full experience, but at least she tried to save her victims. However, she wasn't exactly typical for her kind, hence our friendship.

"Do you remember when you last saw Compton?" I hated having to ask, but we needed confirmation that Kalida was alive.

Her shoulders rose and fell on a heartbroken sigh. "Time m-meant nothing."

"Did anyone else see her?" I asked the room.

"Monday," the young one sitting on the bed said. She added the date to clarify, surprising me. It was the same day I met Streator by the pool. "Miss Compton offered to drive me home after school, but that's not where we went."

Well, this just got interesting. "Did you know Miss Compton?"

The girl nodded, her chocolate curls bobbing. "She's Mister Geier's friend."

"Mister Geier?" I prompted, my expression politely interested. Inside, I was raging.

Another nod from the girl. "My neighbor."

Well, shit. "Does Miss Compton visit often?"

"A few times a week," she replied. "She always called me pretty, so I thought we were friends. But then her darkness took over." The innocence in her voice had me reestimating her age. She resembled a teenager, but humans matured quickly these days and her lack of panic struck me as very naïve. Everyone else in the room wore a cloak of fear. But not this little one.

This girl had probably grown up in a sheltered home with caring parents, making her an illogical choice for a kidnapping. Not to mention the fact that the child was

Geier's neighbor.

She didn't fit the profile. The other girls were young, but at least eighteen, and not nearly as virginal as the girl sitting on the bed.

So why did Kalida pick you?

"Where do you go to school?" I asked.

She named a location I'd never heard of, but I guessed it was a private institution. And then she noted her current level.

Sixth grade.

Eleven, maybe twelve, years old.

Unacceptable.

The urge to deliver retribution overwhelmed me, shooting flames through my veins.

I would inflict a severe amount of pain on Kalida when I found her.

Fuck the consequences.

I swallowed my anger and forced my expression to remain neutral. "Do you live near the school?"

"Uh-huh," she replied and recited her address.

Her trust had nothing to do with my fake badge and everything to do with her general goodness. She reminded me of an untouched angel.

I frowned. *Is that why Kalida took her?* Did she plan to torture the innocence out of her?

My fingers itched for a blade, but I ignored the impulse. These girls had been through enough. They didn't need to see my vengeful side.

A soft knock at the door caused a flurry of movement as several of the women joined me on the floor. Even the girl in the corner inched closer. Their inherent belief in me to protect them warmed my heart.

Several of them touched me as if reassuring themselves that I was still in the middle of them. Most of them hadn't been physically assaulted during their brief captivity, but the familiarity still surprised me. It suggested they saw me as nurturing, which was a bit ironic considering my predilection for violence.

"Is it okay if my friend joins us for a minute?" My

voice was low and reassuring. "He won't hurt you."

A few of the women looked at each other uneasily, while the young one nodded her approval. She was one of the few who didn't move, choosing to sit cross-legged on the bed with an expression of contentment.

"He's safe," she proclaimed with a definitive nod.

This child continued to shock me. "You know my friend?"

She scrunched her nose. "Sort of. He's the one who saved us."

I glanced at the closed door. *How could she possibly know that?*

"The dark one?" a brunette beside me asked.

"Yep," the odd girl replied, sounding confident and not at all ruffled.

Murmurs of approval followed that pronouncement, and Xai inched the door open. He found me in the crowd of girls, and a look of adoration flashed in his gaze.

"My contact is here," he informed in a tone much gentler than normal. "He brought a few medics with him." The child slipped off the bed while he was talking, causing his focus to shift downward as she wrapped her arms around him in a hug. He didn't return it.

"Yes?" he asked. She stood at least a foot shorter than him but seemed entirely unfazed by the lethal air surrounding him.

Far too naïve.

"Thank you," she said.

He patted her head as one would a pet, but his voice held a touch of emotion. "You're welcome, little one." His gaze rose to meet mine, and he smiled. *I'm not completely heartless*, he seemed to say.

I know.

"Are you finished here?" What he really wanted to know was whether or not I found our lead, which meant he hadn't been eavesdropping for once. That intrigued me almost as much as his hand on the little girl's head had. He hadn't tried to pry her off of him yet, nor did his body language indicate he wanted to. The embrace struck me as fatherly, a trait I never would have assigned to him in a million years.

I cleared my throat. "Yes. I believe we're ready to proceed." *And that girl you're hugging is the key.*

"Excellent. I'll let Shane know." He looked down and smiled. "Do you want to come with me?"

She nodded.

He held out his hand, and she accepted it without question. I stared after them in confusion. Nothing about her reactions were normal. Several of the others expressed similar confusion.

I stood with some effort and nearly collapsed as a wave of fear clouded the room. It tugged at my soul, demanding I face them and offer peace. This part of my being had grown stronger over the years and came from my mother's side of the family—an urge to heal.

"Fate has delivered all of you a cruel hand," I said softly. "But she's also given you another chance. Some of you might want to hide from it, to wallow in the past, and I can't fault you for that. But life is shorter than you think. Those people out there want to help you, and they have the tools to do it. Trusting them will be difficult, perhaps harder than the experience you've already been through, but that trust is worth the effort. I promise you can do this, and do you know why I'm so confident?"

I waited for the victim in the corner to meet my gaze, as she needed these words the most. The others in the room hadn't been touched; they were being saved for the auction that never took place. They were the lucky ones who would be able to return to their lives with therapy and go on living. But the woman Kalida had chosen to torture with her Succubus ways wouldn't recover so easily. It would take years, maybe decades, for her to feel somewhat normal, and even then, she would have nightmares.

She peeked up at me through her thick lashes, her expression strained. But a fighter lurked in those eyes. The same one who told me her story despite our short time together.

There's hope for you, I told her with my gaze.

"You're survivors," I said out loud. "That's not a term to ever take lightly, and don't let anyone ever belittle it."

Xai appeared in the doorway behind me. I felt his warmth and devotion roll over me, soothing my need for retribution. *Soon, love*, he was telling me. He knew how I longed to punish Kalida for this, and he would help me.

"The medics are in the hallway. They're here to help you," he said to the room. "They'll present their credentials as well."

I couldn't smile, so all I did was nod as I left the room and noted the female nurses waiting to enter. At least his federal friend had been intelligent enough to bring women. I doubted any of them wanted to be touched by men.

"Where's the girl?" I asked as the nurses closed the door to the bedroom.

He grinned. "With Tax. She's fascinated by him."

"You left her alone with a demon?" I started toward the living area. "Have you lost your fucking mind?"

"Relax, love. She can handle herself."

"She's a child!" And alone with a demon. *For fuck's sake.*

But sure enough, Xai was right. The girl sat beside the blond Tracker with her hands in the air in front of his face. And he looked… amused.

"What is she doing?" I whispered, baffled.

A broad-shouldered man, who I assumed was Shane, stood silently in the middle of the living area. He didn't so much as look our way, too consumed by the bizarre little human on the couch.

"She's feeling his aura," Xai replied. "I believe she's enthralled by it."

I blinked. "What?"

Xai cocked his head to the side and studied me. "You can't sense her?" The look I gave him must have answered that question, because he chuckled. "Oh, darling, come now. It should be obvious. I picked up on it immediately. That's why we saved her from the office before the fire. The Pestilence demon didn't affect her at all."

"She was in the office with the demons?" That explained why I didn't recall her from the other night, though I hadn't exactly cataloged all the victims in my memory. "Why?"

The girl smiled radiantly and broke into our conversation. "You were right, Mister Xai. I like this one."

Tax chuckled. "That's because I don't want to eat you."

She batted at him in a playful gesture that left all three men in the room grinning at her antics. And that's when I saw it.

That goodness radiating from within her.

It reminded me of my own.

A beacon of hope, I'd called it.

My hand slipped over my mouth as it threatened to drop.

No.

Impossible.

But she shined so brightly.

She resembled a cherub.

"A Nephilim," I breathed. No wonder Kalida had taken her. They were rare beings indeed. "But whose child?"

Xai shrugged. "Your guess is as good as mine."

"But surely we would know. We'd feel them on Earth." Yet the only angelic being I ever ran into was Xai. Never anyone else from home, yet someone had fathered this child. And recently, too.

"Unless they went home," Xai murmured. "They come and go all the time."

My brow furrowed. "What?" That didn't make any sense.

Xai cupped my cheek with one hand and drew his thumb over my lips. "This, darling, is what you've never understood." He faced me fully, grasping me with both hands so I had no choice but to stare deep into his fiery gaze. "Demons can portal in and out of this plane every day. What makes you so certain our kind can't as well? That child, Evangeline, is proof. And there are several just like her."

I'd never met a Nephilim and had assumed they were a fantasy, but she proved that to be wrong.

They're real…

"I'm Shane, by the way," the agent added as he turned bright green eyes my way.

His presence slammed into my psyche, causing me to gasp. Xai's arm came around me to hold me steady as I openly gaped at the familiar man whom I'd never met but recognized.

"Well, she picked up on that rather quickly," he mused, looking over my shoulder.

"You're the spitting image of your father," Xai replied. "Nathanial is rather notorious on our plane."

Two Nephilim in one room.

"I need air." I didn't wait for permission but left the apartment and went straight for the stairs, taking them two at a time all the way up to the roof.

CHAPTER TWENTY-ONE

EMOTIONS SUCK

I BURST OUTSIDE and sucked in the afternoon air with greedy gulps.

My hands went to my knees as I crumpled to the ground and curled into myself.

The truth hurt.

It'd been in front of me all these centuries, yet hidden behind a cloud of fantasy.

Seeing is believing.

I took that phrase to heart. Nephilim were a myth created by angels who longed to fornicate on Earth, or so I thought. But it was true, and I'd probably met others without realizing it.

All those beautiful, innocent souls... How many were actually the offspring of my kind?

Demons can portal in and out of this plane every day. What makes you so certain our kind can't as well?

Was he right? Did we have an option to go home? Why hadn't he told me? All these centuries together, and he never once mentioned it…

"Because you wouldn't have left," he murmured above me. "You can only cross back over if it's what your heart desires, Evangeline. And despite everything, I've yet to convince you of that no matter how hard I've tried."

Tears filled my eyes. "You don't know what I want."

"Oh, but I do, love. More than you know." He knelt beside me but didn't touch me. "If you wanted to leave, you would. But you're stubborn, and you refuse to *see*."

Pain lacerated my chest, making it difficult to breathe.

I hated him in that moment.

Despised every trick, every wound, every hurtful phrase he'd ever inflicted upon me.

I wanted nothing more than to push him from the roof and watch him fall.

And yet, my heart ached at the very thought of harming him.

It infuriated me.

I wanted to punch him.

To drag him under me and kiss him.

To rail and rant and scream.

But my body froze in a ball as waves of emotion and pain overwhelmed me. Because he was right.

I'd been so blind.

So naïve.

So ridiculously in love with him that, despite it all, I *still* refused to see what was right in front of me. Because I didn't want to leave him. I didn't want to *live* without him.

Our relationship was toxic, fucked up, and deplorable, yet the emotions he evoked deep within me couldn't be ignored.

"I hate how much I love you," I whispered, my hands curling into fists. "I fucking hate it."

"I know." He grabbed the back of my neck in a possessive hold that provided a strange sort of comfort and forced me to meet his agonized gaze. "You call me selfish, but all I've ever been since your Fall is selfless. Because convincing you not to love me has been the hardest thing I've ever had to do, but it's the only way for you to go home, Evangeline. You've never belonged here."

"That's never been your decision to make," I argued, furious. "You've always tried to force my hand, when all I've ever wanted was to be by your side for eternity. How many millennia have you wasted pushing me away, Xai? And for what? To convince me to go home brokenhearted? How is that living?"

"I don't deserve you, Evangeline."

"Another decision that was never yours!" I tore out of his hold and leveled him with a glower. "My soul knows her mate, and all you've ever done is deny it. So maybe you're right, Xai. Maybe you don't deserve me, because Heaven knows how hard I've tried to prove otherwise, while all you've done is throw me away like garbage."

"Evangeline—" He tried to reach for me, but I jumped to my feet and stepped backward.

"Stop." I held up a hand as he advanced on me. "This conversation isn't happening now. We have a case to solve, and it's my life on the line. Which, I finally realize, is why you've been so adamant to help me these last few days. You realized Zeb could destroy me, which means that you finally understand what life would be like without me.

"And it scares you. So much so that you willingly dropped all your shields and reverted to being the man I Fell for so long ago—but it shouldn't take my imminent demise for you to see that we are meant to be together. That you would be miserable without me because I'm your soul's other half. *That* is the fate you subjected me to thousands of years ago when you made the 'selfless' choice to push me away. Perhaps it is what you deserve."

Or what we both deserve.

I started toward the door, but he stepped in my way. Emotions stormed in his black irises as he tried to hold me in place with his stare.

"Move," I demanded.

"Make me."

His challenge stoked the violent flames dancing deep inside me. The last few days had unhinged the darkest recesses of my soul. I craved blood and death more than I did air.

"You don't want to dance with me right now, Xai."

"On the contrary, love. I always want to dance with you."

I tried to slip around him, but he countered, and I reacted with a kick to his sternum that he blocked with ease.

Fury licked a path through my veins, centering in my heart, and instinct took over. I went at him with everything I owned, my tired limbs striking out and seeking a weakness.

But he knew my style too well.

Or I didn't truly want to hurt him.

The truth eluded me, which only infuriated me more.

"You're holding back," he growled as he followed it up with a leg swipe that put me on my ass. "Stop thinking and fight."

I glowered up at him from the ground.

Angels didn't need sleep to survive, but lack of it weakened us. Me more so than him, apparently. He looked the epitome of ease, while I panted at his feet.

My blade flew from my hand before I realized what I'd done, and Xai caught it by the sharp end.

"You're better than this, Evangeline." He closed his fist around the knife, drawing blood for sport, before tossing it to the ground beside my head. "Hurt me."

"I fucking hate you," I snapped as I jumped to my feet to begin again.

"I know," he replied as he caught my ankle and twisted it.

This time I'd gone for the kick on purpose, hoping he would react the way I anticipated. While he forced me into a spin, I withdrew another knife and sliced it across his cheek. He didn't even flinch, just grabbed my wrist and spun me until my back hit his front.

The blade fell from my palm, clanking against the concrete next to the one Xai had discarded. I only had two more left, and they weren't nearly as accessible. Not that it mattered.

"Don't you see?" His lips brushed my ear with the words, and I hated the shiver they elicited. "Living without you is my greatest punishment. It's what I deserve for your Fall, but your death would destroy me. *That* is what scares me, Evangeline. I've always known life without you would be torturous, but at least you would be alive and safe."

My heel collided with his shin, causing him to flinch enough for me to loosen his grasp and escape his hold. I slipped away and leveled him with a glower. "And what about me? You've sentenced me to a life of loneliness."

"Better than life with me on this plane."

I threw my hands up in the air in frustration. "And who are you to make that choice for me?"

His bloody palm clasped the nape of my neck as he forced me to meet his gaze.

"Your mate," he growled. I tried to push him away, but his opposite arm snaked around my waist to hold me in place. "It's my duty to put your happiness and well-being above mine. Always."

"By leaving me after the Fall? By forcing me into working as an assassin? By leaving me in Hell?" I couldn't help the hysterical laugh that bubbled out of me. This conversation redefined the meaning of insanity. Our volatile relationship had finally reached a breaking point. One I wasn't sure we could ever come back from. "Oh, Xai, don't you see how all those occasions nearly destroyed me?"

"All I've ever wanted was to send you home, where I knew you would be safe and eventually forget me."

"You don't get it," I replied brokenly. "*You* are my home. Hate has never been the answer, Xai. Only death could sever the ties between us."

I grabbed his shoulders to shove him, but my limbs refused the demand. He had exhausted me for the final time. Fighting him never fixed anything.

"I resigned myself long ago to the thought of you leaving me alone on this plane, but never by way of death." His forehead rested against mine on a sigh that suggested I'd exhausted him just as much, at least emotionally. "I can't live without your soul, Evangeline. You're my better half and the love of my existence. Without you, I cease to be."

The words were so soft I barely heard them, but the power behind them shattered the barriers around my heart and stole the air from my lungs.

"I can't do my job on Earth with you here. All I care about is keeping you safe on this plane, which is destined to be destroyed by Hell." He sounded as fragmented as I felt, and it floored me.

Xai had made himself vulnerable. To me.

Perhaps it had always been that way while he hid behind an impenetrable wall of confidence, or maybe recent events had loosened his steadfast control.

"You know I can take care of myself."

"Oh, Evangeline, I know, but you're my heart. Protecting you is as important as breathing." His lips feathered over mine in the gentlest of caresses as he continued.

"You are the strongest, most stubborn being in existence, and I wouldn't have it any other way. But that doesn't stop me from worrying, love. It's irrational and I despise it, and I've tried everything in my power to send you somewhere safe so that I can focus, but you refuse to obey. And that disobedience both enthralls and infuriates me. I can never win with you, and I'm so tired of fighting it."

His mouth captured mine in a kiss that unleashed all the hurt of his words. I clung to him as he gave me everything—pain, frustration, love, fury. My legs buckled beneath me, but he held me steady, as he always did.

My anchor.

My love.

My other half.

This embrace felt different. Each touch originated from honesty and truth and was oh-so intense.

Peace…

A sensation of unity overwhelmed me as his tongue entered my mouth to mate with mine. This wasn't about dominance or submission but about a promise between two connected souls.

Yes…

Xai's blood marked the back of my neck as he shifted his grip. Both of his hands went to my jeans, unfastening the button and zipper and sliding them down my legs with my panties.

I kicked the garments off with my shoes, leaving me naked from the waist down, with the exception of the blades strapped to my inner thighs. Xai didn't remove them. He enjoyed adding elements of risk to our lovemaking, and there was nothing more dangerous than an armed angel.

The humid air reminded me that we were outside and on display to anyone in the buildings taller than this one, but I didn't care. They could all watch. Xai belonged to me, and I wanted the world to know it.

He drew a finger through my slick folds and grinned against my lips. "Fighting always did turn you on," he murmured, approval evident in his tone.

I shifted my hips against his, luxuriating in his thick arousal. "I'm not the only one who enjoys it."

"Only with you, Evangeline."

My fingers slid into his thick hair as I forced him to continue kissing me all the way to the ground. The concrete bit into my back through my thin shirt, rooting me in the moment.

Sweet, delicious pain followed by ecstasy.

His hands disappeared to unfasten his belt and loosen his pants, but his tongue never left mine. And then his palms were on my cheeks, angling me to better receive his oral claim while his cock slid easily into my welcome heat. One strong thrust had him seated deep inside, pinning my hips to the ground beneath him.

"I love you, Evangeline," he whispered. "So much that it hurts."

"I love you too." I shifted to meet his claim and moaned into his mouth. "Harder, Xai."

I needed to feel everything.

I needed him to make me scream.

"Always," he promised. And I knew what he meant.

Whatever I wanted, whenever I wanted it, he would be there, just as he had always been. I may not have seen him or understood his methods, or even agreed with his plans, but he'd never left me even when he pretended to. He cherished me in his own way, trying to force me to return to a plane that would feel empty without him. And that's why I would never leave—I belonged at his side even when he believed he wasn't worthy.

He wrapped an arm around my shoulders to keep me in place as he fucked me into oblivion. Pleasure mingled with pain as the concrete etched a pattern into my back and ass. I would feel the markings for days, even after I healed, but I didn't care. Not with him giving me every part of himself—heart, body, and soul.

"I'll chase you," I threatened, meaning it.

"And I'll let you catch me," he replied before taking my mouth in a violent kiss, sealing the promises murmured between us.

Hot sensations rolled through me as I received him with every part of my being.

No one else could do this to me.

And there would never be another.

Not after this.

My nails dug into his scalp, holding on for dear life as he carried me over into a rapid climax I hadn't even felt coming. It started in my core and spiraled outward to my limbs, causing me to moan his name.

Fuck.

Waves of energy ripped through me as I shuddered beneath him.

I knew he was nowhere near finished with me yet, despite our ticking clock.

Time could go to Hell.

This mission too.

All that mattered was this moment with him.

I kissed him with a ferocity only he could receive and squeezed my legs around his waist. He flipped onto his back, carrying me with him, and sat up with me straddling him. My shirt flew over my head, followed by my bra, leaving me naked on a very clothed man. His pants were only unfastened enough to allow his arousal to penetrate mine, and my only sources of armor were the two silver daggers strapped to my thighs.

My back arched as his lips sealed around my erect nipple without warning. He sucked so hard that I shivered. God, I loved it when he treated me as if I was unbreakable. He never held back, always giving me what he wanted and knowing exactly what I needed. The pad of his thumb found my clit as his teeth sank into my breast.

I clawed at his scalp, holding him to me as he soothed the ache with his tongue. His hard cock pulsed inside me but didn't move in the way I wanted while he continued to torture me with his mouth and hand. My arousal heightened to excruciating levels until I all but begged him to take me again, to continue his claim and sate my rising need.

But he ignored my demands and focused on memorizing my curves with his lips.

"Xai," I growled, frustrated. I squeezed his erection with my inner walls and tried to shift, but a hand on my hip held me immobile. "Fuck me."

"I am," he whispered against my abused nipple. I loved the way it throbbed against his lips, craving both more and less. Such a fucked-up conundrum that equated to our relationship. We were combustible together. An explosion of epic proportions that no plane could contain, and I wouldn't have it any other way.

He flipped me off him and onto my knees, shocking

192

me into submission. "Hands on the ledge," he demanded as he shifted behind me.

I didn't even try to fight it. I just grabbed the railing of the roof and widened my legs for his assault. He wrapped his hands over mine as he slammed into me from behind.

So passionate and raw, and exactly what I wanted.

My knees would be scraped and bloody after this, but I couldn't feel anything except his cock hitting that spot deep inside over and over and his lips caressing my neck. Words of worship fell from his lips as his name trembled from mine.

Anyone watching would have one heck of a show, and knowing that only increased my passion. Xai redefined the meaning of exhibitionism, and I loved him for it.

He shifted my hands into one of his as his opposite one dipped below to fondle my sensitive bud. Sensation overwhelmed me as he rolled my clit between his fingers, applying just enough pressure to torture and please. The confusing mix sent me skyrocketing into oblivion on a scream that everyone in the building had probably heard.

"You've always been mine," Xai growled against my throat as his pace increased. "And I'll always be yours."

"Yes," I breathed, conceding the truth as I pressed back against him.

It was the response he needed to let go and join me in the world where only we existed. His groan was music to my ears as his essence spilled deep inside me, branding me in the most intimate of ways.

He pulled me away from the railing with one arm wrapped tightly around my breasts, and his hand guided my chin backward to meet his kiss. His shaft throbbed inside me as he held me tight, my back to his chest, both of us on our knees. What an erotic picture we created, one I would cherish for eternity.

"I still don't deserve you," he said, his mouth brushing mine with each word. "But I can't live without you either. I never could."

"All I've ever wanted was for you to admit we belong together, Xai."

"Of course we do," he whispered. "But I've never seen the point in admitting the obvious."

"You spent thousands of years denying it."

"No, Evangeline." He tugged my hair to force my head back and meet his gaze. "There is a difference between denial and deflection. Everything I have ever said and done was with purpose."

I tried to shake my head, but he held me still. "But you never chose me, remember? You never wanted me. You claimed love was a naïve notion that I shouldn't expect from you."

"Mmm, all carefully phrased words and questions meant to push you away, and all said with a touch of truth." I flinched at his cruelty, and he grinned against my lips. "I didn't choose you, Evangeline; my soul did. And love is an emotion that doesn't come close to what I feel for you, just as I've never so much wanted you as craved you."

"You're an asshole," I said, irritated by how quickly he inverted all those haunting phrases with a few words.

"I am," he agreed. "But I'm yours, love. Always."

My back burned from abrupt coldness as he pulled away to stand behind me. He held out his hand for mine with a question in his eyes. *Accept me?*

As if I ever had a choice.

I danced my fingers over his and allowed him to help me up from the ground. "I'm still furious with you."

"Good." He wrapped his arms around me and pressed his forehead to mine. "You know how much I adore angry sex."

"Keep it up and I'll bring out the knives."

"Mmm, I love it when you flirt with me." His lips whispered over mine. "But we have a Demonic Lord to hunt and kill."

"You started this," I pointed out.

"And I'll finish it," he promised. "After we deliver Kalida to her father and exonerate you." His kiss lingered only briefly before he smacked my ass. "Now get dressed and don't even think of cleaning up. I like you looking thoroughly fucked. It provides a degree of motivation we are both going to need."

I shook my head. "You're insufferable."

"Tick tock, Evangeline," was all he said as he turned toward the stairs. His pants were already zipped, buttoned, and belted, while I stood naked behind him.

Typical.

I dressed while he observed me from the door with a heated expression. That gaze darkened with promise when I picked up the discarded knives and slipped them back into the sleeves of my shirt.

The man was insatiable.

He stopped me with a hand on my shoulder. I expected some sort of sardonic comment, but he surprised me by pulling my tangled strands up into a ponytail and securing it with a black band from his wrist. Not exactly a hair tie, but it worked.

"I love you, Evangeline," he murmured as he ran his knuckles over my cheek. "And since it pleases you, I'll endeavor to state the obvious more often."

"What may seem obvious to you isn't always clear to everyone else, Mister Cryptic," I replied, grinning. "But I love you too." I nipped his chin in silent reprimand. "And for future reference, you don't need to mark me with blood for everyone to know I'm yours." Because that was why he had exposed my neck. He wanted everyone to see his imprint.

He shrugged. "I'll wash it off you later when we're done."

"Yes," I agreed. "You will."

CHAPTER TWENTY-TWO

LOVE:
A GAME AS OLD AS TIME

"THIS WAS FUN. Let's not do it again for a while," Remy said after dropping us off in the hotel parking lot. "Cheers." He vanished before we could reply.

I stared at Xai over the hood of his sporty car. "I agree with the demon."

"You're not feeling portal sick, are you, love?" he teased as he opened the driver's side door.

"I'm feeling a lot of things," I admitted as I joined him inside the two-seater. Not just about what had happened on the roof, but in the apartment as well. Shane, the Nephilim, had flashed me a knowing smile when we returned and had winked at Xai. Their easy candor confused me, as did the situation in general.

"How did you meet Shane?" It seemed like a good place to start with the myriad of questions streaming through my head.

"He tried to kill me," Xai replied as he shifted into first gear. "He failed," he added with a grin.

"And you let him live?" I already knew he had, but that didn't leave me any less shocked.

Xai shrugged. "He thought I was a demon—guilty by association and all that—and he proved to be quite handy with a silver bullet. Much to his chagrin, however, I woke up irritated and with a headache. But we worked out our differences. Seemed wasteful to destroy such a skilled sniper."

"Silver bullet?" I repeated. "As in pure silver?"

"Indeed. His organization is quite fond of them." Sunglasses shaded his eyes but didn't hide his amusement. He was being deliberately vague.

"You can't say that and not continue, Xai."

He smirked. "Your ignorance is charming, Evangeline."

"Yeah? Well, I'm about to be not so *charming*."

"I love it when you tease me." His hand slid from the gearshift to squeeze my thigh. "They refer to themselves as the Genesis—a play on current religion that depicts their kind in a rather unclear manner."

"I've never heard of them." Which wasn't surprising given that I'd considered Nephilim to be a myth until today.

"Rumors existed, but Shane provided me with the first measure of proof. It seems the Nephilim have networked with one another for centuries, but only as a means to provide mutual protection. They've only recently chosen a violent path, hence my discovering their organization." He danced his long fingers along my inner thigh to my knee and back. "Can you guess why their methods have changed in the last decade?"

I studied his profile. His golden skin glowed in the afternoon sunlight, giving him that angelic appeal I adored so much. That devilish tilt of his lips made my heart race, as did his words and the implication behind them. "Are you implying my retirement caused it?"

"Hmm, no, not exactly." His palm left my leg to shift gears as we entered the highway. The smooth purr of the powerful engine matched the man behind the wheel. Both were sleek, smooth, and sexy as sin.

"You see," he continued, "the Genesis consider themselves to be the protectors of humanity, which, I suppose, is appropriate. It is why you and I are here, is it not?" He smirked, amused, while I considered his offhanded comment.

Xai had never explained to me why he Fell. I always assumed his reason to be a nefarious one, yet his actions of late painted a different story altogether.

He rarely let me see the good in him, but it existed. I saw it today with the child and heard about it earlier from Tax. Xai had literally gone to Hell and back for me, something he didn't have to do. That was not the action of a selfish man but of a protective one.

What a mercurial being you are, dark angel.
Forever changing what I know and believe.

"But as good as you are at destroying rogue demons," he continued, "I don't attribute the Genesis's escalation of violence to your retirement."

"Amazing," I corrected. "You meant to say, 'As amazing as you are at destroying rogue demons…'"

A perfect dimple creased his cheek. "And overconfident as well."

"Are you inviting a demonstration?" I asked sweetly. "Because I'm happy to oblige."

"Always," he murmured. "But all in due time, love." He returned his hand to my leg and stroked the blade hidden along my inner thigh through my jeans while returning to the topic at hand. Not the easiest location to pull a weapon from, but one of the last places someone checked during a pat down.

"The members of the Genesis have placed themselves strategically all over the world. Shane, for example, is a high-ranking official in the Department of Homeland Security."

Interesting detail. "That explains why you called him

about the trafficking incident."

"It does, but I also called him because of Trudy."

"Trudy?" I repeated.

"The young Nephilim." The fondness in his voice prodded at my heart. Xai didn't usually handle small beings well, but he seemed quite taken with this one. "Remy found her in the office where the demons had been meeting. He claimed she was sitting on the desk, waiting for him, when he returned to torch the disease-ridden club. When he called me for instructions on how to handle her, I advised him to put the girl with the others and finish the job."

"Did he know she was a Nephilim?" I asked, curious. Angels possessed auras, but not ones that demons could sense. Hence Zeb's inability to know whether or not I had killed his daughter. My presence couldn't be felt by a Tracker or any other being from Hell. It was part of why I excelled at my job. The underworld couldn't feel me.

"No, but her lack of a reaction to the Pestilence demon unleashing his lethal gift in the club suggested her uniqueness. I confirmed it when I met her."

I frowned. "You called Shane before you met her, though."

"No, I met the young one while you were resting," he murmured. "Then I phoned Shane."

It took me a moment to remember the last time I slept.

Yesterday afternoon, post-sex.

"I feel like I should be offended that you had enough energy to conduct an interview after I passed out." Because Archangel or not, I'd worked him hard.

He chuckled and slipped his hand higher to where the heat radiated from my center. "Oh, Evangeline, is it my turn to be arrogant?"

"You're always arrogant."

"Mmm," he replied, his hand exploring, "but on this, I'm even more so."

I bit my tongue to keep from moaning. My core ached from his attentions earlier on the roof. Unfortunately, sex with the Archangel had left me bruised, something my unnatural healing ability didn't seem equipped to handle. Had I been human, he would have broken me.

I squirmed, but he held me in place with his heavy palm. "You were trying to tell me something," I managed.

"Indeed." He tightened his hold enough to elicit a flinch. Constantly mingling pain and pleasure. My body trembled as he released me to trail those clever fingers down to my knee. I felt both relieved and bereft without his intimate touch, a reaction I refused to acknowledge. Emotions had no business in the task at hand.

"I assume you're telling me all this because you have a theory." Because Xai didn't speak this much without a purpose. He loved to taunt and play games, but everything he did held a significance—like his dominant hold on my leg. It was his way of reminding me of his place by my side. As if I could ever forget.

"Yes. As already stated, the Genesis have placed themselves strategically throughout society. They're small but mighty, and all of them have received military training. And I don't mean basic training, but intense, elite skill sets acquired from Special Forces and other secret branches of governments from all over the world."

"You sound impressed." Which I could appreciate, but he needed to get to the fucking point.

"I am," he admitted. "I didn't sense Shane until the bullet struck my chest, and by then, it was a little late for a reaction."

I emitted a low whistle. Sneaking up on Xai took a skill very few beings possessed. "All right, you have my attention."

"As if that's anything new," he replied with another caress. This flirty side of him rarely came out to play, but I loved when it did. Even if it did accentuate his cockiness. I placed my hand over his in a gesture of togetherness.

"Stop teasing me, and elaborate. Because I know you're telling me all this for a reason."

He flipped his hand palm side up to lace our fingers together and brought my wrist to his mouth for a gentle nibble. A light reproach for my being impatient. If he didn't start talking, and soon, I'd show him the true meaning of the word.

"There's been an influx of rogue demons on this plane over the last decade. I thought at first that the underworld had decided to come out to play in your absence, but I quickly ascertained it to be deeper than that. Apparently, I wasn't the only one who noticed the imbalance." He released my hand for the gearshift again as we approached our exit.

"You're saying the Nephilim noticed too," I deduced.

"Yes, they did, and they've taken it upon themselves to clean up the mess, so to speak. Surprisingly, they're quite good at it, but they won't be able to handle what's coming."

Silence overwhelmed the car as we pulled off the highway onto a main road littered with palm trees and expensive shops. Wealth and status lived here.

"So what's your theory?" I asked, referring to the increase in the demon population on Earth. "Do you think Geier is trying to take back his territory through the use of rogues?"

"It's a possibility," he replied softly as we turned onto a side street. Trudy's neighborhood wouldn't be far now. "But why destroy something you want to own? Those demons we saw the other night indicate something far worse. I suspect—"

Xai's body went rigid, putting my senses on high alert.

The hairs along my arms rose as electricity crackled through the air.

Demons.

A lot of them.

"Ambush," I whispered.

"Yes," Xai agreed.

Adrenaline kick-started my heart, shooting fire through my veins.

Fight, my soul encouraged.

Idiot, my brain chastised. Because why wouldn't they set a trap? I'd been so wrapped up in Trudy and Shane that I hadn't considered the obvious.

"It's the Pestilence demon," I said. "He must have run home to tell on us after we spoiled his little underworld meeting at the club."

Our identities, or at the very least, our *ancestry*, would have been evident after the fight with his demonic buddies. He would have told Kalida all about it, which implied that she knew we had Trudy and that the girl would lead us here.

"We should have anticipated this," I continued, irritated. Because we'd arrived without backup and very few weapons. My senses told me we were more than outnumbered and outgunned.

Xai said nothing as we continued into the neighborhood, driving right into the center of their circle rather than away from it.

I opened my mouth to suggest turning around, when nausea slammed into my abdomen with the force of a freight train.

Hell. Fuck. This shouldn't happen on Earth.

It felt like we were on the brink of entering the underworld. As if Xai had driven us right through a portal to Hell's door, yet we were surrounded by mini-mansions and palm trees.

"We need to turn around," I managed. My insides cramped and my heart rate spiked. No way could I fight like this. "Xai…" It sounded like a plea, and not the good kind.

But he ignored me and kept driving, his posture less stiff than before, confusing me. Every single one of my nerve endings hummed with tension, while he appeared relaxed.

"They're going to take us," was all he said.

"What?" He couldn't be serious. He must have meant that they would kidnap us if we didn't get the fuck out of here. Which was what we needed to be doing. Now.

"It's the only way to learn more, but it might hurt a

bit." He sounded far too resigned for my liking.

Blackness swarmed through my thoughts. Another indication that we were far too close to something, or someone, emanating great evil. Xai always handled the sensation better than I did, as was evidenced by his unnatural calm as he continued to drive.

I scratched at the invisible bugs crawling up my arms as I strived for sanity. "Turn around."

This little two-seater was built for speed and maneuverability.

He needed to use it.

"It's too late for that," he murmured. "You're just going to have to trust me, Eve."

Famous last words, I thought with a mental laugh.

Every time I trusted him, he hurt me.

And always at the worst time too.

Like when I thought we were finally moving forward…

My brain clicked as the truth smacked me across the face and sent a dagger through my heart.

"You knew." My words were whisper soft due to the cotton seeking residence in my throat. "You sent away our backup…" He claimed the others weren't needed for the reconnaissance mission, that he didn't want to risk their demonic auras being felt, but he knew all along that this was a trap and drove us willingly into it.

"It was the logical assumption, Evangeline." He sounded so nonchalant, as if he didn't care at all that his choice was ripping me apart inside.

"We should have agreed on a plan." One that didn't involve black spots dancing before my eyes. The darkness radiating from this neighborhood rendered me useless, which he knew better than anyone.

"I thought we did," he replied as he parked the car right in front of our destination. He didn't even try for inconspicuous.

"You're a bastard," I whispered. He could have warned me, asked for permission to proceed, or done anything other than escort us both into a demon's nest.

But no.

"You're weak." Those two words slammed into the side of my ribs with the force of a bullet. In all our time together, he'd never referred to me as *weak*.

"Fuck you." It came out breathy thanks to our surroundings, which only infuriated me more.

He merely turned off the car and set the keys on the dash without looking at me. His expression was one of irritation, not repentance.

I wanted to stab him, but logic determined my actions.

Xai wanted me to trust him, but I couldn't. Not after everything he'd put me through. Not again. And not while I felt so weakened by whatever lurked nearby.

I slid my phone from my pocket and held it loosely at my side—out of Xai's view—and blindly typed a message to Gwen.

Geier is in Miami. I added his address. *Tell Zeb.*

Because I could see the acceptance in Xai's posture. He had no intention of helping me out of this, which meant I no longer had a partner.

Or maybe I never did.

I'm alone. Again.

I slipped the phone beneath the seat and hoped Gwen understood my fumble-fingered message. If anything, she could use the GPS locator to find my last location. At least on this plane.

The stench of the underworld seeped into my pores, draining my energy in cruel waves. Hell felt close, just as it had that night at the shipping yard and again at the club.

Unnatural. Un-Earthly. Unreal.

"I'm sorry, love," Xai whispered. "But you're going to need your strength."

I didn't see him move, or expect it.

His hand knotted in my hair—not out of tenderness or seduction but out of cruelty. And then my head met the dash. Twice.

And the world went black.

CHAPTER TWENTY-THREE

THE ANGEL OF MY HEART
FINALLY SPEAKS

Yes.

I'm an ass.

But let me tell you a story, one born not of happiness, but of the sorrows of the heart. About the day I Fell…

* * *

"Your destiny is on Earth, Xai." My father folded his arms in a way meant to intimidate me. It used to, long ago, before I realized my power had surpassed that of Mietek, the Archangel of Chaos. "And *her* place is here."

"You've destined me to a plane I have no reason to care for, to a life of solitude, all to protect beings who live only to die." Not the future I wanted, or desired, not when my heart and reason for breathing existed here.

"There will come a time when you will understand your purpose." My father loved his enigmatic reasonings.

"And if I decide not to fulfill this prophecy you've crafted? If I opt to stay here instead?"

His answering smile was sad. "Then the underworld wins."

"By taking over a less-than-worthy realm?" I snorted. "I fail to see how that is possible or how my presence there will deter them."

"Chaos, Xai. It lives in your blood, and only you can use it." His explanation rivaled the others—neither revealing nor helpful. "But she has to stay here."

"Evangeline is not one to heed orders, Father." Her stubborn nature was what first drew me to her. That and her ability to keep up with me. Few others possessed the skill and drive to do so, and oh, how I loved to dance with her. A warrior with feminine curves and a lethal smile that were meant to drive a man wild. And all that golden hair—how I loved wrapping it around my fist in the throes of passion.

"No, which is why you need to end this." My father's words snapped me from my daydreams. "She can't Fall. Not with you."

"And if she does?" I asked, curious.

"Then you will fail." Those four words sent a chill down my spine. They were spoken with such finality that I couldn't doubt the veracity of them.

"Your feelings for her are a distraction," he continued. "One that you cannot afford to let interfere. Not with this."

"And by 'this,' you mean, Hell taking over Earth. The consequence would be what, exactly?" I could tell by the slight flare in his gaze that my question was not the one he expected, but rather the one I needed to ask.

"War," he replied simply.

A war between the realms.

Over Earth.

It seemed illogical to desire ownership of a weaker plane, but then again, the underworld wasn't known for its sound judgment.

"How long?" I asked. Not about the impending battle, but my supposed destiny. "When can I return home?"

My father's lips pulled into another sad smile. "That is unknown, Son. But this is your purpose. To protect humanity."

"And prevent a war," I replied mockingly. "You put a lot of faith in my wings, Father."

"This burden is not for the faint of heart, but I have no doubt that you are the one to see it through."

"Assuming I have no distractions," I added bitterly. "What am I supposed to do there? Meander about and befriend the literal living dead?"

"They are called humans, Xai. And they live longer than you realize."

"Their entire existence is the path to death."

"And do you not feel sad for them?" he countered. "Pity their short time of relevance?"

I blew out a breath, my shoulders sagging. It wasn't humanity I despised, but rather this path that I had no choice but to follow. "Am I allowed to visit?" I asked quietly.

Another one of those pitying looks. "You know that to be impossible, Son. Time is different here. A day on our plane equates to a year on Earth, which is more than enough time for the underworld to start a war."

He grabbed my shoulder in his version of support, but it felt brittle in the moment, and a touch cruel. Because this fate—the one chosen for me, not by me—doomed me to a life of loneliness. But I would go because it was the right thing to do. Even if I didn't understand it or care for the plight of the human race, I believed in honor and purpose, and protecting humanity was my purpose.

"She'll be happy here," my father whispered.

"She'll forget me here," I returned, my heart breaking.

"Sometimes love requires the greatest sacrifice, Son. Your heart for hers." He pulled me into a hug. "But it must be done, or you'll forfeit her life."

His words stopped my heart. "What?"

"Distraction equals war, Xai, and war equates to death." His words were a breath against my ear as he pulled away. "You must do right by her."

* * *

Evangeline Fell.

Her gorgeous, lithe form lay sprawled in the grass, and I ached to go to her. To comfort her. To tell her everything would be fine, that the burning sensation would cease… But I remained motionless, my hands in fists at my sides as my heart broke over and over again.

I'd caused this.

In a moment of weakness, I'd admitted my longing to spend eternity with her, and she followed me.

My sweet, stubborn, strong woman Fell for me.

I allowed myself a selfish second of happiness before shoving it from my mind.

Not two days on this plane, and I could already see that she had to go home. Demons had taken up residence all over the place, dividing the territories amongst themselves and determining ways to live symbiotically with humans.

I finally understood my purpose.

Heaven had sent me here as a warning—a reminder that my kind was watching. The underworld could live here as long as they chose not to overrule the plane. If anyone considered stepping outside the line, I would serve swift, angelic justice as a warning. One Hell would have to abide by, or further retribution would result from my realm.

But Evangeline… She didn't deserve this existence. And my father was right. Having her here was already a distraction, which I couldn't afford. Just feeling her presence in this realm had sent me running, removing my focus from my current tasks and laying it all at her feet.

If anything happened to her here, I would never

forgive myself.

What was I thinking? Suggesting that she Fall for me was the most selfish act of my life.

She needed someone better.

A new lover, one who could be there for her as she needed, to cherish and adore her in the way she deserved.

I couldn't be that man. Not now, perhaps not ever. And I owed it to her to send her home, where she belonged. Where she would be safe.

My heart splintered into a thousand pieces at the realization of what I had to do, the only solution.

She had to *want* to return to Heaven, and that required her soul's cooperation. But my Evangeline was stubborn. She wouldn't leave me so easily, not without a believable push.

Simply telling her how to ascend to Heaven would never work, not with our precious bond holding her back. My darling Evangeline couldn't fly with me tethering her to Earth.

The only way to convince her to go would be to hurt her. To destroy her faith in our love, to convince her that I had never cared for her, and to shatter the connection between us.

It would be the hardest thing I'd ever have to do; of that I had no doubt. But there wasn't any choice.

I refused to forfeit her life as my father had prophesied.

Because, Heaven knew, he was never wrong.

And I wouldn't let fate take Evangeline from me.

Not because of my selfishness.

My hands curled and uncurled as she continued to convulse on the ground. She seemed so cold and alone. The embodiment of my future without her.

But at least she would be safe, and one day, she would forget me and move on with her life.

That would be my solace.

For she would forever live in my heart.

* * *

Perhaps I was wrong that day.

Maybe I should have told her the truth and let her decide for herself, but I did what felt right at the time.

I've spent every day of my existence protecting and loving Evangeline in the only way I know how. She's my heart, the only reason I do anything, and all of my decisions are calculated.

Today is no different.

She'll see that when she wakes, realize why I did what I did, and perhaps hate me for it. I can live with that so long as she's breathing.

I need her strong, alive, and ready to fight.

Because without her, I cease to be.

CHAPTER TWENTY-FOUR

BATHING IN BLOOD ISN'T NEARLY AS SEXY AS ONE WOULD THINK

A DEEP VOICE rumbled through my thoughts. The words were fuzzy and unclear, reminding me of someone speaking above water while I swam beneath.

My head throbbed in protest as I tried to surface.

Something had knocked me out. Hard.

Instinct held me still while I tried to figure out what had happened.

The memory of my last moments awake slammed into my chest.

Xai.

He had deceived me again.

Something about me needing my strength. Damn right I would because his ass was mine when I got out of these restraints.

Wait...

LEXI C. FOSS

My brain caught up with my angry thoughts as my surroundings registered. Metal bracketed my wrists behind the back of my chair, but my legs were free.

Mistake number one on my aggressor's part, not that I was complaining.

"Perhaps logical," I heard Xai say from nearby, "but it carries significant risk."

"All great success requires even greater sacrifice," a man replied in a low, rumbling murmur.

Geier, my memory supplied.

It took considerable effort to fight the shiver that wanted to ride my spine.

The last time I saw the former Demonic Lord was the day Zeb overthrew him. I had stood on the side of the victor, something Geier vowed never to forget. It seemed he'd found his revenge by setting me up for Kalida's murder. Clever bastard.

And now he had me cuffed to a chair.

Fantastic.

"Perhaps true, but it's not your sacrifice, is it?" Xai's voice held a touch of irritation so light that most wouldn't notice. "But as I said, it's an intriguing offer."

"Does that mean you're in?" The familiar feminine purr scratched my insides and shot a jolt of adrenaline through my veins.

Kalida.

Her presence tested millennia of patience. I needed to remain still, but damn if breaking my bonds to throttle her didn't sound appealing.

I craved her blood.

And Geier's too.

Warm fingers danced over my cheekbone before tracing the line of my neck. I knew whom they belonged to even before he spoke.

"Mmm," Xai murmured. "May I say goodbye to her?"

His thumb caressed the dried blood staining my skin, and I sensed he was trying to tell me something, but that had to be wishful thinking.

The asshole had knocked me out after tricking me to

come here without backup.

And here I thought he loved me.

A laugh caught in my throat. I should have known.

Another trap. Another lie. Another betrayal. Typical Xai.

"As long as you don't mind an audience," Kalida replied.

"They say that trust is the foundation for a beneficial partnership." The admonishment in Xai's voice was followed by a sharp pinch to my earlobe. He meant to either convey a message or test my consciousness, or maybe both.

"But," he continued, "as I happen to enjoy a little voyeurism, I'll concede on this point."

"Then by all means." Geier sounded bored. "But she's mine to do with as I please when you're finished."

"Of course." Xai's nonchalant response stung. There were worse punishments than death, and one of them was to be handed over to a Demonic Lord for centuries of torture.

I'm going to fucking kill you for this.

After I took care of Kalida and Geier, anyway.

"Open your eyes, love," Xai said as he curled his palm around my nape. Directly over his mark. How fitting. "I know you're awake."

I did as he requested, but only because pretending would earn me nothing. His molten irises grinned down at me, and I hated how that dark look escalated my pulse. Not in fear, but in arousal. I knew what usually followed that unspoken promise, and he didn't disappoint, lowering his lips to mine and brushing the softest of kisses over my mouth. Such a cruel gesture considering our audience and location, but all the more erotic for it.

My blood hummed in response to the elaborate mix of danger, seduction, and lies. Anger mingled with lust as my soul shook with vehemence and love. Such a tangled web of emotion.

"Open." His tongue punctuated that whispered command by parting my lips and seeking deep entry.

I allowed him two strokes before I bit down. Hard.

He murmured in approval before shoving his wounded tongue in farther and filling my mouth with blood. His fingers slid into my hair to yank my head back, leaving me with no choice but to swallow his essence. Xai had done a lot of things to me throughout the years, but this was new. He enjoyed a fair bit of blood play while fighting, but we never *drank* from one another.

The stroke of his thumb along my throat made it clear what he wanted, and the sharp angle he held me in forced my compliance.

I swallowed.

Sweet and tangy, and purely Xai.

Foreign energy sizzled through my veins, conflicting with my mental response. I wanted to hate him, but my soul refused to allow it, as did my heart. If my hands were free, I suspected one would hit him while the other would hold him closer.

Only you leave me this conflicted, I thought bitterly.

My neck ached from the uncomfortable position and the stiffness of my skin. His bloody mark from earlier felt thicker than it should, almost as if he had added to it. Or maybe he'd bled more than I realized.

I flinched as a similar sensation irritated my wrinkled brow. The sticky consistency painting my forehead didn't make sense. Xai had slammed my head into the dashboard. That should have resulted in a bruise, not a cut, which meant that someone had lathered my forehead with blood that didn't belong to me.

What the hell are you trying to do to me, Xai? I wondered, more confused than ever. *What game are we playing now?*

I tentatively touched my tongue to his and jolted when he caressed me back in an unexpectedly gentle manner.

My eyes flew open to find him staring down at me. Not at all how we usually kissed.

Finally, he seemed to say.

I'm going to kill you, I replied with a glare.

Try. His amusement radiated through me, but I

couldn't catch the rest of his secret meaning. This embrace implied a pact of sorts, not the goodbye he'd indicated out loud.

And angels never shared blood this way because of the power exchange…

I blinked.

Oh.

Yes. His pupils dilated. *Now you see.*

The mark on my neck had never been about possession, but protection. And as he pulled back to let me study our surroundings, the reason for his unexpected gift became clear.

We were in a room reminiscent of a medieval torture chamber, except for the yellow light dangling haphazardly from the rocky ceiling above. A table of dirty tools sat to my right, and there was a heavy stone door in the corner.

I'd seen rooms like this one in my nightmares.

Because we were in Hell.

Literally.

Yet, unlike all of my previous visits, I felt fine because of Xai.

His Archangel bloodline thrived on chaos, and there was no place more chaotic than the underworld. My mother's bloodline flowing through my veins required life, healthy souls, and general happiness to survive, hence my inherent inability to function on this plane. But by coating me in his essence, Xai had essentially covered me with his aura, thereby temporarily protecting and empowering me in the underworld.

"You're weak" suddenly took on a whole new meaning, as did his irritation. It hadn't been meant as an insult but as an assessment that bothered him.

"They're going to take us… It's the only way to learn more, but it might hurt a bit."

"You knew… You sent away our backup."

"It was a logical assessment, Evangeline."

"We should have discussed a plan."

"I thought we did."

The conversation from the car flooded my thoughts,

forcing me to reconsider what I thought I knew.

What plan did he think we'd discussed?

I quickly ran through our long morning, the interview with the victims, our interlude on the roof, and how it had ended.

"We have a Demonic Lord to hunt and kill... After we deliver Kalida to her father and exonerate you... I'll wash it off you later when we're done."

Well, shit.

Xai must have seen the understanding in my expression, because he smiled, confirming my train of thought.

Some fucking plan.

I refrained from shaking my head and settled on giving him a look to convey my frustration.

You and I are having a long talk when this is done.

Because all of this could have been explained to me rather than implied through a bunch of perplexing statements. Not to mention his knocking me out solely to coat me in blood. I would be repaying the favor later. With a knife.

"Enjoy Hell, darling," he murmured, repeating the phrase he used so many years ago, the same one destined to haunt my nightmares. But now I understood. He never left me, and he wouldn't leave me here either. Not without an escape plan. Why else would he go through the painful process of coating me in his aura?

"I suspect there are a few amusements in store for you," he added with a wicked curl of his lips, his message clear. *Have fun killing some demons.* "I so wish I could witness what's to come, but there's a matter on Earth that requires my attention."

Kalida's answering giggle suggested she was looking forward to that mission, but I doubted the two of them had the same intentions in mind. Xai clearly hadn't gotten all the details he needed, hence his need to go undercover as an ally.

Fantastic.

He brushed his knuckles against my cheek before

trailing his fingers down my arm to where my hands were bound behind my back. He pressed a slender piece of metal against my palm out of sight of our audience. *A key.*

I closed my fist around it and glowered up at him. "I'm going to enjoy stabbing you later."

He grinned with anticipation. "Flirt."

"Ass," I returned.

Kalida appeared at Xai's side, her freshly manicured hand wrapping around his shoulder possessively while she stared down at me with sparkling black eyes. Her mother's Succubus genes gave her a curvy figure meant to seduce, while her father's lent to the darker complexion and jet-black hair.

I smiled at her. "I can't wait to return you to Zeb."

It would be difficult not to kill her first, but there were sentences worse than death and her father knew how to deliver them. Being his child did not mean he would take her treachery lightly.

She sidled closer to Xai and pressed a hand to his abdomen as he wrapped his arm around her in a false show of solidarity. His eyes never left mine as emotion smoldered in his pupils. A tell only I would recognize. *Fury.*

"Poor little Evie," she cooed. "You were asleep for most of the negotiation, so let me bring you up to speed." She dragged her nails across Xai's flat stomach in a possessive manner that irritated my feminine instincts. He might be a colossal jackass, but he was *mine.*

"You see," she continued, "Xai just offered you as a gift to Geier in exchange for a new partnership." She glanced up at my angel adoringly, but he didn't return the gesture. "He's upgrading from my worthless father to the stronger player."

I couldn't help the laugh that bubbled out of me. It probably sounded hysterical to them, but that was only because I had tried to hold it down and failed. Because wow. Kalida had lost her fucking mind. There were so many things wrong with her assessment, but I settled on the most obvious.

"The stronger player being Geier?" Humor filled my voice. "That's cute."

The former Demonic Lord moved forward to stand beneath the room's only light so I could properly see him and the ice radiating from his eerie russet-colored eyes.

Like Zeb, Geier was a decent-looking man, but with pale skin and a head of light blond hair pulled back into a ponytail at the nape of his neck. It seemed fitting for his history, since the last time he ruled Earth, Vikings existed. Apparently, no one gave him the updated fashion memos.

"I'm looking forward to teaching you a lesson, Evangeline," he murmured. All calm, poised confidence. Exactly what I expected from his kind. The threat and power lingering in the air sent a chill down my spine. Xai had given me the key to my escape, but even armed, taking down this demon would be no easy feat.

"Alas," Geier continued, "we have business to attend to, as Xai already noted. But I do intend to play with you later. A few hours, or days, down here should weaken you enough so that I'll be able to do whatever I want to you without much of a fight."

He stepped closer and reached out to drag a thumb over my lips, making it clear the ways in which he wanted to abuse me. Whatever humor had brightened me moments ago was long gone as he studied me with his shrewd, calculated gaze.

Geier wouldn't be the first demon to possess an angel fetish. Something about defiling something so pristine and good appealed to the darkest of beings, and the one standing over me was one of the vilest of them all.

Electricity sizzled over my skin as he traced my jawline with the pad of his finger. The uncomfortable zing of energy indicated his evil intentions and overwhelming strength. Even on my best day, in top shape, he would be a challenge for me. Down here I stood no chance, and he knew and reveled in it.

"Maybe I'll take you back to Earth every now and

then to recharge you," he mused. "And just when you feel strong enough, I'll force you back here, to your knees. Where you belong."

Xai smirked at that, and I wanted to smack him. He was the only man I had ever kneeled for, and he knew it. But it was a fucking inappropriate moment to remind me of such a thing, which was the point. He wanted my head in the game and not living in fear of the demon's unveiled threats.

Because despite the key in my hand and temporary protection from Xai's essence, Geier's words unnerved me. The notion of being at his mercy for any length of time terrified me. Especially his taunt about teleporting me between realms. It was my nightmare realized, and the arousal brightening the demon's gaze didn't help the situation.

"Mmm, yes, I can see we'll have a lot of fun together." He let his hand fall, the back of his knuckles just barely touching my breast along the way, before he snapped a finger at the door. Two Guardians stomped in and awaited Geier's command with matching expressions of servitude. "I want her strapped naked to my bed until my return. No one is to touch her other than me. Do you understand?"

"Yes, sir," they replied in unison.

I met Xai's eyes over Geier's shoulder. The dark angel appeared bored, save for the slight flare in his pupils. He didn't appreciate the image of what the lord planned to do to me, but he wasn't going to stop him either. Not because he didn't care, but because he knew he didn't need to.

Trust, his eyes said. He knew I could handle myself, especially with the key to my freedom and the two knives hidden beneath my jeans. They felt like brands against my inner thighs. Not strip-searching me was a mistake, one Xai had helped to facilitate, no doubt.

How did he keep them from sensing the silver on me?
Had they allowed him to enter with blades?
Did the underworld alter their perception of the precious metal?

"Shall we?" Xai asked, gesturing to the door. "Unless we need to supervise the move?"

Geier eyed me speculatively, searching for signs of strength or rebellion. I glowered up at him but also allowed a tiny bit of the fear his presence evoked to show in my expression. It wasn't hard. My soul quivered into a little ball in this realm, and his dominance intimidated the fighter inside my heart. That didn't mean I wouldn't go down swinging—I would—but in Hell, I knew Geier could beat me eventually. And that resignation was what I wanted him to see.

"I'm not concerned," he said after a minute. "We can go." He nodded to his Guardians as he led the entourage out the door. A Portal Dweller stood waiting in the hallway, her expression passive. She held out a hand without speaking, and Geier took it as Xai and Kalida joined him.

Ebony eyes met mine just before the foursome vanished, and in them I saw love. But it was gone too quickly and replaced by a pair of approaching Guardians.

Hmm… Time to play.

CHAPTER TWENTY-FIVE

HELL'S ACCOMMODATIONS
LEAVE MUCH TO BE DESIRED

"HELLO, BOYS," I greeted.

These asshats certainly chose the wrong day to make my acquaintance.

I slid the key into the cuffs and gave it a flick as the two Guardians sauntered toward me. The metal unlatched with ease, and I caught the restraints before they fell to the ground.

"Do you want to chat first or get down to business?" I asked, curious.

They both grunted with disinterest. Typical Guardians.

I shrugged. "Well, I tried."

Their movements were predictable and synchronized. My shoulders fell, as did my head, in a show of weakness as one pulled a key ring from his pocket. I suspected it

221

was missing the one that Xai had somehow stolen and dropped into my hand. He always did have clever fingers.

Demon One grabbed my shoulder with more enthusiasm than necessary and nodded to the other. "I'm good."

"Are you, though?" I asked as I wrapped the cuffs around the knuckles of my left hand. "Because I beg to differ."

The dumb Guardian didn't see me coming until it was too late. I swung my fist upward into his jugular, knocking the breath from his windpipe. His grip left my shoulders to wrap around his damaged throat while the other demon looked on in surprise. I took advantage of his shock and introduced my foot to his abdomen. My right hand met his neck as he keeled over, placing him in a similar position to the other man.

Both of them wheezed as they tried to catch their breath. All humanoids were weakened by throat punches, putting them down for at least twenty seconds, which granted me just enough time to retrieve the knives from my thighs. Not the most eloquent of takedowns, but beggars couldn't be choosers.

"Now, I did ask if you wanted to chat first." I twirled the silver with my fingers and tsked. "And you said no."

"Bit—" The shoulder-grabbing demon's response was silenced by my blade meeting his heart. An easy throw given our proximity. I sent the other one into Demon Two's chest and waited as they both wilted into ashes.

"Eve two, underworld zero," I murmured as I retrieved my toys. I wiped them against my jeans before sliding the metal up the sleeves of my shirt into a more accessible location. "Now to find a way home."

Easier said than done. Xai's blood had empowered me temporarily, but I doubted it would last for long down here. I needed to find a Portal Dweller in a realm designed for confusion and mayhem. It could take me years or decades, which would only equate to a few days or weeks on Earth.

Fantastic.

I searched the room for anything useful. The rusty torture tools on the table wouldn't be worth much in a fight, and there weren't any weapons in the demon's ashes that I could use. Not surprising. Guardians relied on their strength and nothing else.

A peek into the gray stone hallway proved the former Demonic Lord hadn't bothered with additional guards. He probably assumed I would be too weak to put up a fight, something Xai may or may not have confirmed.

"Thanks, *love*," I muttered.

Pretending to be an ally was certainly one way to obtain information, but I would have preferred torturing the details out of them—something I would have said had Xai asked for my opinion. Alas, he chose for me.

Just as he always did.

Like knocking me out in the car and covering me in his blood.

His intentions were in the right place, but he needed to either let me protect myself or, at the very least, communicate his intentions. Because I refused to be treated as a pawn, and that was what he did today. He had used me as a bargaining chip while placing himself in a dangerous situation as a double agent. A brilliant notion, minus the whole leaving-me-out-of-the-loop part. Xai would see it as protecting me—his only weakness— and although I understood that on a logical level, I refused to accept it as reasonable.

I stepped into the rocky hallway. The yellow light dangling from the ceiling gave each end an ominous glimmer.

"Here goes nothing." I picked left because, why not?

All the doors were open and led to similar rooms to the cell I had just vacated. No windows or stairs, just an endless corridor lined with sharp edges and a ceiling that had seen better days.

Xai's blood kept me strong, allowing me to experience Hell for the first time, and I wasn't impressed. They could use some serious decorators down here, and a little sunlight never killed anyone. Not that the underworld had a sun to speak of, but more of a purple glow tinged with blue. Their version of a fiery orb never set, either, giving the illusion of an endless day that only prolonged time on this plane.

All the religious texts on Earth held a touch of truth. Torture, blood, and sin were all common in Hell, but perhaps not in the way a human could comprehend. Souls weren't so much agonized as vilified here. They enjoyed their hazardous games and lethal activities. Thrived on them, in fact.

Hence this endless hallway.

A mind trick, I realized as I passed the exact room I had walked out of however many minutes or hours ago. "Fuck."

I regretted killing the Guardians so soon. One of them probably had the mental means to get out of this literal hellhole. Some phrase or move would open an exit, or maybe a shift of a rock. The walls were intricately woven with a bizarre metallic stone that lacked a name in my vocabulary. Just as silver didn't exist here, this material didn't exist elsewhere. A gray mix of hard substance with subtle cracks that held no meaning.

Tracing the nooks and crannies, I searched for a pattern and found none.

Everything about this place was chaotic and nonsensical.

It was all upside down…

I laughed at the absurdity.

Damn demons.

I raised my hand to run my fingers along the ceiling as I wandered, until I found the latch I needed. A tug revealed a set of stairs.

"Fucking demons," I muttered as I jumped upward and landed seamlessly on the first stair. Everything rotated around me to accommodate the new dimension and path. The gray corridor disappeared beneath my feet as new one appeared lined with blues and reds. Blaring heat singed the air, warning me away from touching anything around me. I moved quickly upward, eyes peeled for an exit. It wouldn't be obvious, but subtle. A knob in a space that shouldn't exist…

Aha!

A black notch on an otherwise smooth stone step.

I waved my hand over it to test the temperature and found it lacking in warmth.

"And away we go…" I laid my palm over it and shrieked as it opened on a tidal wave.

Literally.

Water everywhere.

For fuck's sake.

I started to swim upward but thought better of it and went downward instead.

Toward nothing.

And then something.

I broke the surface with a gasp and a curse. The last time I visited Hell, Xai had left me in some sort of maze with walls. No water or fire, just endless searching. I preferred that over this ocean of nonsense.

Waves crashed all around me, each of them boasting portals to different realms in Hell. At least humans had created maps and technology. Demons relied on insanity to make decisions and move around.

With a sigh, I dove into a random wave and landed on my feet in a field of questionable greenery. My clothes and hair were dry, but my skin felt clammy and my stomach churned. I knelt to gather my breath and regain my focus, but it didn't help. Something about this plane hurt more than the others.

I ran a palm over my face and paused on my forehead.

"Fuck…"

Xai's blood had washed off in the waves.

That's why I felt weaker. His protection was waning…

My hands fell to the ground. It was too brittle and rough to be called grass, but the fresh-cut blades were visually similar. And the hills and surrounding flowers resembled those on Earth as well. But the violet sky was distinctly otherworldly.

Movement to my left had me tensing for a fight.

Two humanoid creatures approached, their figures hazy on the horizon.

There were no trees or rocks to hide behind, nor did I have time to find a doorway.

Not that it mattered. I needed a demon to help navigate this plane and find a portal to head home, so I'd just have to use what was left of my energy to force one of them to help me.

Despite my dwindling energy, I had just enough of Xai's blood remaining in me to stand on steady legs. It wouldn't last long at this rate, but posturing meant everything in the demon world.

I palmed my daggers, ready for a fight, until I realized who approached.

The blond one looked as if he wanted to kill me, but I was too surprised to voice an opinion on that. "What the hell are you doing here?"

"What do you think?" Tax growled, clearly irritated. "Do you have any idea how long we've been looking for you and how many damn realms you've traveled through?"

Remy smirked beside him. "Don't mind him. He's feeling a bit portal sick."

"Fuck you, man," Tax replied with a shiver. "I fucking hate you right now."

"Trackers don't like the water lands," Remy explained, shrugging. "Doesn't look like you did much either," he added, noting my defeated state.

I sheathed my weapons and ran a hand over my face, exhausted.

"Xai sent you."

Which meant I'd been wandering around a lot longer than I realized, which Tax had already implied. Not having to eat or sleep, nor knowing the date or time, really messed with my ability to comprehend anything beyond survival here.

"He sent us a text right before you two disappeared

into the underworld, and we've been searching for you ever since," Remy replied.

"Fuck," the Tracker added with a shudder.

"How did you find me?" Because Tax couldn't sense my angelic aura, and if they followed me here from the ocean, then this wasn't a chance meeting.

The lanky demon pointed at his head. "Bracelet."

I stared at him. "Bracelet?" *Did I hear that right?*

"Tax means the one in your hair," Remy explained. "It belongs to his sister."

"Xai wears it so I can track him when needed," Tax muttered. "And he put it on you." He made that sound like a grave offense, but I was too preoccupied to comment.

I gently prodded the black band holding up my ponytail. Xai had used it to gather up my hair after our interlude on the roof. Which further confirmed he knew that I would end up here and require help to return home.

"I'm going to kill him." Or kiss him. I couldn't decide. I wanted to do both at the same time, and also fuck him. And probably slap him, or cut him, or *something*. Once I regained my strength. Because right now I didn't feel all that great.

"He saved your life," Tax remarked. "But, hey, if you would prefer we leave you in the nether fields, then we'll be on our way."

"I wouldn't recommend it," Remy put in. "Gets cold here at night, and you don't look so hot, angel." Those sharp green eyes held a spark of memory. He had seen me at my worst all those centuries ago, huddled in a dark corner, unsure of my surroundings, and attempting to protect myself with words alone. We both knew that was my fate if I stayed here.

My muscles were already atrophying without Xai's markings on my head and neck, but the ingested blood kept me sane on the inside. At least for now. I'd be a quivering mess soon, but we had time for a brief conversation.

"One question before we go."

"Only one?" The Portal Dweller displayed a pair of adorable dimples that endeared him to me a little more. At least he seemed to like me, unlike the Tracker.

"Where are all the demons?" I hadn't seen a single one other than these two and the Guardians, which felt wrong.

Everything about this place feels *wrong.*

"You've been traveling through the nether realms," Remy replied. "No one lives here."

I glanced around. "Really?" I could understand not wanting to live in a tidal wave, but the tranquility in this field wasn't bad.

"Stay for an hour and you'll see why." The taunt in Tax's voice matched the mischief in his bright gaze.

I took the bait, curious. "What happens in an hour?" Not that I wanted to remain here much longer. My hands were starting to shake, something I tried to hide by shoving them into my pockets.

"It gets cold," Remy murmured. "Really cold."

Tax grinned. "We could come back later if you want to stay and enjoy the freeze."

"You were taken to the pits of the netherworld," Remy continued, ignoring the Tracker's cruel suggestion. "At least that's where the bracelet led us first, and you've been gallivanting about since. Trust me when I say that you don't want to stay here."

"Gallivanting," I repeated. "Not how I see it." I focused on the still-smiling Tracker as an idea occurred to me. "Did you sense Kalida's presence when you tracked me?"

His amusement died. "You saw Kalida?"

"That's a no, then." Damn. We still didn't have physical evidence for Zeb. "What about other demonic auras near your starting point? Did you feel anyone or anything other than your sister's bracelet?"

Recognition sparked in those hazel eyes, but he didn't elaborate; he just said, "Yes."

"Would you be able to track those auras?"

He folded his arms. "I'm not a hound dog."

"You're a Tracker demon."

"And now she's stating the obvious," Tax drawled, his attention drifting to Remy. "Can we leave her here and tell Xai she froze before we arrived?"

I fought the urge to introduce my fist to his head and focused on the purpose of my request. The shaking had spread from my hands to my arms, which meant I didn't have energy to spare on kicking his ass.

"Kalida is alive and working with Geier on some plan to overthrow your current Demonic Lord, or perhaps worse," I said in as stern of a voice as I could muster. "There were two Guardians working with them—whom I already killed—but there was also a Portal Dweller. If you can track her and deliver her to Zeb, she could provide the proof we need to convince him that his daughter is alive."

"Which will exonerate you," Remy translated.

"Yes."

"And what about Xai?" Tax asked. "Where is he?"

"He didn't tell you?" Their silence helped me feel mildly better about being kept in the dark, as it seemed Xai didn't communicate his plans to them either. "He allied himself with Geier and Kalida to learn more about their operation."

Remy cursed while Tax whistled low.

"Idiot," the Portal Dweller muttered.

"Yep," I agreed. "So now we need Zeb." Something I never thought I would say, but this wasn't a typical situation. "Can you take me to him and then help Tax find the female Portal Dweller?"

"I don't need his help," the Tracker muttered.

"Why not?" Remy asked, sounding offended.

Tax palmed the back of his neck. "Because I already know who she is and where to find her."

"Then why did you give me a hard time about tracking her?" I asked, my tired voice lacking the annoyance I felt.

I need to leave this place. Soon.

"Because I don't like you." Tax's simple reply sounded so practical and only increased my frustration. "But," he continued, "now that I know she can help Xai…" He shrugged as if to say, *Well, now I guess I'm okay with helping.*

Damn demons and their screwed-up logic.

"Cheeky," Remy said, amused. "Right, then. Shall we go?"

"Yep." Tax grabbed the other demon's shoulder. "Ready."

"Don't be shy, angel." Remy waggled his fingers at me.

"You both seem to be courting death," I muttered.

"So you keep saying," the Tracker drawled. "Yet, I don't see you delivering on that promise, Eve."

"Keep it up and I'll deliver." The shudder traversing my spine ruined the underlying threat of my words. *Definitely time to go.*

"Promises, promises," he cooed.

His overconfidence floored me. The demon knew I could kill him with a flick of the wrist, even in my weakened state, but he didn't have any qualms about taunting me.

I suddenly understood why Xai had befriended these men. It wasn't their usefulness, though that certainly added to their overall charm, but their general disregard for hierarchy. It was refreshing.

"Let's go." I grabbed the Portal Dweller's other arm.

Remy's eyebrows danced tauntingly as he said, "Hang on, angel."

CHAPTER TWENTY-SIX

THERE'S NO PLACE
LIKE A DEMONIC HOME

I WRAPPED MY damp hair up in a towel and studied my reflection in the mirror. The color had returned to my cheeks, but exhaustion underlined my blue eyes.

Hell had taken a lot out of me. Angels didn't require sleep, but it helped to restore our energy levels when we did. And I hadn't rested much in the last week. Hence the need for a shower when we returned to the Miami hotel. I used it to reenergize while Tax tracked down the Portal Dweller.

I stretched my arms over my head to loosen my stiff muscles before drying my hair and bundling it up into a ponytail with Xai's black band. Normally, I would be against the idea of wearing a tracking device of any kind, but there was nothing typical about our situation.

Jeans, a tank top, boots, and several knives later, I

exited the bathroom and found Remy leaning against the hallway wall. He held out his hand to stop me from entering the living area, where Tax sat sprawled out on the couch, waiting.

The air sizzled with the arrival of another demon, silencing the question rising in my throat.

"You've got some nerve calling me," the female demon seethed as soon as she appeared. She stood with her back to me and Remy, her hands on her hips, as she faced the Tracker on the couch.

"Oh, Clarissa, don't be like that," Tax admonished. "We had a good time, you and me."

I suppressed a snort. He sounded rather arrogant for a scrawny man, although I supposed he was decent looking. The full lips, smoky gaze, and thick light hair added to his charm. But I preferred my men tall, dark, and lethal.

"You're a fucking bastard," Clarissa growled as she lunged at him.

Remy smirked, enjoying the show, while Tax did his best to fend off the furious demon.

"And suddenly I remember why I ended things," Tax muttered. "Anytime now would be great."

"Anytime for what?" she demanded, her fiery personality matching her long mane of red hair. "As if I would ever fuck you again after what you did!"

"I wasn't—" He paused to grab her fist as it nearly connected with his jaw, and jumped from the couch in an effort to restrain her.

Remy's grin morphed into unrestrained amusement as he observed the female teleporting around the Tracker every time he tried to grab her.

"Oh, for fuck's sake!" Tax shouted. "Stop standing there and do something!"

The knife left my hand just as the woman's attention flashed our way. It sank into the divot between her doe eyes, sending her to the ground in a startled coma. The silver blade wouldn't kill her unless I shoved it through her heart, but the metal would keep her unconscious until

I removed it.

Remy whistled. "Remind me not to piss you off, angel."

Tax studied the woman at his feet with a look of irritation. "We could have tried talking to her."

"She didn't appear to be in a talkative mood, Tax," I replied as I pushed off the wall to join him in the living area. "Whatever you did seriously pissed her off."

"You totally pulled a Hell-stand on her, didn't you?" Remy teased, shaking his head. Catching my look, he elaborated. "You know, like a one-night stand, only in Hell, where it lasts a little longer than on Earth?"

"Seriously?" Of all the strange idioms for a demon to invent, *that* was his choice? "Can we go see Zeb now?"

Remy flashed me a dimpled smile. "All work and no play, eh, angel?"

"Stop flirting with Eve and take us to Lord Zebulon."

"If you think that's flirting, then I understand why poor Clarissa was so displeased," Remy replied. He ducked a punch from Tax by teleporting to the other side of me.

I rolled my eyes Heavenward. "It's like working with toddlers. You could at least send me someone to work with." Not that anyone was listening or would care. They'd proved that centuries ago.

Warm fingers wrapped around my wrist, and the room disappeared. My stomach churned as demonic energy rolled over my skin. The sensation of shifting realms and space reminded me of flying, yet it felt *wrong*.

I stepped away from Remy as soon as a familiar room of masculine tones and floor-to-ceiling windows appeared before us. He didn't remark at my brusque move, but his vibrant eyes held a hint of amusement. Naturally, he found humor in my discomfort. Something told me the man rarely took anything seriously.

"Disarm," dual voices commanded from my left.

Well, that confirms we're in Zeb's home, then. Not that I doubted our destination; Tax had proven to be quite a skilled Tracker.

LEXI C. FOSS

"Chill, Dargarian pets," I said as I headed toward the master staircase. I knew Zeb's Chicago home better than my own; I used to live here, after all. "I'm not here to harm your master, boys. But I do need to talk to him, and if you think I'm giving you my silver, then you clearly don't know me very well."

Heat crawled over my arms as one of them sent me a warning shot. Not hot enough to burn, but enough to singe the blonde hairs standing on end. I palmed a knife and turned.

"You do not want to fuck with me right now."

"Drew, she's fine," Remy said, addressing the redheaded demon with narrowed jet-black eyes.

"Where's Xai?" he asked in a low murmur.

"That's why we're here." The Portal Dweller clapped his hand on Drew's shoulder, drawing the Dargarian's focus away from me. "I'll fill you in while she chats with our lord."

"She can't see Lord Zebulon while armed," the other redhead declared.

"Either you let me see him or you end up like her." I gestured to the Portal Dweller in Tax's arms. "Your choice."

"She dares to threaten us?" the Dargarian hissed.

I ignored his complaint and kept walking. Normally, I would wait for Zeb to descend, but we'd wasted enough time already. Xai was in a precarious situation doing Heaven only knew what.

My steps were silent as I headed toward Zeb's personal chambers. I left Remy behind to argue on my behalf and nodded at the Guardians who stepped into my path at the top of the stairs.

"You're going to want to move now," I told them. They looked at each other and then at me. "I won't ask again."

"Let her pass," Zeb said from an open door down the hall. His lapdogs slithered away as a single unit while I followed their master's voice to the bedroom at the end.

I wasted no time and started speaking as I entered.

"We have…" My heart leapt into my throat, halting my words.

Zeb stood beside a four-poster bed, dressed in tailored black trousers and an open dress shirt, with Gwen kneeling at his feet. Her dark head was against his leg as he softly stroked her head. She didn't look at me as I entered, her reverence for the Demonic Lord taking precedence.

"Evangeline," Zeb murmured. "Guinevere informed me that Geier is in Miami and that you might be in need of assistance. Would you care to elaborate?"

He continued to pet my best friend's hair in a soothing manner that left me uneasy. His unbuttoned shirt revealed a chiseled physique, something most women would admire, but my heart rate escalated for a very different reason. There was only one reason a man stood in a state of semi-undress around a Succubus, especially one as beautiful and sweet as Gwen.

Any outward reaction or question on my part would be wrong. Demonic hierarchy didn't apply to me, but it definitely applied to her. I hoped Zeb would never take advantage of his position, but I knew he would and obviously had.

"Evangeline." The impatience in his tone snapped my gaze up to his ebony eyes.

I swallowed. *Your daughter is alive*, wasn't something I wanted to say with his hand so close to Gwen's neck.

"Geier is building an army," I said instead. "An illegal one."

One dark eyebrow inched upward. "Is he now? And what does this have to do with Kalida?" he asked as he wove his fingers through Gwen's hair. She sighed against him, as if content, and I wondered how much of it was an act.

"There's someone downstairs you need to talk to." *Preferably away from my best friend.*

"Clarissa?" he asked, amused. "Care to elaborate on why your silver flows through her blood?"

"She wouldn't have come willingly," I replied. "Which

you already know."

A chill of power swept over me, reminding me that the man before me may appear calm and collected, but his perception and abilities far outweighed that of a normal demon. He would be a worthy opponent in a fight, could even possibly kill me. Few beings on Earth possessed that talent.

Zeb's perception and affinity for strategy were what won him this territory, and he'd only grown stronger over the centuries. His ability to sense Clarissa downstairs was child's play in comparison to what I knew he could do. He played on a level few others could comprehend.

All those twists and turns…

And masterful plans…

Positioning Gwen at his feet between us was purposeful, a way to protect himself while reminding me of his authority here. It was a game of chess with him being the most powerful player on the board, while the rest of us were mere pawns.

It'd been that way from the beginning.

"You already know why I'm here," I realized.

His lack of a reaction confirmed my assessment.

I shook my head with a laugh that I didn't feel. "When did you figure it out?"

"My suspicions piqued after your visit to the shipping yard." He looked fondly at my best friend as he cupped the back of her neck. "Guinevere confirmed them when she told me about Geier. Kalida always did admire that bastard."

He brushed his knuckles over Gwen's cheek before laying his hand palm up in front of her nose. "Are you fit to rise, sweetheart?"

"Yes, my lord," she whispered as she accepted his help up off the floor. "Thank you."

He pressed a kiss to her temple and whispered something in her ear that brought a flush to her cheeks.

Of course she would be smitten with the Demonic Lord. He was attractive with that chiseled abdomen and sharp cheekbones, and his stamina no doubt translated to the bedroom. Her weak legs suggested as much as she clung to him to steady herself, and he wrapped an arm around her waist.

So, what, you came here to save me and ended up in bed with the man? Seriously, Gwen?

"Where's Xai?" Zeb asked, drawing me from my thoughts.

"He traded my life for a position on Geier's team." Saying it out loud sent a shot of revenge filled adrenaline down my spine. It straightened my posture and bolstered my confidence. "It was a charade to garner trust and it worked."

Gwen's cerulean gaze met mine, and in her expression, I saw the fire I loved and adored. She said nothing, likely out of respect for her superior, but that expression relieved me. I hadn't lost my best friend to the wills and charm of the Demonic Lord.

"Undercover?" Zeb mused. "Sounds about right."

The fact that he didn't even question Xai's intentions said a lot about their bond. "You're so certain he isn't double-crossing you after torturing him in Hell just last week?" I couldn't help the admonishment in my tone.

Zeb merely shrugged. "He helped me work out some frustration that would have otherwise been directed at you."

"You're a bastard."

Gwen cringed at my abrupt statement, while the man beside her chuckled. "That may be the case, but it also belies the point. Why did you bring Clarissa?"

Something he didn't know? Fascinating. "She's working for Geier and Kalida."

He nodded. "I see. And you brought her here to provide proof that my progeny lives."

"Yes."

"Then my men have permission to kill her." He said it so casually, yet I knew his pets downstairs heard it and would follow through with the command. "I don't require proof, Evangeline. You seem to forget that I trust your judgment, as well as Xai's."

"Oh, I'm sorry. You mean, when you falsely accused me of committing murder?"

"If I truly thought you were guilty, I would have punished you on sight."

"You did," I countered. "By forcing me to work with Xai."

He grinned. "You can thank me for that reunion later."

"Should I thank you for torturing him in Hell as well?" I couldn't help bringing it up again. The bastard pissed me off with his archaic antics.

Gwen flinched at my tone. Zeb might be her lord, but he wasn't mine. My respect for him hung by a thin thread in this moment.

He buttoned his dress shirt before fixing his chocolate gaze on me. "My friendship with Xai predates formalities. I required an outlet that he provided, but I imagine what bothers you isn't so much my methods as the fact that he offered himself to protect you."

I folded my arms. "Whether you're right or wrong, you punished him for something neither of us did."

"It was never about punishment," he replied. "But enough about the past. Our future is far more pressing. Someone, I suspect Geier, is altering the balance and thinning the walls between our realms."

Xai had asked if I felt the shift in power earlier this week before mentioning the holy blade. A chill crept up my spine at the reminder that Zeb possessed a weapon that could kill me. *We need to steal it from him.*

"You appear unconvinced, Evangeline." Amusement briefly touched the demon's lips. "Why do you think Xai befriended me some millennia ago? Fought with me instead of with Geier?"

Uh... He had misunderstood my hesitation, but I rolled with it. "Because you were the lesser of two evils?"

Xai had never given me a reason, just stated his intentions and acted on them. It had always been that way. I gave up questioning him early on in our relationship because he never elaborated.

Zeb smiled. "Our interests align, Evangeline. We both wish to protect this plane from war, which is exactly what will happen if we don't fix the misalignment of power."

"Indeed," a deep voice said from behind me. It sent a chill of familiarity down my spine as Zeb straightened in surprise. "I suggest we start immediately."

"And you are?" The demon demanded, his voice holding the authority of the one who controlled this territory.

But the being behind me superseded all laws.

Just like me.

I slowly turned to face the angel I hadn't seen in over two thousand years. He looked exactly as I remembered him, with a shock of white-blond hair, striking blue eyes, and a face no older than mine.

"Dad," I managed.

His cold look both melted and froze my heart. "Hello, Eve."

CHAPTER TWENTY-SEVEN

YOU KNOW IT'S BAD WHEN
AN ARCHDEMON SHOWS UP

WORDS ESCAPED ME.

What did one say to a father after several millennia apart?

How are you?

I missed you.

Welcome to Earth.

He took my options away by pulling me into a hug filled with warmth, love, and a touch of admonishment. The kind of embrace only a father could give, all wrapped up with a lethal edge. After all, this was the angel of death.

"Why now?" I whispered. "After all these years... Why are you here now?"

"Because you need me." Simply stated, as if that was the obvious answer.

"Us, actually." Archangel Mietek appeared while he spoke, stirring a gasp from Gwen and alarm from me.

Power sizzled in the air as the male angels asserted their dominance over Zeb in a not-so-subtle manner. I stepped away from my father to see the Demonic Lord pulling my best friend behind him, his posture protective.

The lack of guards pouring into the room suggested my father or Mietek had done something to disarm them. I hoped they hadn't killed them all. Remy deserved better, and the Tracker, despite his asshole tendencies, did too.

"You know why we're here," the Archangel said from beside me.

The demon met Mietek's gaze boldly, recognition dawning as he realized *who* had addressed him. "I do," was all he said.

"Then my son has done his job." Mietek's stature and dark looks were so much like Xai's; even their chiseled bone structure was the same.

The realization for his purpose here pricked my heart. Only one thing would pull the Archangel from his duties in Heaven, and that would be to save his son.

"Xai's in trouble," I said, pained.

"All of you are," my father corrected. "Someone is trying to open a gate."

My eyebrows shot up. "To Hell?"

"That's what Xai and I suspected after the shipping yard," Zeb replied as Gwen peeked around him. "We've been trying to prevent it from happening for centuries, but we both knew it to be inevitable."

Energy caressed the air, announcing a new arrival, seconds before a man appeared on Zeb's chaise lounge in the corner. His vibrant sapphire robes, violet eyes, and white-gold hair painted him as decidedly "other," as did his unnatural looks. No being on Earth possessed skin that perfect, a mouth so potent, or a face that beautiful.

Because that's what he was: beautiful.

Not handsome, or overly masculine, but a thing of beauty that defied understanding. My heart hurt just looking at him.

Gwen fell to the floor in prayer while Zeb bowed his head, but the being didn't bother with him. His focus was on the Xai's father.

"I thought we had a deal, Mietek." His lyrical tones scattered goose bumps down my arms. *Pure, unadulterated power.* "You stay in your realm; I stay in mine." A bowl of strawberries appeared in his lap, and he popped one into his mouth, his expression exuberant. "Mmm, I must say, I've missed the sweetness of this plane. Shall we stay and play?"

Mietek folded his thick arms, legs braced. "Careful, Ashmedai, or I'll suspect you mismanaged your realm on purpose."

Ashmedai's resulting smile stole the air from my lungs. Xai owned my soul, but this being possessed a lethal attractiveness. The kind that brought most women and men to their knees in worship.

Just like Gwen...

An Archdemon, I realized. The underworld's equivalent to Archangels, only far more dangerous due to their sinful proclivities. Bael was the only one I'd ever met, and I didn't much care for the memory. Their kind were hubristic, seductive, and enigmatic.

"Mismanaged my realm," Ashmedai mused. "We shall see. I sense"—he paused as he considered—"a breach in the veil. I believe it's your place to inform me of such things, Zebulon. Care to elaborate?"

"Yes, my prince. The disturbance is new, and I believe caused by Geier." Short and to the point, but said with a touch of reverence. Demonic hierarchy was a bizarre thing. Zeb never once looked up from the ground to address his superior, something a man in his position rarely had to do.

Heaven didn't maintain the same rule structure. We respected our elders, but in a kinder way.

Ashmedai stood, revealing his six-foot-plus muscular frame and focused on Gwen. "You knew this and chose to entertain your baser needs before notifying me?"

The man has a point, Zeb.

"Guinevere brought me Evangeline's message shortly before the angel herself arrived with additional information. Nothing else occurred." Honesty underlined his tone, but demons excelled at lying.

The Archdemon crouched before Gwen and used a finger beneath her chin to force her to meet his glowing gaze. "Is that true, young one?"

"Yes, my prince," she breathed.

I waited, ready to put a blade through this asshole if he tried to hurt Gwen, but aside from a caress of her cheek, he did nothing other than stand to address Mietek. "I hear Miami is warmer than Chicago." His robes morphed into a pair of board shorts and flip-flops. "Is this more appropriate?"

I couldn't help the smile stretching my lips. Mietek and my father had both arrived in professional attire, similar to what Xai always wore, but Ashmedai's choice reminded me of my own.

"You need a shirt, my prince," Gwen whispered. "The humans will be… distracted."

He took in his chiseled physique with a shrug. "Right."

A white shirt that left little to the imagination appeared, and he looked to Gwen for approval. She merely nodded, but the flush in her cheeks said it all. His appearance combined with his unconcealed power had invited the Succubus out to play.

Maybe she hadn't fed from Zeb after all. She looked too hungry.

Then what was that exchange about earlier?

"Shall we?" the Archdemon addressed Mietek.

"You never were one for planning," the Archangel replied dryly. "There are various factors to consider, including mortal lives to protect."

"So you suggest we plot our moves whilst the breach between realms grows?" Ashmedai spread out his hands and collapsed into the chaise again before waving the angel onward. "Please. Do get on with wasting my time, then."

Oh, I liked him. Cocky with a touch of humor, and he had treated my friend with respect. My kind of demon.

As if hearing my thoughts, he winked at me before settling his features into stoic lines and concentrating on the unamused Archangel standing next to me.

Mietek launched into the details he knew, thereby proving that Heaven did monitor activities on Earth. He mentioned Geier's location in Miami, touched on the demon trafficking, and also noted the current location of his son.

"He's projecting," he explained when I gave him a look at that last part. "You would feel it if you opened your mind. He's in immense pain."

"Pain?" I repeated, my mouth going dry. "What do you mean?"

"How do you think Geier is opening the gate?" His condescending tone pricked a nerve.

"I don't know, Mietek. I don't go around trying to create passageways to Hell."

His expression said my sarcasm didn't amuse him. Well, too fucking bad.

"Angel's blood, Evangeline," my father replied. "With a holy blade."

My gaze went to Zeb. "You gave the holy blade to Geier?"

His ironclad control slipped as both eyebrows shot upward. "You think me suicidal? The blade I own is still in my possession, and before you mention my time with Xai in Hell again, perhaps you can now consider the purpose. We both needed to know he could survive it, but I needed to be in the right frame of mind to test him properly."

"So you knew this was going to happen?" Fire licked through my veins as a cool dose of deception followed. "And neither of you thought it would be a good idea to tell me this? It could be *my* blood being used to open a gate right now!"

"Why do you think Xai accepted a position on Geier's

team?" Zeb tilted his head in the belittling way used to address a child. "Counterintelligence was only part of it, Evangeline. He offered his blood instead of yours, just as he always planned to do should the need arise, and arise it did."

"Yes, you've always been a problem for him," Mietek muttered. "Distracting his focus, and now he faces the ultimate sacrifice."

"You say that as if they've ever had a choice." My father's quiet tone captivated me as it always did. "We both know that was never the case, Mietek. They are destined for this together."

The Archangel gave my father a withering look. "Fate's whispers are not destiny, Azrael."

"Perhaps you should try talking to her more," my father suggested. "She's your mate, after all."

"Apologies, but are you going to get to the point soon? I'm dying of boredom over here." Ashmedai had another bowl in his lap, this time blackberries. He popped one into his mouth as he added, "I'm still waiting on a plan, unless allowing the Son of Chaos to die is our plan?"

"They're going to kill him?" A touch of hysteria underscored my words.

I couldn't lose Xai.

Not after everything we'd been through.

I hated him at times, but I loved him more.

Always.

My soul couldn't survive without him.

Ashmedai set the bowl aside and stood again. "The Archangel's progeny will die if we all continue to waste time by discussing what we already know. We can reseal the gate with our blood, Mietek. Just as we did millennia ago. Then it will be up to Zebulon and the others of this realm to clean up the mess. I don't see what more there is to 'plan.' "

"If we are not careful, closing the portal will kill innocents," Mietek replied.

"Innocents will continue to die until we reseal the

underworld," Ashmedai countered. "But, as always, the choice is yours." That last bit was said with an edge. These two clearly had history.

"He's right," I said before Mietek could argue. "They've already started unleashing creatures on this plane who shouldn't be here. I've faced a few of them over the last week, including a Pestilence demon who is still here."

Ashmedai did not look amused by that at all. "Geier will pay for this with his life."

I gave Zeb an expectant look. If he didn't admit to the other culprit in this mess, I would. Because I owed Kalida nothing.

"It seems my daughter may be involved as well," he admitted. "She faked her own death and framed Evangeline, but it appears she's very much alive and working with Geier."

"I see," was all Ashmedai said, but his expression implied they would be discussing that in more detail later. Zeb acknowledged the verdict with a slight nod.

"We need to go." My father's tone held a note of urgency that echoed Mietek's and Ashmedai's expressions.

Something has happened, I realized, but I didn't—

A sharp pain struck my chest, shoving me backward into the wall.

It came from nowhere and everywhere at once, flooding my thoughts with a sense of doom that left me shaking.

I barely registered Gwen screaming my name above the chaos raping my mind.

Reality fragmented and pieced itself back together.

Black and white.

So cold.

Alone.

I shivered.

It burns.

Ice mingled with lava in my veins.

"...drawing energy..." Mietek's voice. Fractured.

Nonsensical. "…now."

Darkness overwhelmed the light.

My stomach churned.

I'm sorry… Xai's voice.

Imagined or real?

I love you.

Always.

Forever.

Everything appeared in a blink of an eye, washing away the voices and sensations.

My body warmed.

Heated.

Too hot.

The pain subsided.

My eyes fogged before clearing to reveal my surroundings. It took several seconds for me to understand.

I was not in Zeb's bedroom but in Miami.

We're back in the shipping yard.

And all Hell had broken loose.

Literally.

CHAPTER TWENTY-EIGHT

DEATH STOLE MY SARCASM

SMOKE.

Fire.

Brimstone.

Demons.

"Fuck," I whispered.

I'd landed on top of a shipping container in the middle of chaos. My father, Mietek, and Ashmedai were nowhere to be seen. But the ground was littered with demons fighting humans.

No.

Not quite humans.

Nephilim.

I recognized Shane's blond head. He appeared to be shooting bullets with an excellent aim. The demons were exploding into ash upon impact, indicating his weapons contained silver. Had I been in a proper frame of mind, I may have questioned that little detail more, but the headache splitting my brain in half forced me to focus my energy elsewhere.

My eyes danced over the crowd as I tested my balance. Something had knocked me off-kilter, and someone had dropped me here in the process.

The pain had been so abrupt, so confusing and heartfelt, and… "Xai!"

I started at a dead run, my soul guiding my feet as I moved. My knives dropped into my hands, slicing and dicing demons as I flew through the shipping yard on instinct.

It couldn't be too late.

He'd better not leave me.

But even as I put all my effort into getting there, I knew.

My soul felt him slipping from my grasp.

Tears streamed down my cheeks as I forced myself toward him even faster. It would hurt later, but I didn't care. He needed me.

Flames licked at my skin.

The stench of sulfur threatened to dissuade me, to slow me down, but I refused to allow it to consume me.

I stabbed something twice and kept going, even when my stomach heaved and my mind shuddered.

It would not be too late.

There.

Blue and purple danced in the distance, a sphere of molten death.

The gate.

Demons poured out in droves, scattering onto Earth like an army of ants and right into some sort of force field my father had created. It zapped them to the ground, where they writhed in agony. I fed off that pain and allowed it to bolster me just enough to dash through the portal into the one realm I hated.

Xai lay just inside, his dying form on a black rock. Kalida and Geier were nowhere to be seen. Not that I looked hard. My eyes were only for my lover. I fell to his side, my hands cradling his blood-drained face. The holy blade pinned his wrist to the Earth. I yanked it out with what remained of my energy and sheathed it against my forearm.

"Wake up," I begged, crying in earnest. "Don't you fucking leave me like this!"

Nothing.

No response.

No heartbeat.

I started to drag him toward the gate, but something struck me hard in the shoulder. It hissed upon impact and scattered agony down my arm.

"I should have known," Geier said as he stepped out of the shadows. "Needless to say, I suspected it. Xai loved you for millennia, but I wasn't about to turn down his sacrifice. His Archangel blood is more powerful than yours."

I ducked just in time to dodge his next throw. "I'm going to take great pleasure in killing you," I whispered.

A wave of energy overcame me as my soul came to life with a vengeance.

Killed.

Mate.

Die.

I screamed.

All the pain, frustration, and love built into it and unleashed, and along with it came a side of me I rarely let take over.

Death.

My mind clouded with single-minded focus, and the world became Geier.

Revenge.

Pain.

Evil.

I leapt at him, weapons drawn, and ignored the pain in my shoulder as I sliced at his face, hands, arms. He wasn't weak like most demons, but strong and fierce, and fought hard to protect himself.

Blood, sweat, and tears covered my face as every angelic cell I possessed went into taking him down.

And he laughed.

Enjoying my weakened form on this plane, he cooed sweet nothings that only a sadist with no remorse would say.

His knife ended up at my throat as he pinned me to the ground, and I went still. Not out of fear or exhaustion, but to look him in the eyes. I wanted to watch him die.

Because someone had joined me.

And he would finish the job.

"Your life is forfeit," I growled.

"Is it?" He grinned, and menace poured out of him.

"It is," my father replied as he drove a blade into Geier's head from above.

I tried to smile at the look of horror on the man's face, but my soul refused. Even as his body froze from the silver touching his brain, I shoved him from me to crawl back to Xai.

So pale.

No breath.

Still no pulse.

I buried my face into his neck and sobbed. "No!" If he left me, I'd kill him again in the afterlife.

My hands curled into fists around his ripped shirt, and I used all my strength to drag him with me to the gate. Fighting ensued around me. My father had left his post outside the gate to help me, and the demons were taking advantage. But he fought them with a precision I envied, giving me the time I needed to pull Xai back onto Earth, where I covered him with my body in the only form of protection I could give.

"Damn you!" I cried and beat his chest fruitlessly.

No response.

Not even a smirk.

Every drop of blood had been drained from Xai's body by a holy blade.

Recovering from that…

251

No. I refused to think about it.

I couldn't.

Not now.

"We need to close it!" I heard Ashmedai shout.

"Get inside!" Mietek demanded as he appeared near my side, his focus on the Archdemon.

My father appeared again, covered in demon gore, his expression exuberant from the fight. It only made me cry harder.

Never had I felt so weak.

So broken.

So alone.

"We need you, Evangeline." My father's soft tones came from above. "You need to help us close the gate."

I stared up at him. "I can't."

"You can."

"Xai—"

"Made the ultimate sacrifice, and it will all be for naught if you don't get up here and help us fight." The sternness in his tone fractured my heart in two. One half lay with Xai, the other with duty and honor. "This is your destiny, child."

I shook my head, confused, hurt, and torn between two worlds. I only ever wanted the angel beneath. Everything else was fun and enjoyment. *Selfish indulgence.*

Death littered the container park, threatening to spread beyond.

The human plane is at risk.

An angel's purpose on Earth was to protect humanity from harm.

I continued to fail them every moment that I mourned.

My lips found Xai's, touching them too briefly as I allowed a final tear to decorate his cheek. Then I climbed to my feet, determination simmering in my blood.

Mietek and my father continued to fight as Zeb and Ashmedai slipped into Hell. I palmed two fresh blades and fed off the lethal air as I killed everything that stepped into my path.

"Now!" Mietek shouted over the roar of noise. His bloodied hands marked the Earth, not the force field, and I followed suit with my father while the Archangel murmured in the ancient language.

Electricity and ethereal energy mingled in the air, creating rain and ice to fall from the sky. Each bead of moisture weakened the fiery orb before us, shrinking the gaping hole until it resembled a small sphere that sparked and ebbed.

A tendril of purple smoke slithered out just as the hole popped and disappeared.

Mietek collapsed in exhaustion, my father with him, but I felt nothing.

No pain.

No fatigue.

Just empty.

He's dead.

Zeb and Ashmedai appeared with two unconscious demons in their arms. They dropped the bodies unceremoniously at their feet.

"Gather them all," Ashmedai demanded. He had swapped his board shorts for the sapphire robes, giving him a regal flair that demanded respect.

"My prince," voices spoke in unison as demons appeared out of nowhere.

The Royal Guard, I realized. An elite class of demons who protected Hell's princes. They were known for their lethality and precision, and he'd summoned them to help with the cleanup.

I slid over to Xai to stand guard over his body as the minions dragged wounded demons over to Ashmedai. Several of the Nephilim walked over as well. Shane spotted me and started forward, only to stop when he saw who lay at my feet. His expression broke at the sight, further driving the knife through my lifeless heart.

He's gone.

"Wake them." Ashmedai's command was for Zeb.

The Demonic Lord complied by yanking the silver daggers from Kalida and Geier's skulls and handing the weapons to the Archdemon. They didn't even sizzle in his open palm. A show of power. Silver didn't harm Hell's princes, just as it didn't hurt angels.

"Earth is under the dominion of the high council, a committee composed of royalty from both realms. Today we have witnessed the most serious treason. Violating the veil between worlds is punishable to the highest degree." Ashmedai continued in the language of Hell, addressing all the wounded demons while he waited for Kalida and Geier to regain consciousness.

I knelt beside Xai, desperate for his touch, and flinched at the ice coating his skin. In all my years, I'd never witnessed an angel's death. The fact that it had to be Xai's…

A choked sound came from my throat, and I muffled it by pressing my face into his neck, breathing in his remaining scent as if to hold on to it forever.

The world around me melted away.

My soul slipped into memories.

Stolen kisses.

Loving games in the sky.

Chasing each other in circles.

Endless quarrels.

I would give anything to go back, to hear his cryptic words and argue over something trivial. Like working for Zeb.

Fuck.

We'd wasted so much time. So many years fighting, arguing over frivolous things. His high-handed behavior no longer mattered.

How could I be mad at a corpse?

I curled my fists into his shirt and fought the tremor that ravaged my body.

To think of him in such a way…

How could you do this to me? I wanted to yell to the Heavens at the unfairness of it all, but he brought it on himself. By sheltering me as he always did. He'd never learned, even in the end, that I didn't require his protection. All I ever wanted was his love.

And I had it. For a brief time, he'd allowed me to see it, but it wasn't enough. I needed more.

The angel inside of me fluttered helplessly, and I freed her to mourn. To fly in the stars, searching for the one she would never find.

A part of me died in that moment.

Lost forever.

To eternal rest.

"Please..." A woman's voice broke into my thoughts like nails on a chalkboard. Kalida had fallen to her father's feet to beg for his mercy.

"My daughter died," he replied coldly. "I don't know who you are, but you are no progeny of mine." The dismissive nature of his words spurred something inside of me.

"You," I whispered, and all eyes turned to me. "You did this." I found my footing and stalked toward her, knife drawn. My control had long since fallen by the wayside, and I couldn't give two fucks about formalities or right and wrong. "Whose idea was it to frame me? Was it yours or Geier's?"

A starry night stared up at me, those Succubus eyes so alluring and yet so deadly. I wanted to carve them from her pretty little head and squish them under my boots. She cast a demure gaze at Ashmedai.

"Don't look at him. I'm asking you the question." I yanked on her hair to force her gaze back to mine. "Tell me."

She swallowed.

Good.

She should be nervous.

"M-mine." Her whisper-soft answer sent adrenaline pumping through my veins, but I withheld the urge to react violently. Not yet.

"Why?" I demanded. Her purpose for hurting Zeb I understood; he killed her mother, and she clearly sought revenge. But why me, and why Xai?

"Jealousy," Ashmedai murmured, answering for the quivering demon. "How adorably human, Kalida, envying an angel's relationship with your father."

Kalida's eyes rolled into the back of her head during his deep dive into her psyche. It probably hurt to have her mind ripped open by a Prince of Hell. She deserved so much worse.

"You used a rusty old blade and left a messy scene behind." Some maniacal part of me tsked, and a laugh that sounded nothing like mine followed it. Because the whole scene was insane. "And you thought you would get away with it? By pitting your father against me? He knows my skills better than that."

I shoved her away and stepped back. Killing her wasn't even worth my time or effort. My blade in her heart would be an honorable way to die, and she didn't deserve that.

Geier knelt a few paces away, head down, shoulders caved inward.

"Such a sad picture," I said, more to myself than to anyone else. "A Demonic Lord brought to his knees. You were never worthy of this territory, let alone this plane. I hope you rot in Hell for all eternity."

So much for my innate desire to seek vengeance.

I couldn't honor them in such a way.

Ever.

My father nodded in understanding, while Mietek appeared torn by the decision.

I returned to my lover, my forehead falling to his as I willed him to breathe again. My angelic soul had yet to return.

Perhaps with her went my desire to kill.

Perhaps it was all in my head.

Shattered summed up my being.

I never thought I would be that woman who relied on a man, but my bond with Xai surpassed all understanding. We were joined together on a plane of existence that prevailed for very few, and to lose him... It forfeited my right to breathe.

My face found his neck again as my arms wrapped around him.

Home.

That's what I wanted, what I *needed.*

To take him home. One last time. To the field of flowers and warmth, where our wings joined as one.

I craved the ability to fly.

Just one more time…

CHAPTER TWENTY-NINE

ONE FINAL DANCE
AMONG THE CLOUDLESS SKY

THE SUN STROKED THE SKIN OF MY BACK, willing my body to reheat, but I ignored the sensation in favor of the ice beneath me. I clung to him with all my worth as my body shook.

On some level, I understood that I'd lost it. That I was sobbing uncontrollably on the outside as I cocooned myself in a world that no longer existed.

I sank deep within that dream as I strove for the one place that always made me happy.

And when I opened my eyes, I was surrounded by the golds and bronzes that I remembered.

A gorgeous azure sky hung overhead, flowers pebbled around me, and violet feathers cushioned my back. Xai rested beside me, his midnight wings edged with silver.

I rolled onto him, peppering his jaw with kisses,

longing to spend just one final memory with him. Even if it wasn't real.

"I love you," I whispered. "Time will never change that."

Eyes the color of onyx blinked up at me, clearly as if in a daze. "Eve?" His hoarse voice hurt my heart.

"Shh…" I nuzzled his cheekbone and sighed as his chest rose beneath me. "I need this. I'll go back soon. But not yet."

Or ever, my soul threatened.

Maybe.

Heaven could send another angel to watch Earth. Xai had more than served his purpose, and I'd already given up so much of my own life. My father mentioned humanity being my destiny, but what if I didn't want it?

That's selfish.

I know.

Just give me a few minutes of peace.

Xai's fingertips danced along my wings, sending a shiver down my spine. It felt so real.

"I've missed these," he marveled. "You're so beautiful, Eve."

A tear slipped from my eye. Because none of this was actually happening. And his words proved it.

He caught the water droplet with his thumb and sucked it into his mouth before maneuvering me onto my back with him on top. "What happened, love? Why are we here?"

More moisture pooled behind my lids, leaking from the corners. He traced them with his tongue and pressed the tenderest of kisses against my temple. "Talk to me, sweetheart."

"You died," I whispered. "You're dead."

His chuckle vibrated my empty chest. "I don't feel very dead."

"Because I'm daydreaming." I trembled beneath the emotional onslaught and worried that it would wake me from my final moments of bliss.

His tongue parted my lips, seeking deep entry in that

way I loved.

I gave myself up to his possession, allowing him to own my mind, body, and soul, and said to hell with propriety. He would always hold dominion over me, and I no longer cared. Because I held the same power over him.

Equals.

Lovers.

Mates.

"Evangeline…" He palmed my cheeks to angle my head for a more thorough embrace, and I let him. My legs cradled his hips, accepting his weight as his hard body aligned fully with mine.

One more time.

I ignored the small voice in my head trying to sprout reason and put every ounce of energy I possessed into our kiss. His lips left mine for my chin before trailing down the column of my neck to the top of my tank top.

He slowed his pace and traced the tips of my cleavage with his tongue. The fabric fell away, having already been ripped by the wings at my back—something I would evaluate later—and then my nipple was sucked deep into the cavern of his mouth. I arched into him, craving more and missing his teeth.

"What are you doing?" I asked, confused by this gentle side of him.

He switched to my other breast, peppering kisses along the way.

"Adoring you…" He placed an open-mouthed kiss on my stiff peak and laved it to the point of ecstasy before sliding down to where his hands were removing my jeans.

"Cherishing you…" He licked a path from my belly button to the apex between my thighs. My jeans slipped down past my ankles, where he kicked them off with my panties, leaving me naked beneath him.

"Worshiping you," he whispered against my sensitive folds. The hot air from his mouth preceded his intimate kiss, sending shock waves of pleasure through my limbs. It startled an agonized moan from my chest.

No one knew my body the way Xai did.

No one would ever replace him.

And oh, that spot...

His finger had slid inside me to play while his tongue memorized my sex. It left me delirious beneath him and unable to focus on anything other than what he was doing to me.

A multitude of sensations tingled inside my lower abdomen.

It felt like torture. It felt amazing.

"Loving you," he said in a low murmur that vibrated my sensitive flesh. I had no idea what he was referring to, but my brain stopped thinking.

I sat on the brink of something powerful.

Electric.

Orgasmic.

"Mmm, that's it." He nibbled my folds teasingly before giving me a deep lick that ended where I needed him most. "Let go, Evangeline."

He sank his teeth into my clit at the exact moment ecstasy slammed into my gut, forcing me off the ground. With his hand on my abdomen, he pushed me back to the grass as he consumed my pleasure with his mouth. I shook beneath him from both the realization that this would never happen again and the intensity of the moment.

His clothes disappeared, revealing a body far paler than usual but still as powerful as I remembered.

"I want to fly, Evangeline." He lifted me onto him, his cock sinking into my trembling heat as I wrapped my legs around him. "Fly with me."

My wings responded to the command as we took off into the crystal horizon, his powerful feathers propelling us skyward while mine steadied our ascent. He kissed my neck as he moved, his happiness branding me deep inside.

We hadn't made love like this in so long... I had almost forgotten how intense and beautiful it felt. Soaring through the cloudless sky without a care for anyone or anything else, just our souls mating on the most devoted of levels.

"I've missed this," he whispered against my mouth.

"Me too." I fought the tears this time and lived in the moment, with him, cherished and at peace. My arms wove around his neck, my fingers threading in his luscious hair as I parted his lips with my tongue. He let me guide our kiss as he gently rocked into me below.

This was not about lust but about passion.

An eternity of promises and love.

I allowed myself to believe it was real, if only for a moment, and lost myself in his embrace.

Hours, maybe even days, passed as we flew at our leisure.

I lost track of the orgasms between us.

They didn't matter.

The bond was what held us together, what allowed our souls to flourish.

"I never want this to end," I admitted.

"Then it won't," he replied.

I longed to believe that.

He silenced reality with a devastating kiss that went on for a limitless time. My body writhed against his, seeking the friction it desired, and I came undone among the stars later that night. His body followed mine, shaking with emotion and pleasure, and still we flew.

Until Heaven's moons dipped in the sky and the sun peeked again. Xai's forehead rested against mine. "They're summoning us."

Yes, I expected that. They would only allow me to dream for so long.

"I wish we could ignore them," I whispered. "Forever."

He chuckled as we began our descent to reality. "We will always find moments to ignore them."

"Promise?" It came out choked with emotion.

"Always," he repeated. "I'll never leave you again, Evangeline. I vow it."

I wished to believe him, but deep down, I knew the

truth. "I love you, Xai. I always will."

"And I love you, darling." He pressed his lips to mine before settling us onto the field where it all began.

We were twenty angel years old the first day we kissed. Right here. In this very spot. And as his mouth caressed mine, I couldn't help but find it a fitting place for us to say our final goodbye.

I held on to him so tightly, terrified of the moment when I would no longer feel him again, but his skin never left mine. It felt so warm and real beneath my fingertips. Such a cruel trick from my imagination.

"You're trembling, Evangeline."

I nodded against him. "I don't want to say goodbye."

He ran his fingers over the tender spot between my shoulder blades where my wings attached. "I don't either, but we'll have to eventually."

"I know," I whispered.

"But maybe we can negotiate a few weeks home before we return to Earth." His suggestion sounded heartfelt and oh-so real that it pricked at my heart. I shook against him, unable to hold myself together any longer, and his strong arms were all that kept me from collapsing.

"I can't do this without you. Don't ask me to." A moment of true weakness, one I had avoided for so long, but I couldn't hide from it anymore. I would never be whole without him. "I can't."

"What are you going on about?" He lifted my chin, forcing me to meet his gaze, and a sudden wave of understanding lit his features. "You think this is all a dream."

"It is a dream. A beautiful one that I don't want to wake from. Nothing will be the same without you."

"You would still be my powerful, strong, resilient Evangeline." He brushed his knuckles over my cheek and smiled. "The same one who managed to portal both of us to our favorite memory in a moment of grief. All these millennia of trying to force you home and it took my near death to do it." He chuckled and shook his head. "I should have known."

"What do you mean?" My fog-ridden brain wanted to read into his words, but my heart refused. It couldn't handle any more trauma.

"Did my body turn to stone, love?"

I nodded. "You were so cold."

"But did I turn into marble?"

I pulled back to look at him. "Stop being ridiculous." Even in my dreams, the bastard spoke in riddles.

"Angels turn to marble when they die. It's not common, and you've clearly not seen it happen, but that's how our bodies process death. Geier brought me to the brink, but our bond brought me back." He cupped the back of my neck.

"I do owe you an apology for my methods. It took the last of my energy to break through your walls and absorb enough strength from you to survive." He grimaced. "I also owe you an apology for not being all that forthcoming on the plan, I suppose."

"If you're trying to convince me that this is real, then you're doing a horrible job of it. The Xai I know never apologizes." And it sort of pissed me off that my made-up version of him did. At least leave me with a bit of anger to hold on to when I needed to grieve.

"That's because I'm usually right; however, in these two instances, I was not. I thought you understood my intentions, but I realized too late that was not the case. By then, I could do nothing but push forward, much to the detriment of us both. And forcing myself into your mind…" He lowered his forehead to mine. "I want to regret it, but I'm too thankful to wholeheartedly apologize. Did I hurt you?"

"You threw her into a wall," a sharp voice stated from nearby. "Knocked the wind from her, but she woke up in time to help us fight."

Xai's grip tightened on my neck. "Father," he greeted through gritted teeth. "I assume you've come to berate me again?"

"No, but I brought you some clothes," the Archangel

replied, and I swore I heard a grin in his voice.

Xai dragged himself away to grab the robes Mietek held for us. We donned the gold-and-white fabric in silence. My brain worked through the events, translating our conversation and this new development.

Is he really alive?

No.

Maybe.

It hurts too much to hope.

"Now, how are you feeling?" Mietek asked as he clapped his son on the back.

"Like I almost died," Xai replied dryly.

"You did." His father narrowed his gaze. "Agreeing to help Geier was a stupid thing to do."

"It was the only thing to do."

"Perhaps. Calling in the Genesis was a good idea, though. They more than proved themselves as worthy assets to our cause." Mietek sounded pleased by that.

Xai gave him a look. "Yes, you've all bred perfect little soldiers." He wrapped his arm around my shoulders and hugged me close. "Is this the point where you tell me I have to go back?"

"No. Azrael agreed to stay and monitor the situation while you recovered. He seems to be enjoying training the Nephilim in the art of war and death," Mietek mused. "Your father has taken a specific liking to Trudy. She's quite talented."

I frowned. "They didn't return her to her family?"

Mietek's amusement left him. "Kalida used a Scrubber on the girl's family, erasing her from their memories. Shane took her in as his own, but Azrael insists on providing her training. You know how he gets when he senses potential."

"She's in for an intriguing upbringing," Xai replied, grinning.

Trickles of thought threatened my psyche.

This has to be real.

You're creative, but this is beyond your skills.

Thanks.

LEXI C. FOSS

"How long do we have here?" Xai asked, his tone serious again.

"Three weeks," he replied. "I suggest you enjoy it."

"If you're trying to imply that Eve is staying here, then think again. You saw what she did. We're more powerful together."

Mietek eyed me curiously. "Yes, how did you manage to portal yourself and Xai back here without help? We had to wake the Portal Dweller to move you from Chicago to Miami, yet you managed to return here unassisted. And you expedited Xai's healing process as well."

Meaning he's alive. Unless my brain had fabricated this entire exchange.

Do I dare to believe?

I shivered despite the heat and focused on Mietek's query regarding how I moved us here. Something I shouldn't have been able to do, or didn't realize I could do, until now. Assuming this was real.

It has to be.

Xai caressed my wing with his, adding his unspoken support.

A show of solidarity.

Love.

I cleared my throat, but my words held a raspy note to them as I replied, "I dreamed of coming home, to spend one last night with Xai."

"Ah, because you thought he was dead. Angels don't die that easily, though Xai came admirably close."

"Admirably," Xai scoffed. "Your choice of word does not mirror mine."

Mietek continued as if his son hadn't spoken. "I'm glad to have some understanding, as I wondered at your bizarre behavior on Earth, Evangeline. Ashmedai would have allowed you to kill both Kalida and Geier, and yet you chose not to." He shrugged. "Oh well, you essentially subjected them to a worse fate at the hands of a pissed-off Archdemon, and Ashmedai can be quite inventive with his justice. I suspect after a few centuries of torture,

266

they'll die anticlimactically."

"It's more than they deserve," Xai added flatly. "If Geier hadn't immediately stuck me with a holy blade upon arriving in Miami, I would have killed the bastard myself. As it was, I barely had the energy to text my location to Shane."

So that's why the Nephilim were at the shipping yard. The clever bastard had considered every angle of the plan.

Assuming this is real.

It is.

"Oh, that reminds me." Mietek pulled one of the offending weapons from his pocket. "I found this among Eve's clothes you removed in the field, and I managed to retrieve the other from Zebulon, but we need to determine how they procured them to begin with."

"A task for my return to Earth?" Xai guessed.

"Or something to delegate to the Genesis."

Xai arched a brow. "Excuse me?"

"Oh, don't tell me you still haven't realized?" His father grinned. "Leading them is your destiny, Son. As it is yours now too, Evangeline."

"You sound like my mother," Xai said, amused.

Another smile from the Archangel. "I do, don't I? Someone suggested that I talk to her a little more, and I did. Speaking of, she'd like to meet with you for dinner later." With that, he turned around to leave. "Enjoy your three weeks. Azrael will be anxious for your return by then, but I suspect cleaning up Geier's demonic mess on Earth will keep him and the Nephilim busy in the interim. Two decades on Earth is a long time, after all."

That evoked a laugh from me and Xai, one that Mietek didn't hear over the rustle of his wings. He took off in a flurry of black and brown feathers, leaving us alone in our field.

"Still think I'm dead, love?" Xai mused as he turned me to face him. "Or do you require more convincing?"

I stared up into his midnight irises as my heart beat an unhealthy rhythm against my rib cage. Heat rolled off of him in waves, caressing my skin and soothing my spirit.

The angel inside me rested at ease with the truth, while only my mind considered reason.

"If this is all a dream, I'm going to wake up angry," I admitted.

He smirked. "Good. Your temper translates well to the bedroom."

"You're such an ass." But that answer was certainly one I expected from him. *He's alive.*

"That will never change, darling."

"Good. Your asshole tendencies make me want to stab you, and you know how much I enjoy that."

He grinned. "Flirt."

I brushed my lips against his jaw and luxuriated in the stubble there.

A shudder ruffled my feathers, one born of memories and the realization that I hadn't lost him. Whatever issues we had, they were in the past. Maintaining grudges would only hold us back, and life was too valuable to fret over old wounds. We still had several kinks to work out, but we had eternity to do it.

Because he was alive.

Here.

In Heaven.

Holding me.

I pinched my side in one final attempt to convince myself of the veracity of my thoughts, and Xai laughed. Because my doubt was ridiculous. My soul would have wilted and died without him, and yet I felt her floating happily inside me, lost in the contentedness of the moment, loving her mate.

I didn't lose him.

"Mmm, I see you do require more convincing," he teased. "Fancy a little sparring?" His gaze smoldered as he looked me over, leaving little to the imagination of how he wanted our fight to end.

"You're insatiable."

"Only with you, Eve." He nuzzled my neck and pressed a kiss against my pulse. "I meant what I said, darling. I'm not leaving. Ever."

"And the bit about improved communication?"

"Hmm…" His lips brushed my ear. "I may need some convincing on that."

I tried to pull away, but he held me against him. "Almost dying wasn't enough?"

"Touché." He nipped my earlobe. "I'll work on my 'crypticness,' as you call it."

"You really want me to draw blood."

He shrugged. "I'm up for a rougher dance if you are."

I responded by trying to swipe his legs out from under him, but he used his wings to balance in the air.

"Catch me, Evangeline." He took off in a gust of wind that left me smiling in his wake.

CHAPTER THIRTY

A SUCCUBUS AND A NEPHILIM—
HEAVENS, I'M TOO OLD FOR THIS

Twenty-One Earth Years Later

GWEN.

She couldn't see me yet and didn't know to expect me.

Three weeks in Heaven felt like little time compared to her two decades on Earth.

A shadow of goodness still radiated from her, pleasing my heart, but secrets lurked in her aura now. Memories we would never share because I'd left her.

Life was all about choices, and I'd chosen Xai over growing with my best friend. She'd moved on the way most did in these situations, but our friendship still felt fresh to me with my convoluted timeline.

"Do you think she still has plans for my balls?" Xai

wondered from beside me, his hands tucked casually into the pockets of his black pants. He'd insisted on purchasing a new suit as soon as we recovered from our Fall back to Earth. The transition had felt smoother this time, but it still stung. At least I knew we possessed the ability to return if we wanted to, just not for over two Earth decades again. So much had changed in our absence, including my best friend.

"What do I say to her?" I asked, ignoring his attempt at humor. I'd left her at a crucial time without any explanation.

Xai settled his arm around my shoulders and pressed his lips to my temple. "You tell her that you missed her."

Gwen laughed heartily at something the auburn-haired man across from her said. His back was to us, but I gathered from their candor that he was a friend, not a usual conquest.

"Come on, love. Nervousness doesn't become you."

"She's my best friend. Or *was*, anyway."

"Time may add distance, but true friendships never die, Evangeline." Another kiss on my temple followed by a sharp smack to my ass. "Move. We have two other stops on the reunion tour tonight, and you insisted on this being our first stop."

I glared up at him. The word *ass* lingered on my tongue, but I swallowed it. No amount of time would ever change his mannerisms. Xai wasn't exactly the tamable type, something I would always adore about him.

"Fine," I said instead and opened the door to the small Tennessee diner. It was located about thirty miles from our old home, suggesting Gwen had chosen to stay in the area throughout the years.

The handful of patrons inside all glanced up expectantly, similar to that first night Xai had strolled into my bar. The irony wasn't lost on me. Round cerulean eyes met mine, flaring at the edges, before Gwen sprung from her seat and threw her arms around my neck.

I hugged her back just as fiercely and startled as a pair of familiar green eyes met mine over the booth.

The man hadn't aged a day.

"Gleason?" I had planned to track him down in some lecture hall over the next few days, but here he sat in a diner with my best friend. "What are you doing here?"

His eyebrows shot up. "What am *I* doing here? Shouldn't I be asking you that question?" He smiled, then nodded at Xai. "It's been a long time."

"Indeed," my dark angel replied.

I pulled away from Gwen to look between the two men. "Wait, how do you know Gleason?"

"Your silver maker?" Xai translated. "He's part of the Genesis, darling. Has been for several decades."

"What?" I gaped at Gleason. "Why didn't you tell me?"

He shrugged. "Honestly? I wanted to see how long it took you to figure it out, and apparently, several decades is the answer."

"You're a Nephilim."

"And there you go."

I shook my head at his condescending tone, then stopped as I realized another connection. "You made the silver bullets the Genesis used at the shipyard that day..."

"Yep," he replied.

"And you're friends with Gwen now?"

"He's sort of my roommate." Gwen shook her head somewhat sadly. "A lot has happened since I saw you last, Eve."

Guilt sliced through my chest. "I'm sorry—"

"Don't apologize. Lord Zebulon explained what happened, and I understand. Xai's the other half of your soul." Her lips pursed. "Well, he's certainly the blacker part, but we can't choose our mates, I suppose."

Xai grinned. "I'm happy to see you still adore me, Guinevere."

She snorted. "You know I think Eve deserves better, but at least you didn't leave her underground this time."

"Actually..." I glanced up at him. "You did."

"With protection," he added.

"But you still left me bound to a chair in Hell."

He palmed the back of my neck. "With a key," he murmured. "A pair of handcuffs and two Guardians is a walk in the park for you."

"True, but Hell's realms weren't."

"Had you waited for Tax and Remy, it would have been a nonissue. But, as always, you chose impatience over practicality." He nipped at my bottom lip. "Someday you'll learn."

"I'll master patience when you master communication."

He grinned against my mouth. "Sounds like a plan, love." His kiss felt more like a promise, one he pulled away from all too soon.

My body went rigid as a demonic presence other than Gwen's tickled my senses. "Aw, do you think they came to welcome us home?" I asked, batting my eyes playfully.

Amusement radiated off Xai even as his expression clouded over. "I do believe we're about to be summoned."

"Zeb?"

He lifted his shoulder in a partial shrug as if to say, *Does it matter?* Because no, it didn't.

"Looks like our reunion is going to have to wait, Gwen." I gave her a small smile. "I've missed you."

"I missed you too, Eve," she said with another hug. "But I've been okay. Lord Zebulon and Zane have taught me a lot about control, and you'd be proud. I use the gardening sheets when the need arises, which, fortunately, is not often anymore."

I laughed despite the morbid topic. "Yeah? Did you run out of rugs?"

She bit her lip. "Maybe. But seriously, you were right about them being useful. So much less…" She trailed off. "Well, you get it. But we need to catch up soon. I sort of sold your bar and our house…"

"I figured." We would have had to move by now anyway to avoid detection. "But I want to know more about Zeb helping you master your control?" I couldn't help the question in my voice because, uh, what?

Her cheeks flushed a pretty pink as she ducked her head. "Uh, yeah." She cleared her throat. "It's actually, well, because of you. And that text you sent all those years ago, which, I guess, is weeks for you. Anyway, when I showed up to deliver your message, he noticed my energy levels were off and commented on my behavior in the region. Apparently, we weren't as stealthy as we thought."

I looked sharply at Xai, who was smirking. "You told him anyway?"

"No, he already knew. But you can thank me later for requesting that he not intervene. I told him you had the situation handled."

"You implied that you'd tell him if I didn't go to Miami."

"Indeed. It was the perfect bargaining chip."

I gaped at him. "You're unbelievable."

"Thank you, love. Now, shall we go? I do believe our escort outside is getting antsy, and it would be a shame to jeopardize such a pleasant establishment." The sarcasm in his tone indicated he wouldn't mind seeing the place remodeled in demon blood. Some things never changed.

I'd never met anyone who infuriated me like Xai. And I wouldn't replace him for the world.

I grabbed him and kissed him hard. It was either that or stab him, and murder was frowned upon on Earth.

His lips curled. "Mmm, I do like where this is headed."

"Yeah? We'll need to stop by my armory first. Assuming it still exists?" I sent that last question to Gleason, who sat with his lanky arms sprawled out on the booth.

"I've kept it safe, even from the Genesis. They prefer bullets over knives."

"Excellent. Bill me whatever."

"Already have, angel."

I laughed. Of course he had. "Gwen, we're catching up properly later. Girls' night?"

"Absolutely."

"Good. See you soon." I gave her another hug before grabbing Xai's hand. "We're going to need a Scrubber," I muttered as we passed a handful of confused humans. They'd all overheard our conversations thanks to the silence in the diner.

"Yes, Gleason will handle it."

I paused at the door and pitched my voice low. "The Genesis works with demons now?"

"Only the good ones," Xai replied.

Is there such a thing? I wondered but refrained from saying it out loud. Because I knew decent underworld beings could exist. Gwen was one, and Remy and Tax were too. And maybe even Zeb, though that remained to be seen. If he did help Gwen rather than punish her, I might be inclined to like the bastard, at least a little.

Still… "A lot could have changed in two decades, Xai."

"Indeed, but I monitored the situation from above. They're well organized, and Azrael has guided them well in our absence."

My pulse jumped at the mention of my father. He would be our last stop of the night. I'd spent some time with my mother while home, but I had missed him terribly. I would always be his daughter first and foremost, a habit of the traits I had inherited from him.

Xai waved his hand over a sensor that opened the door automatically. Technology had more than taken over the plane in our absence. I couldn't wait to relearn how to drive. The new automobiles looked deliciously fast.

"Gentlemen," Xai greeted as we stepped outside. "To what do we owe the pleasure?"

No one appeared or replied, so I twirled a knife for show. "Perhaps we need to properly reintroduce ourselves," I suggested.

"I was hoping that wouldn't be necessary."

"Liar."

He chuckled. "A woman after my own heart."

"Always," I replied. "Shall we?"

"Stand down," a familiar voice commanded as Tax slipped into view, his expression bored. "Why are you here?"

My dark angel smiled. "What, you didn't miss me, old friend?"

"Not really," Tax said, but his grin stated otherwise.

"I did." Remy appeared in front of us with a welcoming expression. "Lord Zebulon, too, will be pleased you've returned. I'd take you to him, but it's punishment week, so he's in Hell."

Xai's smile slipped. "Has it worsened that much in my absence?"

"What?" The Portal Dweller appeared confused, then laughed. "Oh, no. It's not like that. It's *his* punishment week."

"I'm still not following," I admitted. "Whom is he punishing?"

"Kalida," Tax replied, sounding bored. "Every Earth year, he goes to the underworld for a week to watch Ashmedai's guard punish the former Ōrdinātum."

"A week in Earth time or Hell time?" Xai asked. An important distinction given how time varied between our places.

"Earth time," Remy murmured, his expression reserved.

Seven years in Hell, watching his child suffer. "Every year?"

Remy nodded, confirming my question.

"Shit," I whispered. His daughter had been unfaithful to her bloodline and deserved her fate, but Zeb? "Why?"

"Because his superiors consider the breach in this territory to be the fault of the Demonic Lord," Xai explained. "I can only imagine what they're doing to Geier."

Remy and Tax both shuddered, suggesting that they already knew.

I didn't ask.

Some things were too horrendous, especially with Hell involved.

"What's up with the welcoming party?" I asked,

changing to a friendlier subject.

"Curiosity," Remy replied.

"I sensed the bands." Tax nodded at Xai's wrists. "Only one person owns them." His gaze drifted to my ponytail, where a matching one held up my blonde hair. "Or I suppose two now." He didn't sound all that upset by it.

"So are you staying or visiting?" Remy asked.

"Staying," we replied at the same time. Xai linked his fingers through mine before adding, "Our purpose is here."

Tax cocked a brow. "Doing what?"

Xai smiled. "Keeping you in line since it's so clearly needed."

"Happy to see your sense of humor still exists," the Tracker replied. "Right. Well, before you task me with something I don't want to do, I'm going to head out. Call me when you want to have a drink, and it better not be in a fucking Miami hotel. I hate that city."

"Noted." Xai looked to Remy. "I don't suppose you could drop us off in Virginia?"

The Portal Dweller chuckled. "Back five minutes and already asking for favors."

"You showed up before I could call. Not that I have a telephone at the moment, but it's on the list."

Remy showed off his wrist. "It's all in the watch now. Say a name, the person's image appears… Never mind. We'll save the technology lesson. Where in Virginia?"

Xai gave an address for my father's residence and held out our joined hands. The Portal Dweller didn't hesitate. He grabbed hold of us and teleported us in less than a blink of an eye. My stomach rioted at the sensation, having only just recovered from our Fall back to Earth a few hours before. Unlike Mietek and my father, I couldn't just appear unfazed by losing wings again. Their ease with shedding feathers demonstrated a power greater than mine, proving that even the strongest of beings had superiors.

Except maybe Ashmadei.

"Let me know when you're ready for a territory tour. A lot has changed since you two went off to play in Heaven." Remy winked before disappearing, leaving Xai and I standing before a modest home in Alexandria.

The brick exterior and perfectly sculpted yard held my mother's touch. She'd left for hours at a time to spend weeks on Earth with my father, saying she enjoyed it here but preferred home. He would be returning to her side soon. Maybe even tonight.

A woman with soft brown ringlets opened the door before we could knock, a set of knives in her hands. I admired their craftsmanship before taking in her defensive stance.

"You must be one of the Nephilim," I mused. "My father's taught you some tricks."

Her full lips popped open as her body went still. "Eve?"

"That's what they call me."

She bounded off the stairs and threw her arms around me in a hug that nearly knocked me to the ground. Gwen's reaction I understood, but not this strange woman's. When she let me go and went after Xai in the same manner, my hands itched for weapons of my own, but he merely laughed at her exuberance and patted her back in an awkward manner.

"I see your enthusiasm hasn't changed, Trudy."

"I go by Tru now, actually," she corrected. "And I'm sorry. That was terribly unprofessional of me, but I can't believe you're here! I haven't seen you in…" Her brow pinched. "Twenty-one years?"

"Wait…" I looked over her athletic form and felt my eyes inch upward. "You're…" *The cherub-faced Nephilim.* Except she wasn't a little girl anymore. She'd grown into a gorgeous woman with rich brown curls, subtle curves, and long, shapely legs encased in jeans. "Wow."

Time really did fly down here. She had to be at least thirty now, but her ageless face reminded me of my own. No wrinkles or blemishes, which could be normal for a human, but I doubted mortal aging rules applied to

Trudy.

"How do Nephilim age?" I asked, curious. Because Gleason hadn't looked a day over thirty either.

"It's yet to be determined, but so far, it seems they've inherited immortality from their angelic genes." My father's voice floated from above as he stood just inside the door in an elegant suit. Apparently, he also enjoyed men's fashions. I preferred my jeans and long-sleeved shirt. Far more practical.

"Hello, Azrael," Xai greeted. "Thank you for the vacation."

"You deserved it," my father replied. "You both did."

I smiled. "We're ready to get back to work."

"Good. We have a lot to catch up on." He stepped aside to welcome us into the house. "The Nephilim have been quite busy organizing."

"I noticed," Xai replied as we all moved into the living area. "I monitored the Genesis from above."

My father chuckled. "I suppose that's a matter we should discuss first."

Xai sat on the black leather love seat and pulled me down beside him before asking, "What about it?"

"They're no longer called the Genesis," my father replied.

"Indeed?" Xai sounded amused. "I was never a fan to begin with, but what have they chosen now?"

Trudy perched on the arm of a chair across from us and crossed her booted ankles. "We chose a name more befitting of our origin, or rather, our existence as the children of angels."

I shared a look with Xai. Neither of us had a clue.

"What's the name of the organization we're here to lead?" I asked, curious.

Trudy smiled, slow and sultry, as she prolonged the suspense, her excitement palpable.

Then she uttered three words that perfectly described the group of beings who would shape the future of this world and protect humanity for the centuries to come.

"The Dark Provenance."

EPILOGUE

I SENSED HER IN THE DARK, waiting to pounce, but pretended to admire the night sky instead.

We picked this home in the mountains because it reminded us of the Heavens. So dark, peaceful, and remote. Perfect for this little game she wanted to play.

I waited for the sound of metal slicing air and caught the blade just before it would have hit my shoulder. Always by the sharp end. I liked the way her silver made me bleed.

"Welcome home, love," I murmured as I turned to face her. She followed up the throw with several impressive maneuvers that backed me into the edge of the balcony. I caught her ankle and tried to flip her, only to have her go in the opposite direction and try to knock me off balance.

Six months of constant sparring with the Nephilim had certainly enhanced Evangeline's strength and skills.

She grabbed the handle from my hand and tore my skin as she cruelly removed the knife. I hissed at the pain while smiling.

"I've missed you, Evangeline." She had left for a visit with Guinevere three days ago, and it'd been agony without her. Not that I would admit it out loud. Suffocating the daughter of death went against the grain. She required freedom to fly.

"Prove it," she dared with a swipe of the bloody knife. *So feisty.*

My hardening cock made focusing difficult, but I managed to catch her wrist and rotate her in the way I wanted. Her shoulder blades slammed into my chest as I forced her to drop the weapon, but rather than cave to my demands, she ducked and rolled, taking my foot with her.

I braced myself for the fall, landing with ease on my back, and smiled as she straddled me. If she expected me to fight her off me, then she had another think coming.

My fingers wound in her hair, forcing her down to meet my kiss as I welcomed her home properly with my mouth. She moaned against me, her supple form relaxing as I dominated her with my tongue.

Even from the top, she submitted, not that I needed it. Her warrior soul was what drew me to her. She never backed down from a fight. As was evidenced by the fresh blade pressed to my throat.

I ignored it while I continued worshiping her mouth and wrapped my arm around her lower back to hold her in place as she tried to rock against me.

"How was Tennessee?" I whispered, prolonging the moment.

"Interesting." Her tongue traced my bottom lip. "I think something is going on between Gwen, Zane, and Zeb."

"Yeah?" That didn't surprise me. The Demonic Lord possessed a weakness for Succubi, and Zane had been in love with Guinevere for over a century. The Incubus never told her, though, which was a shame considering the feelings were mutual.

"I don't think I like it, but she seems happy."

"Mmm…" I rolled her over and settled my hips between her open thighs before nuzzling her neck. "Maybe one of them is her mate." *Or perhaps even both.*

"I don't think demons can have mates," she breathed and arched into my hardness. The knife gently slid across my throat to my back, where Eve deftly sliced through the back of my sweater.

I should have known better than to leave her armed. "Careful, darling. You know how I feel about quid pro quo."

"That's what I'm counting on," she murmured as the sharp edge sawed through my belt. I caught her wrists and pinned them both beside her head.

Her coy smile nearly undid me.

"I love you, Evangeline."

She ran her boot-clad feet up my legs, ending at my thighs. "I love you too, Xai."

"Just making sure we're on the same page, love, because I'm about to destroy you." *In the most pleasurable manner, of course.*

"Good," she murmured. "I wouldn't have you any other way."

THE END

USA Today Bestselling Author Lexi C. Foss loves to play in dark worlds, especially the ones that bite. She lives in Chapel Hill, North Carolina with her husband and their furry children. When not writing, she's busy crossing items off her travel bucket list, or chasing eclipses around the globe. She's quirky, consumes way too much coffee, and loves to swim.

Printed in Great Britain
by Amazon